THE HEYDAY
IN THE BLOOD

STOC DYNNWYD YMAITH
LLYFRGELL COLEG MENAI
WITHDRAWN LIBRARY STOCK

PARTHIAN

LIBRARY of WALES

D1353176

Geraint Goodwin was born in Newtown in 1903. He started writing at an early age, his first success being at a local eisteddfod. As a young man he made his living as a journalist with the *Montgomeryshire Express* before moving to London, where he wrote his first book, *Conversations with George Moore*. He was diagnosed with a tubercular condition in 1929 and, after treatment at a sanatorium, travelled abroad to convalesce. He used his travel experiences in his next book, *Call back Yesterday*, which was published in 1935. It was followed, in 1936, by his first work of fiction, *The Heyday in the Blood*, which enjoyed immediate critical acclaim. Three more books, *The White Farm*, a collection of short stories *Watch for the Morning* and *Come Michaelmas* followed, the last of which was written during an increasing struggle with ill-health. Although seriously ill, Geraint Goodwin discharged himself from a sanatorium at Talgarth in 1941 in order to return home to be with his young family, who at this time were living in the market town of Montgomery. He died shortly afterwards. His untimely death brought to an end a brilliant literary career which had barely had time to begin. He was married with two children, a girl and a boy.

LLYFRGELL COLEG MENAI LIBRARY
SAFLE FFRIDDOEDD SITE
BANGOR GWYNEDD LL57 2TP

THE HEYDAY
IN THE BLOOD

GERAINT GOODWIN

PARTHIAN
LIBRARY OF WALES

Parthian
The Old Surgery
Napier Street
Cardigan
SA43 1ED
www.parthianbooks.co.uk

The Library of Wales is a Welsh Assembly Government
initiative which highlights and celebrates Wales' literary
heritage in the English language.

Published with the financial support of
the Welsh Books Council.

The Library of Wales publishing project is based at
Trinity College, Carmarthen, SA31 3EP.
www.libraryofwales.org

Series Editor: Dai Smith

First published in 1936
© The Estate of Geraint Goodwin
Library of Wales edition published 2008
Foreword © Katie Gramich 2008
All Rights Reserved

ISBN 978-1-905762-83-5

Cover design: www.theundercard.co.uk
Cover image: *Head of Dorelia McNeill* (1881-1969)
(oil on plywood) by John, Augustus Edwin (1878-1961)
© National Museum and Gallery of Wales Cardiff/
The Bridgeman Art Gallery

Typeset by logodædaly

Printed and bound by Gwasg Gomer, Llandysul, Wales

British Library Cataloguing in Publication Data

A cataloguing record for this book is available from the British
Library.

This book is sold subject to the condition that it shall not by way
of trade or otherwise be circulated without the publisher's prior
consent in any form of binding or cover other than that in which
it is published.

LIBRARY OF WALES

FOREWORD

In August 1935, Geraint Goodwin wrote to his mentor, Edward Garnett, 'I have got such an inferiority complex (not just mock-modesty) about all I write.... They always say the Welshman is full of bounce, but it is very untrue.' Goodwin's definition of himself as emphatically a Welshman, but perhaps an uncharacteristic one, may stand as a succinct introduction to this fascinating and unjustly neglected writer.

Born in Newtown, Montgomeryshire in 1903, Goodwin made his name initially as a Fleet Street journalist but by the mid-1930s he had determined to abandon what he regarded as hack work in order to try to fulfil his ambition to be a writer of creative fiction. As soon as he did so, his imagination was drawn to the Welsh border country of his early life. Turning his back on London, and warmly encouraged by Garnett, Goodwin began to produce the short stories and novels that give vivid life to a part of Wales hitherto not figuring largely on the literary map.

Despite Goodwin's self-doubt over his own skills as a writer, he held some quite definite views on contemporary English fiction, as he expressed forcefully to Garnett in the same 1935 letter: 'I did not think much of the English section of *Best Short Stories of 1934*. They all seemed to be so polite and... in such very good taste... You felt at the end of them that the authors all dressed for dinner.' Goodwin himself set out to write a distinctively Welsh fiction which would be an antidote to the genteel, dressed-for-dinner fare of many of his English contemporaries.

His first, autobiographical novel, *Call Back Yesterday*, was published in 1935, closely followed by the more fictional *The Heyday in the Blood* in the following year. Indeed, just six months after confessing his writerly 'inferiority complex' to Garnett, the latter was writing back to the fledgling author with warm commendation on the complete manuscript of *The Heyday in the Blood*, saying 'I congratulate you... I think... you have written... a book of real force and flavour – one with roots in the soil – a creative book.' Other critics concurred with Garnett's judgement when the novel was published. Howard Spring wrote in *The Evening Standard* that 'Mr Goodwin has in him the makings of a novelist of the first importance'. Interestingly too, Spring places Goodwin in the context of the recent literary history of Wales, contrasting his work with that of Caradoc Evans: 'What bitterness can do for Wales, Mr Caradoc Evans has done. Now comes Mr Goodwin to show us what love can do.' *The Observer*'s critic later compares Goodwin's writing with that of his Welsh contemporaries, Glyn Jones and Rhys Davies, concluding, apparently rather mystified, that 'there is something happening in Wales'. Only Cyril Connolly in *The New Statesman* is somewhat dubious about an author whom he describes as 'a violent and lyrical young Welshman'. Maybe Connolly suspected that Goodwin did not dress for dinner.

The Heyday in the Blood is set in the late 1920s/early 1930s in the fictional Welsh border village of Tanygraig, a place which is described as being 'off the beaten track'. Its presiding spirit is Twmi Tudor, the pub landlord of the Red Lion, which is the central space of the novel, a space where the locals converge to drink, debate, joke, fight, gossip, and sing. Goodwin was aware of creating an image of Wales which contradicted the stereotype of the sober 'nation of Nonconformists' so cruelly caricatured by Caradoc Evans but, as he pointed out in a 1936 letter to Garnett, 'the picture of Welsh life [in the novel] is true nevertheless, albeit it is not *all* Wales'. The patrons of the Red Lion are an unruly bunch, kept in line by the formidable and sardonic Twmi who is himself not above a spot of poaching or baiting of the local constable. Indeed, there are some scenes in the novel which are pure, highly enjoyable and rumbustious slapstick.

And yet there are other dimensions too. The Red Lion is both a space for farcical comedy and an idyllic pastoral retreat, a 'place of birdsong', lying 'deep in the trees like an old nest'. This more lyrical aspect of the novel is centred upon Beti, Twmi's daughter, a passionate and sensitive young girl, torn between two contrasting suitors, her reckless, fearless cousin, Llew, and the poet and bankrupt miller, Evan. Beti, Evan and Llew are embodiments of the novel's titular 'heyday in the blood', a quotation borrowed from Shakespeare's Hamlet, who speaks, one cannot help but think ironically, of the 'heyday in the blood' being 'tame' in a woman of Gertrude's age when he upbraids his mother in the infamous 'closet scene'. Actually, the 'heyday in the blood' is much in evidence in most of Goodwin's characters, whatever their age, which perhaps accounts for

Cyril Connolly's distaste for what he saw as the excessive 'violence' of Goodwin's writing. His characters, including his heroine, Beti, respond to 'the urgent, unanswerable shout of Nature', much as the neighbourhood's mares respond when Border Prince, the great shire horse, makes his periodic visit to the Red Lion. Beti is, moreover, a girl torn not only between two lovers but between alternative futures – the choice of staying or going, a traditional Welsh way of life which is being slowly eroded and threatened by outside forces or a new life in England, which embodies modernity and freedom. Beti is conscious of living at a temporal and spatial border: 'The old way of things was ending; she had come at the end of one age and the beginning of another. Wales would be the last to go – but it was going.'

To this end, Goodwin continually juxtaposes the rural and the urban, invariably preferring the rural. Beti, for instance, hates the town, which she sees as 'a shovelful of cinders, smouldering and dirty', while the 'jentlemens' from Manchester bring a harsh commercial attitude with them, along with 'something foul and dirty' which contrasts with Beti's unsullied freshness. The 'jentlemens', though, include a Jewish businessman, caricatured in the unsettling terms which are all too prevalent in Anglophone writing of the 1930s. Interestingly, though, Jewishness is perceived by the Welsh locals in the Red Lion as a problematic identity not dissimilar to Welshness. Dici Weasel cannot understand how a Jew can be English, 'for an Englishman can't be a Jew!' Wati Penygraig later tells a story about taking 'a real toff' fishing, only to find out that his client is actually a Welshman, when he starts swearing in Welsh on losing a fish: 'Tamn it all,' exclaims Wati, 'a ploody Welshman for you, and not a toff at all!' His companion, Dai Tweed, commiserates: 'These London-Welsh looks just like jentlemens though'. This rumination on the implied parallels between the Welsh and Jewish relationship to the English class system is reminiscent of other Welsh writing of the period, such as Alun Lewis' 1942 short story 'Almost a Gentleman'.

The Red Lion is visited not only by 'jentlemens' from England, who come for the shooting and fishing, but by 'two shonihois from the South', in retreat from the poverty and suffering of the Rhondda, and en route to seek work on the 'Mersey Tunnel'. Twmi shows his Welsh working-class allegiance unequivocally by regarding the 'jentlemens' with considerable disdain, while giving the persecuted Communist 'shonihois' free lodging, food and boots, for: ' "Cot tamn it all" said Twmi in a fury. "You Welshmens aren't you – not ploody tramps!" ' This telling encounter with the Welsh from 'Down South', which is clearly 'another world' to the inhabitants of Tanygraig, invites comparison with a similar episode in the narrative of another Welsh novel, Eiluned Lewis' *Dew on the Grass* (1934). Goodwin must surely have been aware of Lewis' work, not least because she also was originally from Newtown and had progressed from a successful career in journalism to publishing a bestselling work of fiction based on her own childhood experiences in Wales. Yet the class and political allegiances of the two authors could hardly be more different, as reflected in the episodes in both novels where indigent characters from the Welsh Valleys venture into the rural landscapes of mid-Wales.

In Lewis' novel, the man from Cardiff who towards the end of the novel trespasses onto the sacred ground of the churchyard is treated explicitly as a 'tramp', whereas in Goodwin's, the shonihois are welcomed as Welsh heroes. Nevertheless, the two novels share an elegiac and lyrical tone in evoking a Wales which both writers saw as fast disappearing. And, despite their ideological differences, Goodwin may have been inspired by the success of his compatriot in mapping that particular and idiosyncratic corner of Wales which they both regarded as home. Both works may be seen as contributing to the flowering of the Anglophone Welsh novel of the 1930s, and as evidence that 'something' was indeed 'happening' in literary Wales.

One of the highlights of the novel occurs in the beautifully written Chapter XI, where Evan is hard at work on his Eisteddfod poem on the set subject of 'Peace', while the local foxhunt is in full cry through the village. Evan, unable to concentrate, goes into his deserted granary, where he weighs himself on the disused scales and finds, to his dismay, that he has once again lost weight. At this point, the hunted fox strolls into the granary to take refuge. Evan sees the parallels between the two of them, creatures at bay, threatened by death, and he protects the fox by locking the door on him and throwing away the key, as his antagonist, Llew, violently demands his prize. The scene is reminiscent of a central one in Margiad Evans' 1932 novella, *Country Dance*, where the rival suitors, like young bulls, do actually fight each other over their claim on the central female character, Ann. In Goodwin's novel, though, Beti bravely stands between the two men to prevent a fight.

In the hands of a lesser writer, this encounter could be pure melodrama but Goodwin creates a vivid and memorable scene which simultaneously dramatises the youthful 'heyday in the blood' and places it in a poignant local and international context, at a time when the whole of 'Europe was like a bear-garden', 'though a great many people in Wales still believed earnestly in the cause of peace'.

Goodwin wrote two further novels after *The Heyday in the Blood*. By the late 1930s he and his young family had moved back permanently to Wales. Sadly, however, Goodwin was able to enjoy the critical acclaim for his work for only a short period. Having suffered periodically from tuberculosis for most of his adult life, he died of the disease in October 1941, aged only thirty-eight. He left a handful of novels and short stories which are still extraordinarily fresh and vigorous, among which *The Heyday in the Blood*, both tragic and richly comedic, may serve as a fitting epitaph and a worthy addition to the Library of Wales.

Katie Gramich

THE HEYDAY
IN THE BLOOD

CHAPTER I

Beti had gone out to see the kingfisher. She went tripping out over the old lawn, her feet sinking into it and with each step there came that strange resilience from the earth; it felt as though she were going to take flight.

It was a very old lawn; perhaps a hundred years old. It had mellowed down in its texture so that the grass was no longer hard and pliant. The wood moss spread around it, and the haws from the beech trees were still around the great boles in brown, ripe crescents, unswept from the autumn and lasting through the winter. No one cared for the lawn except to mow it now and again, and yet it was one of the most wonderful lawns in that part of the country.

To run barefoot across the lawn with the dew on it, leaving white footmarks on its glistening front, brought a furtive joy all its own to Beti. Backwards and forwards she would run, the moisture gathering around her feet, cold and sharp and yet soft to the touch. Sometimes she would fall on her knees and rub her face in the dew. It was an old-time recipe for the complexion but she did it for its own sake.

But no one was to know. And no one was to know that she was going to see the kingfisher. She had seen it many times from her bedroom window, flying out from the waterfall to the brook. She knew it was the kingfisher by its low drumming flight, straight as a rod, and then the final curl. But there was only one way to see a kingfisher, and that was from behind – to follow its flight through. The flash of the passing bird was not enough. It was like a shooting star – the colours seemed to explode and before she had lifted her eyes it was all over. But to follow the bird through, to watch the light gather on the drumming wings and the colours glisten like so many facets, finally to blend and liquefy and so enshroud it as a nimbus... that was to see the kingfisher.

And she wanted to see the kingfisher – the colour and the loveliness of it on this first brilliant day of spring. She knew that if she climbed along the bank to the waterfall it would fly out from among the boulders, the water dripping from it and the thin spring sun lighting it.

She had got to the end of the lawn, moving stealthily and furtively, when her mother's voice came out shrill and high. 'Beti, Beti. Where *arr* you now?'

She hurried back, head down, panting.

'Here, Mam,' she said, breathless, at the back door.

Her mother stood there, an old apron about her. She was tall and thin, tight-lipped and sour, and yet with eyes that had once been very beautiful and still could be so at thirty.

2

'Your dad iss in the cellar, calling. There is someone knocking, something awful!'

Beti hurried through the unswept bar, lightless and shrouded with the undrawn curtains. It was like a church after a service in its lifelessness. She opened the door leading into the cellar and into the darkness.

'Hass it gone time?' her father grunted.

She stepped back and looked at the clock.

'It wants half an hour nearly.'

'Near enough. But watch out first!'

'Shall I open then?' she called down.

'Yess, yess,' he shouted irritably in between the hammering. 'Take the tamned hinges off and be quick.' Then he bellowed out from below. 'Wait! Haf a peep first.'

She drew the curtain aside from a window which gave out on the yard. A man was standing on the stone step, his horse tethered to a beam on the porch. He wore a bowler hat and his black coat, patched and worn, came down over his breeches.

'It's Dici Weasel – all dressed up,' she shouted down.

'Tell Dici Weasel to wait then.'

'He's hammering again, Dad. Something awful.'

'Tell him to WAIT,' he bellowed. 'Got tamn, do I run a house for Dici Weasel? Who is Dici Weasel tell me? There iss more holes in hiss pockets than in hiss head.'

'You tell then,' Beti shouted back.

'I tell! Ay, I tell, you see!'

Her father came lumbering up the cellar stairs, cursing. 'What iss this house, ay? A parlour, ay? And so we got to dance to Dici Weasel's asking, ay? The ploody scarecrow that he is.'

3

He was a huge man with a paunch that the homespun waistcoat only half covered. The lower buttons were left undone so that it seemed that he was oozing out of his clothes. He walked with a waddle. His hair, with the red-rust sheen on it, was going thin, and a great moustache, like a mane, covered his mouth. His eyes were very bright and lively for one of his size. The face was cruel in an old rogue's way, but the brightness of the eye redeemed it. He seemed to fill the room by his very presence.

He opened the door a crack.

'What you want?'

'Come on, boss. There iss no harm now.'

He opened the door wider with great reluctance.

'What about that fishing?'

'Highest bidder now. All fair and above board. No one say different.'

'I offer quid. All right. A quid for how many trouts? Two dozens perhaps in half a mile, and those two dozens as thin as twigs. The skins of their pellies iss touching their backs. A quid I say. Lot of money a quid. And who goes over me and offers thirty bob? Two schoolmasters as don't know what end of a rod it iss.'

'Highest bidder; all's fair,' the farmer went on.

'Fair!' bellowed the innkeeper. 'Nice hedges you'll be having in a bit with two clumsy louts stamping up and down the brook. They not put their foots down twice in same place.' He wagged his finger solemnly. 'Platchin' you'll be, Dici – this year, next year, sometime, always. Mark my words now. And the difference from two louts and my jentlemens is how much? Ten bob a year.'

4

'Well, come on boss, now,' said the farmer plaintively.

The innkeeper, having worked off his fury, let him in.

'Ay! Come in! What about Peepy-Tom?' he said, relenting.

'Phut! Peepy-Tom! He's no cop for a man, boss.'

'Cop for his own dirty shadow behind him, that man,' answered the other vindictively. 'A licence iss a licence, else I bet you he wouldn't hang about. No indeed! I would be putting a charge of shot in that big hass of his as soon as see him.'

'Now, now. Peace on earth: peace on earth,' said the farmer sanctimoniously, sniffing into his mug, his long nose hidden and his fair moustache twitching. Dici Weasel was his nickname.

'Peace in hell with that long-leg-ged pugair about!'

'There's a sweat you arr in, all for nothing,' answered the farmer.

'Sweat!' went on the host filling his glass and cursing stolidly. 'Daro. What am I, to be drawing beer at breakfast for?'

He drank out of his own glass, a long gulp and subsided in a sigh. No one worried about his rudeness, for no one had ever known him polite. Twm, the Lion, in a way, was a fixture, as solid and immovable as the house over whose destinies he presided. Everyone in all that part of the country knew Twm. People would drive out of the town in motor cars, just to get him under way no less than for the fare provided. But the trippers came in on sufferance. They shared his hearth and the hearth was home. If he did not like the look of anyone he would tell them to go away, and if he enjoyed anyone's company he would sometimes pay the reckoning. The village of Tanygraig was off the beaten track; not even the big new road to the coast came within six miles of it. It remained throughout this generation as in the last.

He was standing in the window looking out to the village.

'Ay. There's a beauty for you.' He caught the farmer by the hand and led him to the window.

'Well, well, well! It's a great pity. Yess, indeed.'

'Shutapp, man!'

'He's done his best, whateffer, poor lad.'

'His best, ay. And what iss best? I tell you this wance and not two times. No one run pusiness on thin air. No indeed!'

They looked across to the mill. It was called the mill, but such revenue as there was came from the general store, a vague windy place, with peeling walls and flapping sacking, hiding the daylight from the windows. It squatted there, on a bend of the square, like a roosting hen. From the back, day in and day out, came the crooning of the mill and the splashing of the sluice, the occasional curse of a wagoner loading. Then the mill would stop. It seemed then as though the finches in the currant bushes and the sparrows chirping round about, the starlings lining the eaves, their burnt-black feathers atremble, their voices high, sharp and tuneless as a taut bowstring, would all come to life, for only then could they be heard. Then the slow gurgle and the rush of the sluice-water and the settling drumming would pass off into a distant hum. It was part of the village, this never-ending hum; without it the silence seemed unreal.

But this morning it had stopped altogether and no one knew when or how it would restart. And the miller – Evan the Mill – a tall youth with long fair hair and a small moustache like a mark, which showed up the pallor of his face, stood before the door, looking out on the village, facing his defeat with a courage that surprised him. He wanted to bury his head in shame, to go away to hide – to go anywhere away from his own village, his own people.

The furtive nods, the unasked questions, touched him to the quick. And yet he had to bear it out: something told him so. The courage that came to him, came like the fresh spring wind itself, was something unguessed at. He did not wish for it, but it was there. The stand he had to make was an unreal thing – as unreal as the shop – and yet something told him to face the music, to brave it out. Why? And to brave what out? He stood there against a stone post watching the villagers dribble by in twos and threes. They knew already.

Before Evan one of the village children, his peaked face crowned by a great cloth cap, worn and patched, was slowly poking in the powdered yard, watching the stick-end move through the dust with the cloudless carelessness of the child mind. That was *his* world, with all its rapture, this little bit of burnt stick and the powdered dust: that and no other.

Behind him again was the granary, shining in the sun. Against the netted windows, sparrows were beating frantically in little clouds of dust, drumming on the wire face with their wings, fluttering round and round in a whirlwind of chaff and flour.

Evan reached inside for the key and, unlocking the door, lifted the birds gently in his hands one by one and then threw them up with a toss into the open.

'Ay,' said the old innkeeper bitterly. 'Playing with dicky birds is about his mark an' all.'

'He done his best, poor fellow,' answered Dici stoutly. 'And it's come on his head whateffer. The old man had more there, I am thinking.'

'Ah. Too much, the old pugair.'

'Now: now! Let bygones be bygones. But diawch man, there's a poet he is – give him his due. Lovely, man, limpid as a stream. I bet you now, and Evan go for the National Chair and he win, hands down.'

'Phut,' said Twmi with a gesture of disgust. 'What good to him, ay? Limping streams be damned. You watch limping streams, I tell you: limping streams and limping trouts too!'

'And if Evan haf someone behind him now – a good woman – off he go now like a... like a streak.'

He shot his hand up in emphasis, just missing the innkeeper's mug. Twmi grunted in disgust and spat on the stone floor.

'Someone like Beti now,' went on the farmer.

'Wa-at?' shouted the old man, the words coming like a thunderclap. 'Wa-at?' he said again, slamming his mug down on the table, his rogue eyes narrowing.

'I only said someone *like* Beti. No offence now, no offence.'

The farmer patted him on the back affably. He knew that he had overstepped the mark.

8

'There's your pint now. Drink it up and be off. Be off, you hear,' said Twm.

'But no offence now: no indeed.'

'What you say then for? Beti do what she like when I tell her. But she marry a man, see? You know what a man iss, ay? A *man* I say. Think that wan out. Him!'

He snapped his fingers and then took a long draught, glaring over his mug.

'Him!' he went on, mumbling into his mug. 'I like to see him, that's all. Only see him!'

Twm went mumbling about the bar, into the little bar parlour and out again, like an old bear suddenly roused. He drew another pint and emptied half of it at a draught, and then brought his hand backwards across his mouth with a long sigh. His anger was subsiding with the cool ale, as it always did. He moved over to the window again.

'Daro!' he said. 'Look here now! Look at this thing coming. Am I a home for lost dogs, or what?'

The little man who pushed his head round the door-end like a rat sniffing, was Wili Lloyd the Hut. He had a thin red face, touched with blue, like a monkey's chaps, and his eyes were weak and rheumy. He rented a hut from Twmi and had it wheeled down the road. There he mended clocks, when he had the clocks, but they very seldom came to him. It was his pride that he had never done any work in his life and he argued that no free man should work. As a young man he had gone to Australia, which was the one place where he had had to work, and so he came back. And out there his Australian wife, after a few weeks of marriage, had left him to his own devices – which were not many.

He wore flash breeches and a check cap and he never missed a day with the beagles. He smoked 'whiffs' when he could afford them, little cigars at three-hapence a piece, which he stuck rakishly in his yellow teeth, spat a lot and smacked his leggings in a sporty way. That was among people whom he did not know. Otherwise he was always humble, for he had 'touched' most people at some time or another.

'Hi, you,' shouted Twm. 'What you want, ay? It iss not time. Take your funny head out now this min-nit.'

He looked around for something to throw.

'Duw. Just wan now, Twm. Just wan. I spit that hard at work. No spit left.'

'Come here. I tell you something,' said Twmi glaring. 'Catch hold, Dici.'

Dici led the little man before the settle where the host, hands on knees, was spread out expansively, his waistcoat rising and falling in his anger.

'I tell you wance, twice and foreffer. You hear? More than two quids it iss you owe. What you think I do for your nonsenses, ay? I give you wan week from this day, and then – out you go. I make a chicken house of her. Where clock ay, where Beti's watch ay? Where jentlemen's half-hunter left from the last grouse, ay? Where, I ask? Too soft I been. I give you huntin' and whiff-whiffs.'

'Be a sport, Twm. Wan little drink,' said the little man letting the stream of abuse fly over him. He took out a woman's purse, frayed and worn, and held up a sixpenny bit. 'Ready money,' he said.

'By Cod, it iss,' said the old man in wonder; 'You shall haf this wan and no more.' He paused on the way to the cellar. 'You not see Peepy-Tom?'

'Pah! He iss miles away. Drop dead now!'

'On his bike?'

'Bike!' said Wili. 'I tell you something. If I say a heifer kick out the hind wheel at Brynglas auction, what you say then, ay?'

'I see what I see,' said the old man suspiciously. 'Iesu Mawr!' he shouted halfway across the bar. 'Talk of the devil...'

He waddled across to the door quicker than anyone had ever seen him move before. Then he turned round and shoved his great posterior against it.

'Quick, Dici – that glass...'

Dici made to have one last gulp but the old man shouted. 'On the floor, man. On the floor with it!'

Only then did he move away from the door.

The policeman hammered away, not knowing it was unlatched, and the old man shouted.

'Who iss there? Cod tamn, no peace for the wicked. What you want, ay? Go away this min-nit. Bar not open yet.'

'All right Mr Tudor. Me it is: P.C. Ifans. Open at wance!'

Twmi pulled the window curtain aside and peered out. 'Diawl ario'd so it iss. There's early you arr. Come in Mister Ifans, come in.'

The policeman, lean and angular, with a dark, sardonic, sniffing face, walked in. He had to bend to enter the porch. Then he took his helmet off very carefully and brushed around the lining with his bandana handkerchief.

'Goot morning, jentlemen,' he sniffed. 'Not disturbing you I hope?'

'Not at all: not at all,' said Twmi. 'Pleasure,' he added as an afterthought. The others looked down at the ground sheepishly.

'And perhaps I can ask what you got in those glasses?'

'Glass,' said Twmi.

'Glasses,' replied the policeman.

'You arr a wan,' answered Twmi, wagging his finger roguishly.

'I ask you again.'

'Get away, man. Joking you arr!'

'This is fery, fery serious, Mister Tudor.'

'Shutapp man,' replied the innkeeper good-humouredly.

The policeman took a step forward like a keeper in a den of lions. He was watching all places at once. 'Well. We will just have a look, ay? Just to make sure, like.'

Twmi went to reach him a glass.

'Don't touch,' shouted the policeman.

The old man jumped back as if he had been shot and made a great play at rubbing his hands. The policeman reached for the glasses gingerly, fondled them and then sniffed them.

'This is beer all right.'

'Shutapp man. Don't be silly,' Twmi was holding back his laughter.

'Where is it, ay? Where hass it gone? Ah!' he said as his foot slipped and he held on to the table to save himself. 'What iss this on the floor, ay?'

He got down on his hands and knees and began to sniff.

The old man got down on his hands and knees as well, and then Dici. They were moving on all fours across the floor, the policeman and the innkeeper head to head like a couple of tups butting.

Dici, his self-control gone, reached for one of the dart arrows and gently pressed its point against the expanse of serge trousers. Up went the policeman's head, knocking the little table backwards and sending the glasses flying. The crash was heard all over the house.

'By Cod. Now you done it, boss. Damages I am having. What iss a policeman for – all hass and no head! Get up this min-nit and stop that daft game,' Twmi roared.

The policeman, white and drawn with anger and shame, got his head from between the table legs.

'By Cod, Twmi. And you Dici. You will smart for this I tell you. I got head like elephant. You see, you wait!'

He stuck his helmet on his head, unable to face them, and rushed out of the door, slamming it after him. Then he was on his bike and out through the yard and along the road. They saw his helmet-top pass along the hedgerow, jerking forward as he struck on the pedals in his violence.

Then Twmi, watching him out of distance, put his hands on his belly and began to laugh. It began in a wheeze and a choke, and his body shook with it, a low intaking breath that, after a pause, was allowed to escape like steam. It was himself laughing, his whole being exuding mirth, which seemed to envelop the room. And Dici began to laugh too, high-pitched and hysterical like a screech owl.

For the routing of a policeman had some hidden, far reaching significance. It was as though an invader had been

13

beaten off and discomfited; something from the outside that had been set going. The battle, fought often and often, was between staid and unalterable authority and the native cunning. It was, in its way, a game and a delight. The old man would continue to serve drinks out of hours as long as he could stand upright – simply because he could not help himself. He would risk his licence for a complete stranger and for a trifling farthing profit, rather than conform. Twmi's instinct – the Welsh blood in him – ran to poaching as a duck to water: it was innate. He could not poach himself for the simple reason that he could not run fast enough and it was a great grief to him. But the inn was a nest of poachers, and was indeed a sort of clearing-house for game.

He had all the thrill of poaching, the spiritual afflatus that went with it, under his own roof. But a great deal of the really happy spirit had gone out of the fight – for there were regular fixed principles in this pitched battle between cunning and authority – with the transfer of Peepy-Tom to the area. The policeman pitted cunning against cunning. He was himself a teetotaller. There was no flesh to him; it was all bone. And the old man, who had few dislikes, was driven in consequence into some sort of malice against him.

That was why the policeman's rout had brought with it such joy. But Twmi, holding his belly, his eyes streaming, suddenly caught sight of Wili, back to the hearth, sniffing down his nose and making a show of laughing with his mouth.

'Hi, you!' he roared. 'Hind wheel off bike, ay? I give you hind wheel!'

He lounged around the table and shot out his foot, missed and staggered against the settle. Wili went round and round the table gingerly.

'By Cod! What you know, ay? Put app job, no? Out you go! I count three.'

He glanced around the room, his eyes glaring, in search of something to throw. Wili made a bolt for the door in four little hops like a rabbit.

'Iesu mawr – there's a Judas for you,' Twm shouted, beside himself. 'Out you go now, for that. I teach you something. She iss a hen house now all right! Out you go now – dirty poss-cards an' all.'

He walked through the porch and out on to the road, watching Wili hurrying away. The little man was going at a great speed, stopping just short of a run and looking round furtively like a slinking dog.

'I give you whiff-whiffs. I give you huntin'. You hunt the slipper in a min-nit gwas. I ska-tair all to the four winds.'

He shook his fist at the retreating figure. For a moment he stood there sunning himself, for it was the first fine day of spring. To the west the land rose up into the sky: to the east it opened up into the valley which gave on to England, field on field of loamy earth which ran off into a haze. Far away a little plume of steam curled over an engine that was shunting petulantly at the 'junction' set in the fields. But the noise of it travelled right up the valley, although it was miles away. First there was the curl of steam and then, much later, the noise of the engine as it travelled through the still air. That and the brook, very lively with the sun on it, and the dark molten sheen of a 'fresh', were almost the only noises.

It seemed to Twm in a moment of clearness that there was something wrong, but he did not know what. Again he let the noises come up to him, and again; but this time, with a certainty, came the knowledge that something was wrong. He was worried beyond himself and put up his great head like a dog pointing.

In moments of doubt his first instinct was to look for his own. He walked to the brookside to look for his geese. They would always be waddling in the shallows or, with a commotion of wings, drying themselves on the bank, or perhaps sailing in slow convoy, flopping from pool to pool, down the brook.

But now they had gone. He walked along up the bank, pushing his way through the low-hanging alders, until he heard them far up the brook. The water came down muddy.

Then he remembered. The mill had stopped. They had no longer to breast the mill-race, and had gone farther up the brook, now unnaturally still in this place, in search of food.

It worried him to think of the mill stopping. It was not right. And perhaps one of the geese would get caught up in a night-line, for the village lads were always setting them up there. But this was a small thing. The mill had stopped and it had no right to stop. It was part of the natural, instinctive life around him. If they touched that, then they touched him. Just to give up the ghost was not a man's way at all. And that young man up there had a foot in a world that was unreal to him. That he could not endure. Life to him was something real and instinctive – to be lived. And those who reached beyond their appetites, who inhabited this other world, were unreal to him. The only unformed fear he had was of what lay beyond life.

The miller's father had been one of the old school, and between them there had existed one of those long and bitter feuds that are a feature of Welsh village life; him, in his heart, he could respect. But the mere mention of the son's name called up a bitterness that would have surprised him if he ever thought of it.

He walked slowly back to the inn, his head full of musings. Dici's chance remark had unloosened his bitterness. It worked within him, however much he tried to shout it down. But Beti was like him, he tried to tell himself. She knew a man when she saw one.

CHAPTER II

Spring came to the Red Lion in a hundred ways, which Beti knew and awaited.

There was the kingfisher, and the fine sheen of green on the scrub which reached up behind the house, so fine and evanescent that it seemed as though the scraggy, twisted blackthorn had been tarnished overnight. It seemed less substantial than a shadow – but it was there. And then in the meadow over the brook, her father's horses had gone wild. They went charging over the turf, tails up; the booming of their hoofs in the distance coming over to her in the still air like far-away thunder.

The snowdrops had gone from the old lawn – their patterns slowly mouldering in the earth. They had been planted no one knew how many years ago, and they were a part of the house. They formed a clumsy crown and sceptre and below, in bold letters, the word: WELCOME. They were white and chill as the winter itself, though Beti would not have been without them.

But the daffodils were different – not the large, ornate daffodil of the town garden, but the little wild plant, small and sturdy, which shot up in clusters around the borders. It had no more to do with the grand, cultivated plant than the shaggy mountain pony, which her father had on the hill, had to do with a show horse. It belonged to the earth, in its vivid colour, its small flaming cup of gold, rain-washed and clear and violent in its beauty. Those, too, had been planted before anyone remembered, but they were always the same; they neither spread nor died away. They were always there, in their brilliant clusters, with the first thin sun of the early spring.

And with it all the old house awoke. The place was atremble with the high piping chorus of birds. The doves were back in the beeches, with their soft muted cooing, their endless unseen fluttering in the tall branches; the chaffinches and the tits were in the bushes; the missel-thrush with her speckled belly met one, head cocked, at every turn. The swallows had come back to their sun-baked mud nests under the eaves, throwing a spike of shadow beneath them, as, with a shrill twitter, they darted to and fro against the spring sky.

The Red Lion slumbering there under its down-blown smoke, fenced around with trees which reached out, but never encompassed it, was a place of birdsong. It was more felt than heard, as the dropping tinkle of the waterfall at the bottom of the garden. And that, too, taking one abandoned leap through space, from the moss gully above, had its own especial noises. In still weather it came down

19

like a fine shred, breaking on the rocks in that almost soundless tinkle, to shoot up in a cascade so fine that one only saw the sun glisten in it. But a wind blew it backwards and forwards, causing it to play a tune of its own.

For there was no traffic at the Red Lion, and the natural peace possessed it. One was conscious of a motor car, but one was never conscious of the birds. The motor car broke into the quiet and shattered it, destroyed the unsensed rhythm of it all. And for that reason a motor car seemed ten times as noisy, its engine ten times as spiteful as it was. This faint, unalterable twittering of the birds which merged into a cloud of sound, the low hum of the mill and the sharp, metallic tinkle of the brook, were the only real sounds the house knew. Everything else happened; these never happened, for they were always there.

No one knew how old was the house. New wings had been built since the original foundation, and it spread itself out in its warm-coloured brick amongst the trees, with no beginnning and no end. And then, bordering it, were the barns and stables and outhouses, the cobbled yard, the sties. One could wander about all day long and there was always something fresh. It was too big for an inn, and yet it was not an hotel; no modern embellishment touched it.

But its rude comfort was very real. Those who went there went again. Its ham and egg teas were a byword among the townsfolk. Nowhere in all Wales were there such ham and egg teas. That was the only speciality it made, and that was one forced upon it. More flitches and more hams went up on the rafters until, early in the year, the great stone-floored taproom looked like a street overhung with pennants. A tall man could not walk upright among them. The ham and bacon was, of course, home-cured. How, or why, it should attain its particular flavour no one knew, any more than how water in one district is so very much better than in another.

But there was no ham like it – it had the sharp rich tang of the earth in it. The great hams hung up there with their coarse-cut borders, the saltpetre glistening in the lamplight, and then, cut to the horseshoe, showed a moist gleaming pink of lean, a colour all its own, deeper and richer than a salmon cut. It was cut off in thick slices, and the eggs were searched for in the nests; then all put on the great pan that hung from the spit. Over a fire – of pine and peat it slowly compounded its own flavour, filling the house with its pungent smell.

Everything in the Red Lion 'happened'. The visitors came and went as night followed day. However noisy they might be – as the charabanc full of shonihois from the South who had remained for two days when the axle broke on the corner – they could not touch it. The peace, so rudely broken, settled down again like the sea opening and closing. The life went on with the seasons, in time with the seasons – the full violent flowering of the wild daffodils with the first thin sun of the spring; then the deep heavy leaf of summer, when the trees came up to the house as in a flood; the rich bronze and gold of autumn with its thousand tints, and winter with its dark fragile network of branches, the pale, shooting flower of the snowdrops on the frost-gleaming lawn.

Beti watched her mother down the garden hanging out

21

the linen. It had come out of the ottoman above the stairs, where it had lain through the winter all interleaved with sprigs of lavender. It had that dull white texture which rain-water gives and it was going on the shrubs, face to the· sun, to give it that bleaching that only the sun can give. And with her Gwenno, the maid of all work, was struggling with the feather beds, the soft breast-down plucked from their own geese at Michaelmas and Christmas. There were no hair and spring mattresses at the Red Lion.

For next week the 'jentlemens' were coming, and Beti's heart shrank at the thought. This was the spring to her, and that was the spring to her mother – the linen and the mattresses to be aired, a whole wing to be cleaned and scrubbed, for the 'jentlemens'.

They too had 'happened', but now they came every Easter for the trout fishing, every August for the grouse. They had rented a stretch of the brook, a reach of the mountain, through her father. It was a big source of the inn's income, and her mother knew it.

Beti did not blame her mother, but she respected her father the more. For he showed them not one atom more respect than he did to anyone else. There was no 'sirring' them for him. If they liked the place they could come, and if they did not, then they could stay away.

And he, rough and ready and even vulgar, had established some sort of unspoken authority over them, though they paid him and he was in a way dependent on them. They would come and sit in the taproom after dinner and take a seat on one of the benches by the wall, trying to humour him and trying to ingratiate themselves. It was a nod or a grunt from him, moving around the place like a presence, which gave them leave to tell a dirty story to the company, which was their way of establishing themselves. And often enough it would be greeted with a polite titter, for few understood these imported stories. The brand of humour they brought with them was something apart and unguessed at, just as the local humour fell flat on English ears, for the worth of a story was in the telling and in its naturalness. It might be bawdy or it might not: but bawdiness did not make a story.

They were shut out morally from the taproom where the men foregathered, but to Gwenno and to Beti's mother they were the 'jentlemens'.

Beti disliked them for many reasons. They caused needless work with their boots and shoes, which wanted cleaning many times a day. Then they occupied the best part of her own home. Also they spoke with a funny accent, and their faces were white and puffy, with lined blue rings under their eyes. And there was one thing she could not forgive – their dressing-tables were loaded with pomades and grease and hair-oil, which gave her an actual sense of physical revulsion. That a man should scent himself, even his hair, was something totally beyond her: that a man should have anything but that sweat-smelling, earthy odour of the fields was something wrong and even wicked.

Mr Birbaum and Mr Shufflebotham came from Manchester. They were something big in business, but what it was no one knew. Once they brought with them their junior partner, a young sprig of a man in brown suede riding-breeches, who made Beti uneasy whenever she entered the room. One day

23

he caught her by the hand and drew her to him. She plucked her hand away and struck him across the mouth, her eyes flashing.

She stood there trembling, with no word said. But she would have killed him then and there if she could have laid hands on anything. Then she rushed out of the room. Outside she burst out crying; she was inconsolable. But she would tell no one what it was about, not even her father. She rushed off to the mountain, face to the fresh mountain wind that always blew across it, and walked around for hours. It was a way she had when she was deeply grieved, and it always restored her.

She knew nothing about men or their ways – she was as exultant and fresh and clean as a spring flower – and this was her first taste of it. For all the coarseness of the bar, there had never been one suggestive word said to her. And yet there was nothing furtive about sex, about the facts of life. They were as plain as a wide open door. But they were not dressed up and embellished and made dirty – and that was where her knowledge stopped short.

The Red Lion was one of the calling places of Border Prince, the great shire hired out on subscription to the farmers. Who ever thought of giving it any more significance than the coming of spring, the rain, the sun of summer, the ploughing, the harvest? The great stallion would come prancing along the road, dwarfing the man who led it, a rosette like a star on its forehead, its proud head curveting, a sheen of sweat on its great sleek coat and its tufted hocks, proudly stamping and pawing. For a whole day the place echoed to the whinnying of mares brought in from the farms around. There was no more to it than that – the urgent, unanswerable shout of Nature.

If that was life, then Beti knew all about it, but of the furtive, pawing nastiness of the young man in the brown suede riding-breeches she knew nothing. He could no doubt have taught her a lot, had she been so minded, but instead, she struck him in the mouth and went up on to the mountain to clean herself. Those men assailed her like a foul breath: they brought with them something foul and dirty and smoke-fretted. They spoke another language.

She asked her mother what a 'leg-show' was, and her mother did not know. But Beti had some idea that it had some naughty significance – this showing of legs – and she no more lifted up her skirt as she tore across the lawn; not until they had gone and life assumed its old way. Never before had she known of any reason why one should not lift up one's skirt when one wanted to run fast. But these men brought with them a knowledge of the world, and every fresh discovery was like a smudge across a clean page.

'Beti, Beti. What *arr* you up to now? Come and help with the clothes this min-nit.'

Her mother was shouting from the bottom of the garden, staggering under the weight of a clothes-basket.

'Yes, Mam. This min-nit.'

She went running down to the end of the lawn.

'We arr behind-hand awfully. I wish you would *think*, I would. The jentlemens here next week and where *arr* we? Gwenno iss doing the work of two, she iss.'

Beti set herself to work with a will, though her heart faltered. And she could hear her father's boisterous laugh in the taproom and the slow breath-taking wheeze which followed it. Her mother's world was finite and brittle – the house trim and orderly like herself. But her father, vulgar as he was, inhabited some other place. There were no boundaries to his world – wherever it was.

CHAPTER III

With her two baskets laden, their snow-white linen coverings drawn tightly over them, Beti was off to market. They had been pushed into the back of the high Rallt trap and she had climbed up between the farmer and his wife who overflowed in her wide black stuff dress over the near board.

The farmer drove – a gaunt old man, with a high collar and a square hard hat, which was pressed down over his spreading side-whiskers that invaded his lined, out-thrust jaw like furze on a field. His wife was ripe-faced and buxom, and her enormous bust seemed on the point of bursting through her stays, and overflowing like a flood. Between them Beti looked very slim and wisp-like. They were neighbours and they always took her to the town.

The journey was always a tight squeeze, for neither gave ground, and when they turned a corner their posteriors encroached on the seat unwittingly, making it less

27

LLYFRGELL COLEG MENAI LIBRARY

comfortable still. And the old mare never hurried; she broke her trot just when and how she pleased. She knew every inch of the road· and she arranged things as she liked. The farmer never used the whip, though he always carried it in his hand; instead he would point out unfamiliar things with a waving sweep just missing their heads. The unfamiliar things were the little bits of gossip on the road, the fly on a root crop; Ifan the Hafod ploughing at last; a moucher from the town, cutting pegs in a wood; the sprouting green on a rick. The whole passing pageant of moor and dingle, hill and valley went before them in review.

There were two market days in the week, but they were different in every way. Tuesday was the big market, when the whole countryside flowed in; the men were there then, alongside the women, and the Smithfield was open. The roads would be chock-a-block with beasts, reeking of sweat and dust and sheep-dip; flock on flock the whole way, moving there before them in dirty white clouds, the steam rising, the dogs barking, the sheep baaing and the men shouting.

And all the gigs and traps were loaded with produce, for on this day the dealers came from the big towns of the Midlands, with great lorries drawn up on the kerb, fenced around with stockades of coops and egg boxes. Heads and necks, tail feathers and cockscombs, stuck out through every crevice, for it was mostly a live market, and, although the prices were lower, there was a quick turn-over.

But on Saturday it was the little town's own particular market – the townspeople's own right and province. To this the men seldom came – it was something for the women alone. It was their own particular right to raise what they could on the small, unconsidered trifles of the farm – geese wings, and penny bunches of thyme and mint; jars of honey, and a chicken or two, plucked, scalded and trussed, and garnished with a little sprig of parsley.

All day long the townspeople came round and picked, and hawed, and twisted breastbones, and went and came again, until at the end of the day the farmers' wives had little enough time for their own shopping. Some of them came in by trap, but some of them rode in, their baskets on either side of the pony like panniers, the feed-bag hanging from the saddle.

And then, beyond these markets, came the four great fairs of the year, which outshone all else as the sun the stars.

But this day was Saturday, the smaller of the markets. As Beti saw the little town at the valley's end, spread out under its cloud of smoke, fuming there in the bright green of the fields that encompassed it, her heart sank. It lay there like a shovelful of cinders, smouldering and dirty. And she dreaded the long, weary vigil in the market-hall, and the tight-lipped, vindictive stalking to and fro of the buyers.

But her first visit was to old Benbow, the cooper, and this was always a good beginning. As they brewed their own beer, her father had a lot of business to do with him, and she was a frequent caller. Most times she took with her a rabbit, and sometimes, on special occasions, as when the old man had made some effort to defy time, a hare. But this was always hidden in the depths of a wicker basket, and she enjoyed uncovering all the accumulation of stuff on top and laying the things one by one among the shavings on the workbench, and then yanking out the hare by its hind legs and holding it up before his delighted eyes.

'Ah...'

He would look up at it with his weak eyes, for ever watering, and say no more. Then after a while he would shuffle off to a cupboard and bring out a glass, wiping it round with his sleeve.

'And now, m'dear, let's see what *we've* got.'

He would hobble off into the little back room, his body doubled, his knees bent – hobble off to where old rum casks stood in a row, a thin frill of foam, like a fungus, around the bungholes.

'Elder-bloom... for a lady.'

And he would fumble for the tap with his shaking fingers. Then he would sit down before her and watch her sip it. The old man would sit there entranced, his skin shrivelled with age, a single drop always gathering on the end of his long, beaked nose, for which he forever searched. He would sit there and watch her, his heart gladdened at her wild, exultant beauty. It blew the thin, small flame of him into life.

It was wonderful to think of this old man, well over eighty, coming down to the little workshop day in and day out, summer and winter, working, working at his barrels. He was the sixth of his line, and was the last.

'Nobody makes barrels now, m'dear, it's all gone and done with. Slap-dash... slap-dash... that's the way o' things.'

He sat there in the faint light which filtered through the

netted window, his feet buried in shavings and hung around his head the taper augurs, the adzes, a croze and downrights which he had used for sixty years. He sat there on the old 'horse', such a one as the Egyptians used, and shook his head sadly. He had an old, worn-out chivalry that clung to him like a tattered coat. It flattered Beti, who had some innate sense of the proprieties. That was how it ought to be – this separateness as between man and woman. It was the old flavour of life which was being lost.

And then he would tell her stories of his great days in the Yeomanry. He would reach up to the fireplace, where, against the soot-blackened wall, was an old, faded photograph of him in the yard of the Plough before he sailed for South Africa. He sat up there, stiff as wire to impress the camera, a seat which no man ever took, his slouch hat cocked recklessly, his bandolier around him, and his carbine held out at arm's length. The horse had come from up near her home, and he never failed to remind her of it. It gave a touch of intimacy to these unending stories, like sauce to a heavy dinner.

For it was hard going. His mind, fuddled with age, went wandering off. His lone ride across the star-clear veldt became an Odyssey; there were lions and tigers in the scrub, and turtles and crocodiles in the water-holes; pythons, brightly coloured, their coats gleaming like wet paint, infested the ground, and every imaginable bird of prey clouded the air.

But still he went on and on, and with distance the adventures multiplied; the single-handed fights were dropped like unwanted luggage, and whole skirmishing

31

parties engaged, until eventually Botha was routed when Trooper Benbow dashed out of a farmyard with a clatter, a two-horse reaper behind him.

The Boers, he would explain, thought it was a tank, and, as one, took flight to the mountains!

Beti was always glad when he got to the reaper, and the Boer War was over, for she had to get to the market-hall in good time. She always refused a second glass of the elder-bloom because it sent her head humming like bees in a lime.

The only good thing about the market was that she had her regular customers, and there was no need to worry overmuch about the prying and pawing of the townspeople. There was something furtive and dirty about it all; they would not say yes or no, but would hum and haw and grumble, would twist the gristle breastbone in their forefingers backwards and forwards; would taste the butter from her little tasting-leaf, not once, but many times, moving their jaws up and down like a cow chewing the cud, and perhaps they had lived the week through on fish and chips, though the poorer they were, then the more extravagant and finicky.

'Shin bif, shin bif, they want, but they wunna look at shin bif,' an old drover, not quite right in the head, would say, pushing his way through them, moved the while to evangelical fervour.

And the townspeople were always hostile. There was no bridge between these two worlds. They sniggered at the price of things, and always spoke as though the farmers made a huge profit on everything. Some of them were downright rude. One old man would go stamping through the hall all the morning, insulting the women who sat there on the benches, banging his stick on the stone floor to gather a crowd.

'A pretty penny they got by 'em, I'll warrant, and we can starve... and them none the wiser.'

And yet he was worth perhaps ten thousand pounds and he made it all out of the farmers, for he was a corn chandler before he retired.

But Beti did not worry about them; she had her own pride. They were 'townies' and something apart. The word 'townie' was the worst reproach that could be made. A 'townie' dressed differently, spoke differently, lived differently, and knew nothing – that is, nothing that really mattered.

The market-hall was a great draughty place, with a glass roof, like some huge conservatory. The benches ran back to back down the entire length, a hard oak seat and the bench itself like a shop counter, on which the baskets went, and on which the produce was laid out. The floor of cement had been worn shiny with the passing feet, so that it was like an ice rink. Small boys were always dropping fruit stones and apple cores on it, and staid old men would keel over flat on their backs, and there was always someone fanning one such with an old newspaper. And when the Town Clerk went through with his malacca cane, and his gardenia, someone would buttonhole him, telling him what had happened, and he would assure them that the Market-Hall Committee should be told, and he would always do so.

The market-hall floor was the cause of endless deliberations. Once they sprinkled sand over it, but the dogs – the curs and mongrels of the town, who looked upon the market-hall as their own especial province – watered it so industriously that by midday the local boardman had to come with his broom to sweep it up.

The stalls ran down the side, and above them, on their roofs, were the relics of farm sales long ago; tricycles and penny farthings, deep in dust; old churns and bedsteads; casks and corn-bins; chiffoniers and tables – all moulded with age and but half-distinguishable in the litter.

And adjoining the hall was the butchers' market, from whence came the endless chopping and shouting, and the snarling of dogs who were always darting in and out, under the trestles, in search of bones.

It was a world apart, the market-hall, for all people came there; rich and poor, the professional man and the moucher; the county folk and the mill hands in their shawls and grease. There sat the buxom farmer's wife, solid and static at her place, and beyond her the hovering, endlessly searching, brood of women from the town.

And Beti, having paid her penny tariff, took her old place and set out her baskets, hoping that the day would not be a long one. Her heart sank as the minutes went by; the place had that strange, depressing effect on her, as of a tomb, of corruption and death.

It would not be long, she thought, before her cousin came, and she would have a bit of talk with him. She liked to pull his leg and take him down a peg or two, for he thought no end of himself, and he stalked before her just like a game-cock, with his ruff up. But she could always reach that little bit beyond him, for her mind was very quick, and she could catch him out in his postures.

And yet – that was not all of him, either. It made her heart turn over to see Llew come swaggering across the hall, slashing on the benches with his stick and making the old women jump; always with a swagger, even in his walk, a certain pride within himself, a certain spring in the step, and a swing in the shoulders. She had never seen him slouch, like other people did; his spirit filled his frame and radiated it.

He was all fire and light, with a temper like a flame – a cochyn, as they called these red-heads in Wales. And with his tall, loose frame, and his hatchet face, the light dancing blue eyes, which yet could go as cold as stone, the quiff of hair rising and falling over his brow, he looked for all the world like some young, arrogant hawk, with a crest nodding.

And he always sent that exultant glow through her, that sharp, trembling catch at the stomach – and for no reason at all.

For he was her cousin and she knew all about him and the family familiarity took all the edge off things. And there was a lot to know about Llew, and a great deal of it was far from good. The latest news was that he was after a young married woman in the town, and her husband, who worked nights on the railway, had found his stick in the kitchen and had threatened to horsewhip him when he saw him. And yet he was not yet eighteen – not yet a man.

This latest story filled Beti with a vague fear and wonder. He was a man. But ach y fi how nasty it all was!

And then he came stalking through the market, his red head threading its way through the crowd. He had got a big stick this time, a hawthorn that he had cut himself, and he cracked it down between her baskets.

'There's funny you arr,' she said casually, though it had made her jump.

'Where's Mam's chicken? Come on now! She is waiting.'

'Keep cool! Keep cool!' She lifted it gently out of the basket.

He went briveting through the other basket while she was wrapping the chicken, to see what he could find.

'Have be, Llew.'

She punched him hard on the shoulder. She wanted to hurt him and she punched him harder than she need have done.

He held his shoulder and pretended to blubber.

'Fool!' she said, flushing. There was no holding him in these silly moods of his.

'What is the matter Beti fach?' He chucked her under the chin. 'There's nasty you arr today.'

She pushed the chicken into his hands but he would not go away.

'I will give you another wan in a min-nit, you see!'

He began to blubber again. Just then there was a tremendous commotion under the benches, the confused snarling and snapping of two dogs fighting. Beti lifted her feet off the ground in terror. A crowd gathered round and old men with umbrellas began furtive prodding, and a drover belaboured the dogs with a stick. A little Sealyham had leapt at a collie's neck, but the bigger dog had rolled him over in the sawdust and they were now indistinguishable in the mêlée, and there was pandemonium.

36

This was life to Llew. He rushed forward as the dogs rolled into the open, and hovering round, suddenly snatched the smaller dog by the tail and with a deft movement drew out of range. Then as the collie rushed in, he caught him by the scruff of the neck and held him on high. But the collie's long legs dangled downwards and the Sealyham, done out of the fight, leapt at them and held on, his wide jaws closing like a clamp, so that Llew held the two dogs at once.

The women began to scream, the old men renewed their attacks with umbrellas. But Llew was as cool as ice, as though it were the most ordinary thing in the world. He reached down and caught the Sealyham's front paw and squeezed it till the jaws relaxed their hold, and then, as the dog fell to the ground, gave it a lift with his boot and sent it scurrying away. The fight was over. He wiped his hands as though to have done with the whole affair, while the crowd looked on in admiration. It was life and breath to him this part of it.

When he walked back to Beti he was still very full of himself. He waited for her to say something, but she did not. She knew Llew too well.

'What is the big stick for?' she asked, getting one in.

'Mind your business... or I give it you across the back.'

'There's brave you arr! Aren't you a wan!'

'Shutapp,' he sulked. Then changing front asked: 'How is uncle?' Like her father, Llew only inquired about the men of the house; the women were just there.

'Quite well... thank you for asking.'

'I will be up soon.'

'For no good I am sure. Nothing to offer *you* there.'

He sensed her meaning, and took a lofty air. He bent down and whispered in her ear:

'I bet you I empty Llyn Llydaw. You can come. Got a lovely "otter"... best I ever made. A sackful of fish in no time!'

'There's better company, I dare say.'

'Pooh,' he said taking the slight easily. 'I am not asking twice. Please yourself, Beti fach.'

He took up the chicken and stalked away. She felt sorry afterwards that she had been so rude, but it would do him good to be taken down a peg. She would go with him to Llyn Llydaw when he asked her again in a proper way. It was a wonderful prospect, the journey over the mountain to the great tarn lying there in its frayed rim of peat, the face of it agleam. She could hear the gulls screeching as they rose in a cloud off the water and were blown up in the wind like confetti; the triumphant honk-honk of the wild geese in line above; the endlessly sluicing lap-lap among the stones, and the clear ice-cold mountain wind that swept one backwards. Llew, in some way, made the place more real. The prospect of it all took possession of her and the market-hall and the furtive paw-pawing of the people who walked endlessly round the benches were forgotten.

It was late when she was able to hurry away to the Carnegie Library to change her books. This was a ritual every Saturday after the market – the journey to the old disused factory where the library was housed. On the floors, piled up like egg crates, were boxes of books going out to the village institutes, philosophy for the most part –

Hegel and Spinoza, Schopenhauer and Locke. And Beti herself, a village girl, had read a great deal of the best fiction of Europe, for it was all there.

The librarian, all in black, would raise his head over the boxes and caw a quiet caw like an old crow:

'A good pook this wan.' And he would fondle it to him as though loth to give it up. 'What is that wan with you? *Tor-rants of Spring*! Dear me... a lovely name. *Tor-rants of Spring*!' He would push his spectacles up on his nose and heave a deep sigh.

'Sign here now,' he would say, coming back to earth, and pushing forward the ledger which he kept open with his spectacle case. 'Let us keep poetry in this old world of ours.' He would pat Beti on the back, his kindly old eyes moist. 'Let us keep our eyes on the lovely things, Beti fach. For life is a lovely thing; ah yes... a lovely thing!'

And while the free library of the town was chock-a-block with the trivial litter of a thousand books, late Victorian novels for the most part, to be picked up and read, read and dropped, this county library was like a spearhead which drove into the very quick of European culture. While in the Border towns the dramatic companies rehearsed their second-rate farces and all the rest of it, in the Welsh villages there was Ibsen and Strindberg; and while the Border townspeople were busy with the *Cingalee* and dressing up for the occasion, the Welsh choirs had Bach and *Elijah*.

But Beti did not know anything about this as she hurried to the Plough yard and the Rallt trap.

CHAPTER IV

Whether the 'jentlemens' came or not, the life of the Red Lion went on just the same. It was a pebble, one or two pebbles in a pool, and that was all. The ripple, the commotion subsided into the depths; they were there, or they were not there, and it did not matter.

For nothing changed; the old place defied change. Twmi had grown fatter and his hair had grown thin around the top, forming a brim round his head as of loose straw, but that was the only difference the years meant. The same people were there on the oak settle year after year. There was always something fresh, some small commotion, on the surface, but the life of it went very deep and was, in a sense, changeless.

But it was not the same to Beti. The whole place changed with the 'jentlemens'. They were there or they were not there; life was one thing or the other. And yet she had no reason to dislike them – not the elder men – except that they made life different. She could not forget them as her father did, they were too big a part of her world for that.

And now Mr Birbaum, warming his back against the fire, had spoken to her when she was clearing away the dinner things.

'How old are you, Beti?'

'Nearly eighteen, Mr Birbaum.' She would not say 'Sir'.

'Humph!' he said. No more than that one 'humph'.

'Tell your father I would like a word with him,' he added, and no more.

But he patted her on the back in a patronising way and winked.

'Leave it to me, Beti,' he said. She had not the least idea what he meant. But she delivered the message faithfully to her father, none the less.

He looked up from the company and said: 'He knows where I am. What you think?'

'But, Dad...' Beti wanted to know what it was all about. 'What you think?' said the old man, his gorge rising. 'You want me with brass buttons?'

It was no good to argue. But she listened from the kitchen to the time Mr Birbaum would come out and join them as he always did. It was something to do with her, she felt sure.

But the bar was full, and there was great fun going on. Wili the Hut was there now – he had been forgiven – and was talking 'big' about what the Master of the Beagles had said to him. He always talked 'big' when he had the chance, mumbling in his throat as though he had a stone in his mouth, putting his finger through the armholes of his waistcoat and lashing his leggings once or twice in emphasis.

'Shutapp man,' said Twmi in disgust. 'Leave the poor man be now,' wheezing through the bar with a trayful of drinks.

'... so daro he slaps me on the back and says "Wili"... intimate like... "you arr the best, the very best judge of a dog in the whole county".'

'Li-aar!' said Twmi nonchalantly, feeling in his corduroys for change.

'Wa-at did he say?' asked 'r hên Shacob, reaching forward his thin old head, and cupping a hand like a claw around his ear. He was a very old man and very deaf. Those who sat next to him had to repeat the talk, and there was always a process of moving up the settle as though he had the plague. But Dici Weasel was there now and there was no getting away. He showed his teeth.

'About a dog,' he shouted into the old man's ear.

Shacob was satisfied with scraps of talk, just texts, and he filled in the rest.

'Wa-at? About God?' said the old man.

Dici snorted. 'You tell,' he said to Wili. 'He won't be knowing any better, so you can tell all you know.'

'I got you now,' shouted Dan the School to Wili. 'What's a Dalmatian with you?'

'Wa-at?' said Shacob.

'Dalmatian,' shouted Dici, in a temper.

'Damnation, say you?'

'Oh, damn, yes!'

'Pooh,' said Wili casually. 'Smart you are, and all. That's not

42

a dog, man... that's a ploody gippo as comes with pegs. Think I don't know, ay?'

'Hark at that!' Dan turned triumphantly to the company. 'There's knowledge for you. Twmi... 'he shouted to the old man who had come up from the cellar, blinking at the light like an old bear. 'Twmi, what's a Dalmatian?'

'A Dalmatian!' said the old man. 'Humph!' he scratched the back of his head. 'A Dalmatian? Well, good God,' he said in a fury, 'anybody knows what a Dalmatian is, there's ignorance!'

'There you are, see!' shouted Dan. 'What did I say?'

But Wili's discomfiture was covered by the sudden entry of Moses Powell Bakehouse, with a titbit that could not wait. He slammed the door behind him, sending the rings on the curtain rattling, and rushed into the middle of the company spread around the great hearth. They all laid down their mugs in expectancy, for Moses always got the best things long before anyone else.

He was a little dark man, with a bent back and a thin unhealthy face, a sparse black moustache, furtive pouched eyes, with a touch of malice in them, and a thin sniffling nose.

'News, pooys,' waving his arms as though to gather them together, but he delayed the news, whetting their appetites and no more, until their anxiety reached a crescendo.

'Out with it, Moses.'

'Wait a bit... wait a bit,' his hands upraised as though bidding them to desist. 'Can't a man have a drink in quiet?' He lifted the mug to the light and then began to drink in

43

slow gulps, judging the effect the while. It was a supreme moment. No one could judge the news he brought, and everyone hung on his words. For the news might be trifling or it might be anything. It might be the greatest scandal that could be, for all they knew. They dared not pooh-pooh it until they heard; until then they had to treat him with respect, with reverence. It was hard to come by anything good, though there was always a chance. Until those times, which he lived for, Moses had to do with the small bits like a dog nosing out a titmouse.

But the small stuff kept his reputation alive, which was all he could hope for, and he collected the titbits most industriously, grading them according to their worth. Some were to be discarded at the end of his round, some to be passed around the square and dropped at cornel clapian but the best to be retailed at the Red Lion, for as an artist he demanded an audience.

The great events were the girls in the family way; there was nothing to touch that, both in approach and climax, but these again were graded, for there were girls and girls. The pure girl, whose reputation was untouched, at whom no gossip like mud had been splattered, who had enjoyed the sanctity of a good home and God-fearing parents, that girl whom the most malicious hand had to leave alone – that was his chance. Then he was really superb. A nod, a wink, a pause, a good deal of dry coughing into his hand and the ponderous wagging of his little head and the brushing away of a tear.

'Oh, dear. Pity it iss, great pity; white as driven snow she wass.'

'Who, man? Damn it all, be a sport now.'

'Lovely girl, she wass... fit for the best in the land. Just like a flower.'

And so he would go on and on, playing on his audience as sure as any musician on the keys. He was like an old bat in his death-like fluttering, inhabiting some dark, life-defying world of his own. And the pure, clear tumult of life he settled on as a blight.

But what was coming was small stuff, they knew. He did not make such a fuss over something really good; he knew that a good thing would sell itself. Still, they waited for him, for with Moses one never knew.

'Dai Jones,' he said after a while, brushing a hand backwards across his mouth and wiping away the drops that clung to his moustache.

They had all gathered round.

'Lost his goat,' he said.

It was the end. The company relaxed like a spring loosed.

Dai's goat was a good deal, it was true. No one had ever seen a goat before, except the one the Royal Welch Fusiliers had as mascot, the one that used to eat Woodbines. Dai had brought this thing among them for a reason no one knew and set in his by-take beyond the mill bridge, where it went round and round endlessly on a piece of rope. All the village used to go and look at it, with its ancient old man's face and its tuft of beard.

'A dirty thing, ach y fi,' they said.

But Dai refused to get rid of it. He liked to think he had an original mind, and though it was of no use to anyone, it made people talk. He had bought a Jersey cow for the same

45

reason, though the pasture was too hard and it died in a month. But no one but a man with an original mind, he said, would have thought of buying a Jersey: any fool would buy a mountain-black or a cross-bred. He had painted on his cart plate: 'David Jones, Original Farmer'.

'There's for you. Lost his goat,' said Moses to his half-hearted audience. He had missed fire and he was angry.

'Wa-at?' asked 'r hên Shacob, cupping his ear and leaning forward.

Dici looked at him sideways and snorted again. Then shouting into his ear word by word said:

'Dai Jones... lost his go-att.'

'Duw, Duw, what you say? Cut his thro-att?'

'No, man,' said Dici, his gorge rising. 'Dai... Jones... lost... his... go-att!' He pulled the old man's ear flap down as he shouted.

'Dear me, cut his thro-att, has he? Did he cut it badly?' said the old man in a maze.

'Oh, tamn. Cut his ploody 'ead off!'

Dici, white at the gills, walked over to the other side of the room and sat down under the musical box, but Twmi jumped up as if he had been sprung out of his place.

'You silly ass!' He reached under Dici's buttocks and withdrew a tin disc. 'Look what you done now.' He took it over to the light and tried to straighten it, cracking it backwards and forwards like a tin lid.

'Well, who plays it?' said Dici defiantly. 'Only the shonihois from the charabanc. It iss not music.'

'Shut your mouth app,' said Twmi, his eyes blazing. 'I say what music iss, not you.'

46

They put it on the table and Wili had got a poker and was stabbing at it, while Twmi went to the kitchen for a flat iron and then pounded at it unmercifully. But the disc was curled and cracked beyond redemption.

'There's a mess for you,' said Twmi ruefully.

'It's English, though,' said Wili, lifting the fragment with tender care.

'The English haf music, man,' said Twmi with contempt, 'How you think they sing if not, ay?'

'But no cop,' said Wili consolingly.

'Good enough, I say, for a penny-in-the-slot. What you expect, man, the *Messiah*?'

'The *Messiah*...'

They all looked to the door. Seth Rowlands had come in like a blast, beating the air with his arms and shouting. He was a little man, though thick-set, with a long head and close-cropped red hair like thin rust, a wild roving eye with a glint in it.

'Tut-tut, Seth is off!' they said. They always said 'tut-tut' when they saw him, because he was daft, though in reality, much wiser than many of them. He came from the next village, and slept in barns and lofts round about, but would never stay in any place long. He was the natural fool, with the natural's peculiar acid edge to his wit when he was provoked over far, and he needed careful handling.

But he was great company, for all that. Only once had he been before the magistrate, charged with being drunk and disorderly – he had taken a running kick at Peepy-Tom's behind – and in the court he pleaded disorderly, but not drunk, and was fined five shillings. As the sergeant, in evidence, said he had an excellent character, he took out his purse and offered to pay ten shillings, which was all he had, so pleased was he with this tribute coming from so unexpected a quarter.

And the company were glad to see him, because when they got him going a bit, he would start to sing, and he fancied himself as a musician. But of them all, only Twmi understood him: he never pulled his leg. There was a warmth in the old man's eye as he saw him, for in some strange way they were one of a kidney.

'The *Messiah*...' Seth shouted again, getting worked up. 'I tell you! Wait till next Prelim. You beat us all right in "Behold the Lamb", but, by Christ, we sing you to hell in "Glory be to God".'

'Sit down... sit down. Haf be!' said Moses. This competitive spirit as between the villages always led to trouble.

'There's only one thing in music,' went on Seth. 'You must give a note its full value, like... doh, ray, me, soh... oh... oh... oh,' he warbled, waving his hand over his head like a hawk fluttering.

' "Trumpeter, what are you sounding now?" ' said Twmi, reading from the label of the broken disc. 'Well, that's his last trump whateffer.' He flung the disc into the fire, staving it into the ashes with his heel. He was enjoying the fun, breakages or no breakages, and his face was aglow. He was like that – a thing would have to go very deep before it rankled.

'Doh, ray, me, fa... fa... fa...' went on Seth, his head up like a hen drinking, his eyes closed in ecstasy.

48

'Like an old jay,' said Twmi, jerking a finger at him.

At this stage the company always said in loud whispers how Seth had a voice of *rare* quality, and how, if he only had it trained, he would be another Ben Davies; and Seth would pretend not to hear, but clear his throat in readiness.

'Let's haf penillion now,' said Moses. The penillion was a traditional tune for the harp with the words extemporised and most often topical, and often bawdy.

> I wass haf a sister Bella
> She wass haf a South Wales fella...

'Whist: whist,' broke in Dici in alarm. 'Remember the jentlemens.'

'Nice man, Mr Birbaum,' said Moses unctuously.

'But what I can't see, now,' said Dici in his inquiring way, 'iss as how a Jew iss an Englishman.' He paused and scratched his head. 'For an Englishman can't be a Jew, now. Iesgyrn... it hass me beat, it hass.'

'They are the chosen race,' answered Moses. 'They can pick and choose, like.'

'Hush' said Wili, 'here he comes.'

Mr Birbaum came in from the door leading on to the old wing, carrying a bottle of whisky which he and Mr Shufflebotham split every night at dinner. He was a middle-aged man with a paunch which was as yet but a protuber-ance, a white creased face and ringed eyes like an owl's. He nodded affably to the company, held out his hand in protest to an offer of a seat, and took a place on a bench alongside the wall.

'How do you do sirr?' said Dici, with a nod. He was given the still self-conscious welcome of a people who could not but be polite. But the joy of the place had gone out like a fire damped.

'How hass things gone down the brook today!' went on Dici.

'Not bad; not bad. A few leetle ones. But they were taking a siesta I think.'

'Yess, yess,' said Dici looking wise. 'But I tell you, sirr, as how there's nothing to touch a coch-y-bonddu. Little black fly with a 'ackle as comes off the alders: Welsh fly, the coch-y-bonddu... gone all round the 'orrld it hass. The march brown iss goot but not *azz* goot. They eats a Welsh fly first like.'

'Vell, vell,' answered Mr Birbaum. 'It is all the same to me. The countryside is so beau-tiful.'

'Not pad,' said Dici modestly. He was upholding the conversation.

'Not bad!' answered Mr Birbaum coming alight. 'You vant to put it on the map, make it go, like the Sviss do. Nobody knows about it! Vales for the Velsh! I believe in Vales for the Velsh... but you can have too much Vales for the Velsh.'

'Yes: yes,' said Wili breaking in, in his best voice. 'Too insulated we arr... and that's straight.'

'Vhat is business vidout Nature... especially in the spring?' went on Mr Birbaum.

He beckoned to Twmi in a confidential way and led the way back to his room. Twmi shuffled after him, swearing under his breath. Mr Shufflebotham had gone to bed having tired himself out thrashing the water. Twmi stood there, his face bemused. He guessed it was something important, or he would not have gone.

'Now Toome: sit down, sit down,' Mr Birbaum began, handing him a cigar. Twmi bit the end off and spat it into the fire and then lit up. He enjoyed a good cigar: his irritation eased off a bit.

'This is a leetle business chat,' the other said almost roguishly.

'No... a little friendly chat.'

Twmi sat there, imperturbable, blowing the smoke in blue gusts around him. In awkward company he sat, immovable, lifeless. He was giving nothing away.

'About Beti...' The father's eyes narrowed and a glint like a spark came in them. 'She is wasting her time.'

'What hass she done?' asked Twmi, his voice going strange.

'No, no, Twmi.' He patted him on the back affably. 'Beti is a good girl.'

'Humph,' said the father. But the grunt was more eloquent than speech.

'You think it over,' said Mr Birbaum. He had come to the end before he had begun. The going was too hard for him. He would have liked to say what was on his mind and got it done with – that his sister in Golders Green had written him to find a country girl when he was next in Wales. Country girls were cheaper than town girls, were not so flighty, and were satisfied with half the time off. That was what there was to it.

'Service...?' said Twmi in the same voice and with just the lift of an eyebrow.

51

'Oh no,' said Mr Birbaum, relieved and affable. 'She would be quite one of the family. My sister in London has beeg house, beeg car, beeg garden. Golders Green is right in the country with its own shops, tubes, buses... everyting.

'Think it over,' went on Mr Birbaum with the same affable pat. He felt that he had gained ground, but was not sure.

'Me think it over?' said Twmi. 'It's Beti's think. It's her funeral.'

That brought Mr Birbaum's affability up sharp, but perhaps it was only Twmi's way of putting it.

'There's no hurry,' he said at the door.

'Right you arr,' answered Twmi, in that give-away-nothing tone.

He said nothing at supper until he had finished. It was his custom to have a raw onion with cheese: afterwards he carefully rinsed out his mouth with a little vinegar and then chewed a sprig of parsley.

Beti kept her eyes on her plate. She had seen her father go to Mr Birbaum and knew only too well that something was coming.

'Wants her to go to London,' he said casually. He nodded towards the 'jentlemens' wing. 'The Jew wan.'

The mother stopped dead in her stride, in the act of clearing away.

'Talk sense!' she said.

The old man was nettled.

'Chance as a skivvy. Now you understand?'

'You arr always putting things in the wrong,' went on the mother shrilly. 'What did he say?'

'What I said,' answered Twmi stolidly. 'No more: no less.'

'He could have asked me,' said the mother, her face taut.

'So he could: so he will, I daresay,' replied her husband with fine contempt.

'It's a chance,' she said tentatively. She had caught firm hold of the idea but she could only stretch out a feeler as yet.

The old man pushed his chair back.

'What you think, Beti?' her mother asked condescendingly. It was the first time they had noticed her existence.

Beti looked down at her plate, her forehead wrinkled in a frown. Her heart, which had seemed to leap up at mention of it, had now steadied: she could hear it drumming.

'I don't want,' she answered.

'There's a wan!' shouted her mother in exasperation. 'A chance like this and what she say: "I don't want". There's ungrateful you arr.'

She went on and on in her shrill high voice.

'Haf be,' roared the father, as he got up to go. 'Beti do as she want.'

The mother waited until he had gone out and then began again.

'Leave me alone, Mam,' said Beti, worn out with it all. 'I will think: I will indeed.' She was on the verge of tears.

CHAPTER V

Beti was in the yard having a 'look'. Having a 'look' meant that she was doing nothing and when her mother's shrill voice was raised, as it would be, all she could say was that she 'was having a look'.

But she did not like to be in the house these days: her mother's frown, her forced silences, were always a reproach. She was made to think that she was letting them all down, was doing something terrible, by not jumping at Mr Birbaum's offer. This thinking it over was far worse than saying no right out: it kept with her all day long like a guilty secret. The first thing when she woke up she remembered Mr Birbaum, and then it all began to work in her mind like bread rising; all day long she tried to keep it away from herself, but it always came back. There was no joy for her now – not until she said no, and then her mother would always hold it over her. So there would really be no joy ever again. And it was all because of Mr Birbaum, that nasty man. Everything served to remind her of Mr Birbaum: she had never really disliked anyone before.

His great blue limousine was backed in the coachhouse with a plaid rug thrown over its shining snout, and the old brake had been moved out into the yard for the hens to roost in it. The old cord seats were rotting in the dew and it was in a fine mess. And this was their brake! Why did her father let things like this happen? It was so unlike him.

When the big blue car started up, sending out a cloud of oily smoke into the eaves, the swallows, as one, darted out with a screech. Perhaps it was the noise, perhaps it was the smoke, or perhaps, thought Beti, they too did not like Mr Birbaum. But the little ones were left there with their naked necks and heads, like a handful of bone spoons, showing over the rim of the clay-crusted nest. If they were poisoned by the smoke who would care? Mr Birbaum and the other English 'jentlemens' were just like the smoke: they made the air smell. They took something away from it all. She stood there with a bitterness in her heart she had never known before.

Above her, over the stable door, was the gibbet – toll of gun and gin and trap – on which she had never dared look. That had been the only bad thing about her home, but now the badness was spreading like a foul breath. She forced herself to look up; why, she did not know. Clamped there, the nails deep and rusted, were the relics of many creatures once alive, now shrunk and mummified and shrivelled up in death: here a claw, there a skull; a wing nailed out with that transparent sheen of the living bird, got from the sun, still on the feathers. The mask of an old dog fox grinned down, a nail between the eyes, and the brush of another with the soft silver glint of dew in it; a hare's foot and a stoat bent double, impaled through the belly, the brown coat hanging off. There were magpies and carrion crows, old and sightless, and jays, from which the wing feathers had been torn, the wide spade foot of a badger with the earth still clinging on the claws: a hawk, a polecat.

For the first time in her life her mind went out in horror. She could not think or reason. And the fear in her, beginning as a far-off whisper, reached a shout, gathering strength as a flood, until she stood there trembling, her wide eyes staring and her mouth dropped open and moving helplessly. Panic had come to her, she would have screamed but no voice came.

'Beti! Beti!'

Her cousin had come into the yard on his bike. He jumped off and slid it along the wall and rushed to her.

'There's a fright you give me. What's the matter, Beti fach? What's the matter now?'

Llew caught her by her hands and chafed them in his own and turned her round to face him.

She stared at him, unknowing, with her large, lustrous eyes.

'White as a sheet, you arr! Who has hurt you?' He pivoted around with that quick animal poise of his, his body braced, hands clenched, his eyes, steel blue, going hard.

There could have been no one like Llew just then. His violent young self all aglow, quick and resolute, with that instinctive positive way of his; he brought her back to herself as no one else. She felt the life in him, in his hard grasp as he caught her hands and pressed them upwards: then a hand on the nape of her neck pressed her head down roughly.

She felt ashamed of herself now. She wanted to cry but she would never cry before him. Instead she bit her lip, her face working. And all the while he stood there, peering at her, his face bemused.

'You can leave go now,' she said in a pout.

'Nearly went off on the spot,' he rejoined, not knowing how to take her.

'I did not then,' she said, stamping her foot. 'Go away.'

'Pussy ke-eatt, pussy ke-eatt,' he said teasing. He chucked her under the chin and then jumped back.

'Go away, will you?' she said. She ran after him and tried to kick him but he caught her by the foot and made her hop about the yard.

'Where's uncle?' he asked.

'Find out!'

He went to untie the fishing rod from the cross bar of his bicycle.

'No you can't, then!'

'For why?' He looked up at her in question.

'Because *they* haf come.'

'Daro!' he said, striking the butt on the floor. 'My luck, of course.' He stood there pondering a moment. 'I can sit by the brook,' he said. 'There's no harm.'

'No, Llew, don't,' she pleaded. 'Dad will be fine and angry.'

'It's not his brook,' he said fiercely.

'Who then?'

'God's.' He looked down his nose at this bit of sanctimoniousness.

'There's swank,' she said, catching hold of the end of the rod case and tugging at it.

'Funny you arr,' he replied, swinging her round.

'I'll tell,' she laughed.

He suddenly let go the rod and caught her round the waist and then, crooking an arm under her knees, lifted her off the ground. She kicked and pulled his hair but he stalked across the yard and dropped her in a truss of straw in one of the barns.

'That's for you,' he said covering her up. 'Too frisky you arr.'

'Llew,' she shouted. 'I'll tell you something.'

'Yess. I know,' he said guessing her dodge and piling on more straw.

'Just look,' she said, with the straw in her hair. She was happy again, beyond thought; her eyes, the index to her whole self, alight with joy and with that glint in them that came when she had forgotten herself.

'Beti,' he said, breathless as a thought struck him. 'Go and find the spear. That's a girl.'

The spear was a popular weapon among poachers. It was shaped like a trident, with three prongs, and was made by the local blacksmith at a fixed price of eighteen pence, though there was a bigger and more expensive size for sewin and salmon. The haft was usually made of ash, giving more pliancy on the hard bed and being easier on the wrist. With ash you could follow through on a fish, how-ever hard he lay, and then with a flick of the wrist he was out on the bank. But the spear was only of real use on a gravel bottom.

'No,' said Beti. 'There's wicked you arr. Like a monkey up to tricks.'

'It's in the loft with the nets,' he said. 'Think I don't know, ay?'

'They're all over the brook; yess indeed.'

'Like two old sows in a trough,' he replied bitterly. 'There's the mill-pool, whateffer.'

'No. Nor there,' she said pensive.

'He's gone smash,' he said, as a thought struck him.

'Stale news.'

'That will fetch him down a peg, I bet you.'

'For shame, Llew!' She was standing there on one leg, stroking the old oak post of the door, and her mind had gone off.

'Why for shame?'

Beti did not answer. It was no good answering.

'Beti! Beti! Where arr you?' It was her mother's voice, high and shrill from inside the house.

'Yes, Mam,' she shouted and went tripping off.

'I'll be waiting,' said Llew. He was going into a sulk. Beti and he were growing apart – or growing closer together. He did not know which. But they were children no longer and, as childhood went, something had gone out of their lives, leaving this uneasy space that worried him. They could not romp and play as they had done, always this uneasy quiet which would descend like a blight making them for the

59

time self-conscious and unsure. It was as if a stave had been driven in between them.

But Llew never allowed thought to worry him. He took life as it came. When things did not work out to his liking he sulked: and he was sulking now. He kicked his boots irritably against the stable door and then, seeing the big limousine, he wrote a rude word in the dust across its body, then drew a pig, giving the curly tail an extra flourish. They had spoilt his day for him.

But when Beti came running out again, and with her hat, his face lit up as it always did on seeing her.

'Fine and nice,' she said. 'Where you think? Dai the Tweed!'

'I haf not come for to run errands,' he said haughtily.

'Oh Llew! There's nasty you arr today.' She linked her arm through his and half pulled him away.

But he was glad all the same, partly because he felt the old, intimate feeling for her welling up in him again, and partly because he had a few private investigations to make at the old tweed mill, having to do with the run of fish at the weir and such like. Also there were three hours to dinner, and if his uncle saw him doing nothing he would set him digging the garden or slicing swedes on the cutter, jobs in which the young man took no special delight.

So off they set, the little knot of resentment in him unloosening before her light-hearted laughter. She seemed to take on the colour of her surroundings; she was like this spring morning itself, all sunlight and shadow – spring with the bewildering promise of better things, of a life to be.

The tweed mill was over the watershed, a mile down the

road and then a lane's length away from it. It lay there quiet and cloistered in a shroud of green, the beeches high up around it like a fringe, and then the whole track of the brook overloaded with foliage. A few dwarf oaks like hair lay along the banks, which were lush with growth-hazel and blackthorn, as yet tipped with green, and the long rich grass and ferns. Like the village, it seemed an oasis in the bare upland country, which ran off into the shrouded mountains round about. From above you would have seen this slot of green and the tumbling waters of the brook, sprayed up like lace, and the old buildings with their moss-encrusted roofs like great stones by the brookside.

The mill was very old, how old no one knew. There were two buildings, the factory and the mill proper. They were coated with a soft white wash which peeled and caked, and the little row of cottages before the factory, in which were the finished goods, were white too. They seemed to have sunk into the ground and staggered back, like a man in a bog, and were so low that you could put your hands on the slates.

Here were made the hand-woven Welsh tweeds as they had been made for centuries. But now visitors in big cars sometimes pulled up and made a tour round the old place, as though it were a menagerie. Around the factory the brook was spread like a hand with the fingers out, with the gleaming water tumbling over the rock. Out in the sun were the baskets of wool that had been brought in from the mountain and which was waiting to be sorted. It was graded into six lots but only the first two were kept, the others going to Bradford.

The wool came from the little mountain sheep that lay out on the mountain uplands in all weathers, with no ornate fleece, handfuls deep, like the Border breeds, but one made hard and pliant and durable with a texture compact of the very wind and air, the rich pure air of the mountain. And the dyes, too, were local and older than anyone knew. Within, it was being spun and carded with the rich sweat-smelling air of the fleeces, heavy as a cloud, all about.

But it was to the mill that they went, which lay farther down the brook and across a wooden trellis bridge which shook beneath them.

Llew leaned over the rail, his quick eye taking in all the water. The spring sun went down into its depths, coming through the shrub in spirals of light. The sunlight within the water was a very wonderful sight which kept him there. Like quivering twigs, with an almost unseen tremble of the fins, the little mountain trout were breasting the current, now and then rising in a flash to a fly and then dropping back to their places in the stream. Beside them, as they stood there, the old wheel was gushing, the water dripping from the old timbers and sparkling in the sunlight; down the millrace it came with a squelch, churned into foam, and with slow deliberate rushes. They had to shout to make themselves heard.

'Oh, Llew,' she said. 'I don't want to go. Indeed I don't.'

'Go where?' His thoughts were elsewhere and he paid no attention.

'London.'

He had not heard her, so interested was he in what lay

beneath him. She shook his arm, hurt that he should pay no attention to words of such awful import.

'LONDON.' She shouted in his ear.

'London?' he answered, uncomprehending. He turned and faced her. 'Pulling my leg, ay?'

'Indeed! It's Mr Birbaum.'

'Are you going?' he asked in the same matter of fact way.

'No,' she said. 'No, no, no!' stamping her feet on the bridge and sending down a shower of moss.

'There's daft,' he said with a fine contempt. 'Watch me stay!'

That was Llew all over; she ought not to have told him. But she was hurt all the same.

They went into the mill. There were two looms, one at each end, but they both stopped when they entered. The looms looked the same, but the difference was profound: the one was 'hand' and the other 'machine'. The 'machine' came off the water wheel which was regarded as 'power'. An old woman weaved there, a fringe of grey hair dropping over her long white face. She had quick, bird-like eyes which gave the face life and were for ever lighting on the shuttle which clattered above her. She was Mrs Evans, a widow and was very old. She had been at that loom for fifty years and because of the movement of her foot on the treadle was known as Mrs Evans-Lightfoot.

But Llew went straight over to the hand loom where was seated a great friend of his. He was a little man, dark as night, with a long nose and eyes so quick and brilliant that they never seemed to settle. Watkin William Williams – Wati as he was known as, lived at a little cottage 'Penygraig'

63

halfway up the mountain, with an ever-increasing brood which were allowed to run wild. No doctor had ever seen them and no one but the district nurse had helped them into the world, yet there were no finer children to be seen. Wati never spoke of them – they 'belonged'. His hands were very thin and long but moved with a quiet strength, and he moved in the same sure way.

He was quite a famous man in his way, for he was accounted the best fisherman in all that part of the country. His rod was a poor thing of bamboo such as children use, with a self-made hazel switch as an end piece, but with it he could drop a fly where and how he liked, and as lightly as thistledown. The foreman, Dai Tweed, was accounted the second-best fisherman, or the best, according to the school of thought. This rivalry which was thrust on them broke down a certain familiarity. The foreman, having more money, could send to London firms for flies, whereas Wati tied his own, and was therefore always glad to lay hands on a woodcock or a cock pheasant or such like. But when they had a killing pattern they always shared it between them.

In the late summer when the sewin came up from the sea and the pool below the weir was alive with shadows, the water at its head in a commotion with the leaping and splashing, they would forget old rivalries and hurry down.

'Wati! Quick man. They haf come!'

They would plunge in, with net and spear, into this shimmering multitude which floundered below the weir, waiting for the fresh that would enable them to leap up in their knowledgeless search for the spawning grounds, and commit great slaughter. Sometimes there would be a pile of fifty or sixty fish on the bank at a time, which would be smoked in cottage chimneys and so last out the winter.

Beti saw with real pride the greeting they gave Llew: he was one of them. It was just a toss of the head and a gleam in the eye – no ceremony. If the most famous person in the world had come in, Wati would have made a dumb show of respect: but because Llew was a *real* sport – had his own native instinctive touch, that untaught thing – and was moreover a lad with a fine edge to his spirit, he had a place in his heart. It was something unspoken and understood, but Beti noticed it.

Wati was telling a story to his boss with great emphasis and much waving of hands. He was very excited about it all. Dai, who was much taller and lighter, slower in movement, was leaning against the loom, nodding pensively as he tasted it.

It seemed that Wati had been asked to show a doctor from London the stretch of brook, which he did gladly enough, in anticipation of the free drink at the end of it all.

'No good at all, man,' he went on, imitating his casts, 'but diawch, what a rod! Like – like whipped silver; ten pound I bet! Two hours he was at it. But mind you – a real jentleman. Waders he had, and he pulls the flies out with a pincers. There's a toff for you. Not wan word did he say and I was glad, like. What was I, plain Watkin Williams and board school education, to say to a man like that – a *real* toff, see? Well, we get to Tynwrta pool and wan comes at it with a splash would go ten miles. Oh tamn, he strikes too hard!'

Dai leaned back as though released. 'Tut, tut,' he said.

'You wait,' went on Wati, his eyes alight. 'More to come. What did he say, ay? What you think? "Arglwydd mawr! Uffern dân! Diawl â myto i!" Tamn it all: a ploody Welshman for you, and not a toff at all.'

The little man crashed his fist on the loom and spat in his annoyance.

They all sat back and roared with laughter.

'There's for you,' said Wati ruefully. 'Two hours and "sirring" him all the time.'

'Too bad,' said Dai, serious. 'These London-Welsh looks just like jentlemens though. Fery funny!'

'Well, I tell you something,' broke in Llew. 'Beti here iss going to London.'

'Who said?' Beti blushed to her neck.

'There's the chance for her,' said Llew.

'Never,' said Wati in admiration. 'Well, you take it, Beti. Fine place London. I wass there in the Army – passing through like. You know The Load of Hay – first public on the left just past the lamp post. There's a place for you! Bar all the way round and no spitting, no.'

'Well, Beti,' said Dai, speechless. 'There's posh for you.'

'Suppose I don't want,' answered Beti, timid in all this commotion.

'Oh, tamm that!' said Wati, exasperated. He was starting the loom again. 'Fine place Wales – to come back to. Don't you be daft now, Beti; you do as I say.'

But Mrs Evans had come over, gathering the shawl about her bent shoulders.

'There's Welshmens,' she said in a fine frenzy. 'For shame

66

on you I say. Cymru am byth indeed. Come on, Beti fach,' she went on, putting her arm about her, 'leave these nasty old men. Ach y fi!'

She led the way to her loom, where she had a little blue tin can of hot tea, and she poured out a cup. Beti stood there head up and lips atremble. She was on the point of tears. It hurt her to hear the men talk like that.

'Never mind bach. Sit you down.' She stroked the girl's tumbled hair with her old hand.

'There iss only wan thing, Beti fach, in all this wide 'orld. Life iss too soon as it iss. Oh, bach be happy!' Her keen blue eyes kindled at the thought. Then she looked out through the old broken panes to where the beech boughs were plunging in the spring wind, and then beyond them again as into distance. 'I wass happy,' she said; no more. Then with a clatter she set the loom going and pretended to be busy.

'There, there. There's soft I am.' She tried to reach at a tear with her loose elbow, but it avoided her and trickled slowly down her face.

On the way back Beti did not speak. Llew was examining a fly that Wati had given him and then, since he had no cap, hooked it into the inside lapel of his jacket.

'What's gone wrong?' he said at last, when this important business was finished.

'Why must you go and tell?' answered Beti too hurt for words.

'Pooh. No offence.'

'It will be all over the place now,' said Beti.

'Well?' he went on irritated. 'If it was me now....'

'It would be *quite* different,' Beti answered bitterly.

'Well I never.' He was genuinely surprised. He was not going to make it up to Beti, all the same, over so small a trifle. They walked on in silence.

'You arr too high strung,' he said as a final shot, remembering the reproach that was always flung at her. 'Time you grew up it iss.'

They were just in time for dinner when they got back. The midday meal, except on special days, was taken in the taproom at the far end. Twmi thus presided over two worlds at once, his family, and the men who dribbled in, and the talk went backwards and forwards like a shuttlecock.

Eating with him was a rite. He dispensed with table manners; there was no nibbling and sipping, sipping and nibbling. He would stick a bib under his neck, unloosen his waistcoat, and holding his knife and fork upwards, wait for the dish as though the self had gone out of him. Broths were his favourites – the vegetables straight out of the earth. There was some other self to him that Beti only guessed at, but often and often, as she would catch this glimpse of him, wiping the wet earth off the turnips or parsnips, his face ageless and, as it were, empty, the thought would come to her that in some way her father was a great man.

But today they were having tatws llaeth, which was a great treat. It was the Welsh dish of new potatoes dropped into a bowl of buttermilk and eaten with a spoon. The potatoes were there, with the skins on them, the steam rising, and a great dish of buttermilk from the dairy was ready to be ladled out.

Twmi looked up as the lad entered in that intimate way

of the family. He was proud of him in his heart, but he took great pains not to show it.

'Hi gwas!' he shouted. 'You watch!' He waved the ladle accusingly.

The lad, who never knew what was coming next, and to whom one warning was as good as another, took his place sheepishly by the wall.

'I warn you,' said Twmi again. 'You got a rod in pickle for you gwas.'

'Have be,' said the lad, fencing.

'A marked man you arr. You watch Mathias, the keeper, that iss all. I say no more.'

He wiped his hands sententiously as though having done with the whole business.

'You're a wan to talk. I tell you something too. You watch Peepy-Tom I say.'

'Now then! None of your cheeks.'

'Yess, indeed, the boy iss right. Lose your licence you will for every tramp there iss. Where arr we then?' broke in the wife.

'Cau dy geg!' Twmi shouted banging the ladle on the table. 'I will not be spoke to in my house. You hear?'

A storm was brewing. Beti sat mute and silent in her place, bowing her head before it. What a morning it had been! Llew was a regular storm-cock, wherever he went there was sure to be trouble. The least word and he was all a-bristle.

But at that moment their attention was distracted. That moving, ever changeable life at the inn, which was life to Twmi, came up like a wave and engulfed so small a thing as this table cross-talk.

69

Old Shacob had come in, and on his heels Dici, kicking his boots against the step to loosen the heavy mould that clung to them.

Dici, for want of another listener, shouted to the old man 'There iss rain on the way for sure.'

He had cleared his throat to shout it again but Shacob unbuttoning his coat, took out a tin trumpet from an inside pocket.

'What you say?' He aimed the free end, after much skirmishing, at his companion. Dici was so alarmed that he forgot his bit of talk.

'What iss that thing with you?' he said. He took a step forward and tapped it suspiciously with his finger nail.

'No need to shout,' answered the old man casually. 'It do deafen me.'

This was too much for Twmi, who had left the bosom of his family to join in.

'A bugle!' said Dici. 'Wonders never cease. What for iss that thing?'

The old man's knobbled head shook as though it were on wire; he rocked his stick backwards and forwards.

'It iss comfort whateffer,' he said, beating time with it and fixing them with his old rheumy eyes. 'It iss like this. Ever since Marged Ann go on Sunday school treat to Aberystwyth....'

'Go on, man,' said Dici.

But the old man was only pausing for breath. 'Every morning, eleven o'clock, she goes down to siop for two pennyworth of ginger nuts. All right, you say. But wait now. What happen?' His voice went up into a thin wail. 'I get crumbs in my yeahs all day after – like splinters they iss.'

He waved the trumpet aloft in triumph. No one had ever seen him like this before.

'Ay,' broke in Dici unconvinced. 'But you *hearr* her now.'

The old man shook his head knowingly. Then he felt in his waistcoat pocket for a little cork, and winked, solemn as an old owl.

'To turn a deaf yeah,' said Dici in admiration. 'There's wisdom for you!'

'Wa-at?' said Shacob, fumbling for his trumpet.

'To turn a deaf yeah,' shouted Dici.

'Ay,' answered Shacob. 'It iss better that way.'

Twmi had stood there, hands in his pockets, back to the fire, with no word said. But it was as if he was absorbing it all, his head up, the old shadowed look in his eyes. There was only the suggestion of a smile, brief as a passing shadow, on his face.

He went to get their drinks, and when he returned he carried a dinner plate on which the 'jentlemens' had deposited their morning catch. He came in, holding it before him, and then very gently with thumb and forefinger lifted up the fish one by one.

'Not a trout among them.' Then recollecting, he added: 'Ay. Just wan, and he too young to know better.'

He spread them around in a circle with a gesture of contempt.

'Samlets,' he said with a toss of the hand.

The samlet is the fry of the salmon before it leaves the spawning ground for the sea, brightly marked and spotted but with black bars down its sides. It is no larger than a sprat and always ravenous.

'There's a five pound fine for every wan,' said Dici.

But Twmi was still looking at the plate.

'Snatched from the breast!' he mused. Then coming back to himself he turned to Dici.

'Will you be having any salmon roe with you now?'

Salmon roe is the most deadly bait for trout, and is prohibited by law.

'A jar or two maybe,' said Dici knowingly. 'For them?' He jerked a thumb towards the 'jentlemen's' wing.

'For them!' answered Twmi with ill-concealed disgust. 'Fly they iss.' He dismissed their orthodox fishing with a casual nod.

'Ay,' said Dici, 'jentlemens always ketch fish the way no one else does. Part of the game.'

Just then there was a great commotion in the yard. The whole roomful of people, as one, shot out through the door. It had so happened that the 'jentlemens', returning to lunch had left their rods standing against the yard wall, and one of these rods was being trailed around with much flapping and clucking by Twmi's big Leghorn cockerel. The rest of his harem, a motley of Plymouth Rocks, Wyandottes, Orpingtons and game birds, were following him at a distance, their necks stretched out, their heads cocked. And the rod went careering away in a series of jerks, now straightened, now sprung double, while the reel kept screeching.

It was Llew who, his eyes dancing at this fresh excitement, ran forward and put his foot on the butt and then, following the line along in his hands, clasped the bird in the midst of its contortions and brought it back under his arm.

It had swallowed the hook, and Twmi, seeing at a glance what had happened, took out his clasp knife and carefully slit the gullet downways with one deft movement, drew out the hook that way, and then turned the bird loose, very little the worse for its adventure.

He held the hook up before him; a red brandling worm, ringed around, was wriggling on the barb.

'Uffern dân,' roared Dici, beside himself. 'There's a funny fly for you.' He held the pit of his stomach. 'Fly they iss!'

'Ay,' said Twmi, his face empty. 'This wan's a dung fly.'

To Mr Birbaum, who came running out from behind the house in a flurry, he said:

'We saved the rod.' He handed him the split cane. 'The fly iss in a bad way.'

He tweedled the hook in his fingers with the worm still wriggling.

'You want a lead shot on this wan,' he went on, 'to weight it down a bit. They takes it low down, see.'

Mr Birbaum laughed a little nervously. It was Twmi's way, he thought.

'I vill pay for the bird,' he answered, at a loss for words.

'Get away man,' said Twmi affably. He cocked a thumb over his shoulder to where the bird was gaping, a ring of hens around him. 'Back at work in a bit you see!'

Mr Birbaum laughed again and took his rod away with him: the company dribbled back into the inn.

'There's rude you arr,' said his wife. 'Haf sense!'

'Hell to them,' said Twmi stolidly, as he planted his feet down.

CHAPTER VI

Beti had been churning, but the butter would not 'break'. The old blue painted churn, with its bright brass fittings, had been going round and round for an hour. It was hard work, too, for one so slight, but she did not mind this. The dairy, stone-flagged, with an old latticed window with a wild elder before it, was the quietest place in the house.

She could think about all sorts of things there, because when she was churning there was nothing to do but think. The body went lax, but for the weight on the one arm, and the mind went floating off. The trouble was that it went leaping about like a flame in the wind, no sooner touching one thing than it was off to another. There was no weight to it at all; it went off into space.

It was only when the butter did not 'break' after an hour or so that she dropped out of this fantastic place and came down to earth like a stone. You *felt* the butter as it 'gathered', the solid weight of it on the handle of the churn, on the pressure on the palm of the hand. The exhilaration of that moment, so long awaited, was one that neither time nor custom ever destroyed. But when it did not 'break' all sorts of doubts and worries came crowding in, breaking up the peace of it all.

And now the butter did not 'break', but Gwenno would be down soon to take her turn. She was the village girl who had come in as extra help – broad as a bullock with strong rough hands and a round, red face, raw and ripe as a pippin. Gwenno had no fears at all; nothing worried her.

Beti wished she was like Gwenno; she felt that her mother wished so too. But her father never reproached her by word or look, though the Tudors were all as sturdy as oaks. But then it was no good thinking of her father; there was no beginning and no end to him.

The old churn squelched away. It had been a hard week and she was very tired. The 'jentlemens' made a lot of extra work, and, yet the routine of the farm, of the house, went on just the same. Monday was the washing day. There was a great cistern in the yard cut out of solid stone and fed by a spout from a spring. The lead spout was knocked sideways and diverted into the yard and the great cistern filled with water from the boiler. The three women would stand around patting and clouting the clothes as the Breton peasants do. It was the same summer and winter, even though the yard cobbles were filled up with ice. And then there was all the mangling and the ironing.

Wednesday was brewing, but this was the men's affair, although the women had always to be ready to give a hand.

Her father would stand, knee deep in malt, a shovel in his hand and the sweat pouring down his face. The mash was steeped from a great copper boiler, and all day long the steam rose up from the brewery door like a cloak blown upwards. It was the real Welsh cwrw, pure and wholesome, with a tang to it all its own. There was no coddling with, no chemical in, that brew. What the earth gave went into it – that and the clear spring water. When it was all over the mash was tipped out into the pigs-kit, and the pigs made the night sound with their snoring, lying there in a drunken stupor until far into the next day.

It was always made on Wednesdays in nice time for the church bells to ring over it. This was a custom always observed. But there was only one bell, and that did not always ring. And it was not unusual on a Sunday morning to see Twmi, having waited an hour to peg the barrels, rush down the village in his shirt sleeves hitching up his braces as he ran. He would hammer on the door of Job the Grave until it shook.

The old sexton, as like as not busy on a football competition, would raise his steel spectacles and peer through the curtains to see Twmi beside himself, and shouting.

'Cot tamn it all, man, haf you no respect for the Sabbath? Go and pull bell this minnit.'

Baking always followed the brewing the next day. The barm which was skimmed off the brew had been saved – for nothing was ever wasted at the Red Lion. The barm and the wholemeal and the old brick oven deep in the wall, made hot with blazing gorse, gave the bread its own flavour. There was none like it. Some of the white powdered ash that the besom had not cleared clung to the loaves.

All these things the townies thought very novel, though they were as old as time. They could travel across England in a day in their motor cars – as some of them did – and yet they would come and stare and brivet about the old place as though it were all very wonderful. Little wonder Twmi treated them with contempt.

Churning came last of all, and that was why Beti was so very tired. And the next day the 'jentlemens' were going and she knew what that meant. She would have to say yes or no, now – and no would be as bad as yes. There would be no peace any more. She had tried not to think about it and sometimes for a whole day she would almost succeed in pushing it out of her mind. It would keep coming back in gusts.

As the time drew on this feeling became worse until now she felt really sick with dread.

If her father would only let her know what he was thinking. He said nothing. Was it that he did not want to quarrel with her mother, to continue to ignore her: or was it that he did not care? Or was it that, resolute as he was himself, he had a fear of giving advice, was afraid of feeling, and preferred to play the fool?

But Gwenno came in and broke up her reverie.

'There's funny,' she said, giving the handle a twist and feeling for the butter. 'That's twice in a month it iss. Witched we arr for sure.'

'Hush,' replied Beti. She did not want her mother to hear.

'And the new heifer lame,' went on Gwenno, her eyes wide open. 'You know as well as me Beti,' she said in reproach.

'You try. It will come. Only slow – that's all.'

Gwenno was not reassured. But this chance of a bit of talk with Beti was too good to be missed.

'Look,' she said. 'Fine and nice!'

She fumbled at her neck and drew up from her bodice a ring, hung there on a piece of packing thread.

'Why don't you wear it?'

'Pooh. Dad would have me packing I tell you.'

'Who iss he then?' asked Beti.

'He works on the haulage,' said Gwenno proudly. 'A real toff!'

'Be careful Gwenno! Toffs are the worst.'

'Oh Beti fach,' she laughed and put her arms around her. 'You talk as if you know.' She began to laugh outright. 'You arr a wan, you arr. So com-ik!'

'Gwenno... Don't do anything.'

Gwenno bristled.

'Do what if you please?'

'Anything,' said Beti again, at a loss for words. 'Wait, Gwenno. Only wait! There iss plenty would like you, indeed there iss.'

'Oh, I see!' replied Gwenno drily. 'Like all the others arr you? If he iss English, well what? Who arr you to say? A jentleman he iss. Yess, yess! And I am going to be a lady.'

She fondled her engagement ring in her coarse red hands and lifting her print blouse, dropped it down again into its place and held it there.

Beti said nothing. She looked very pathetic standing there and Gwenno's heart was touched.

'Beti fach,' she said softly. 'There's sorry I am. Just fancy – old friends falling out.'

She patted Beti on the back consolingly.

'But you go, too,' she went on, suddenly serious. 'Wait indeed! I like that. I ask you now – wait for what? A nice place to wait in, this! Till we arr old Beti, and worn out. Yr hen gaseg that does both things. There's your waiting for you, in a nut-shell!'

Gwenno caught hold of the churn handle and gave it one or two vicious swings in her anger.

'You go now,' she said over her shoulder. 'They will be shouting any minnit.'

Beti walked back into the house, sad at heart. Gwenno was the last person she would have thought of to talk like this. They were all saying the same thing – her mother, Llew, Wati, Dai; everyone except her father and he said nothing.

It might be that he was worried – but about what? Their financial position was not good, but it was better than many. Farming had gone to pieces there, as everywhere else, and the most that Twmi, himself a fine farmer with a native pride in all he touched, could hope for was not to lose money. There was the inn, that just pulled along on its ordinary custom, though a single false step and there would be no renewal of licence at the next brewster sessions. It was the visitors, big and small – the people whom he despised to the depths of his soul – who stood between him and the bankruptcy court. That was the false position he was in – to be a monkey-up-a-stick to the people who had

79

the money to spend. And if he could suffer fools gladly, thought Beti, then surely she could.

The old way of things was ending; she had come at the end of one age and the beginning of another. Wales would be the last to go – but it was going. Even the old tweed mill no longer relied on the farmers around, but on foreign royalties and the English aristocracy, and people like Mr Birbaum who had out-grown readymades. The flour mill had gone because of the multiple shops which were coming into the market towns, with their self-raising flours and all the rest of it.

Perhaps all the young people were right to get out – to save themselves while the blood was young, and they had the strength to do things; Llew, who had his eye on the main chance, and not Evan the Mill, who could not stand the pace. Perhaps these were the truthful ones after all – the ones who did what was best. Beti always saw a thing fairly and straight like her father, but it made her very sad.

Her father was just going out into the fields when she went in. He had been up since early morning at the lambing, and was off again.

'Let me come, Dad?'

She suddenly felt a desire to be with him: she felt more sure of herself that way.

'You stay and help your mam,' he shouted from the door.

'Only this once,' she pleaded.

'I say no. No iss no.' He softened and added. 'Be a good girl now.' He gave the pony a dig.

He was out in the road, his dogs around him, when he shouted back:

'Here's company for you.'

Her father smiled in that dry way of his. They had their own humour which they could transfer one to the other, often without a word spoken. 'He's jumping up for joy,' he shouted as he gave the mare a touch with the crop and rode away.

But Beti in her heart was very fond of Ben the Post, and that was what her father meant. He was an old man with steel spectacles and two or three days' growth of beard, which clung to his face like hoar frost. His eyes were very sad and always occupied. He was always complaining. His eldest brother was a professor at one of the great American universities and one of the world's great authorities on Celtic research, while his second brother was a distinguished figure in the church and had been for years in the running for a bishopric – and Ben, the youngest, was a postman. They said the brains had given out when they came to him, but that was not really true, for he was, in his way, a great scholar. He had once written a paper on Lotze's theory of reality during the Gilchrist lectures, which had been warmly commented on by some big man.

As a philosopher, he never divulged the post, which was a great loss, for it was the best part of local gossip; but to atone for it he was always prepared to enter at great length on his aches and pains, which were not of great interest to anyone but himself.

And he began right away, as Beti brought him the beer.

'Oh dear,' he said, 'people do make a fuss – and for what? Another letter I got this morning.' He fumbled in his breast pocket for the official letter. 'Twelve miles round

81

sometimes, and for why? You want to know? Eight full miles sometimes iss what – tamned old circulars about pills for thinning, and pills for thickening, patience medicines and whatnots. Hay-pennies every wan! Up the hill to Pwllglas, down again: up, down. There's a life for you. O tamn I said – post offices or no post offices. I tie a bundle of the nasty old things to tail of the old red cow on bottom meadow, and she take them up with milk, or ska-tair them to the four winds. O tamn! More letters from post offices. Complaints something awful!'

He stroked his hand over his chin meditatively.

'All for nasty old pills,' he said. 'Ach y fi.'

Beti always had to listen to something like this. Her natural sympathy would set the old man going, and he had to have his head until he had finished. But it took her out of herself.

'And these poots now, what the post office gives. Postmens iss not fairies I know, but just look! There's hog nails if you like!'

He stamped them on the floor in his annoyance.

'These old tarred roads and my bad knee and all. Bang-bang; thump-thump she goes against the good wan. Diawl you know what! I gets wild! I lifts the good wan and I gives her such a clout.'

He took a long gulp out of his glass now that he had worked off his annoyance. He brushed his hand backwards across his mouth and heaved a deep sigh. Then he said,

'What iss this Beti – about you going?'

'I never said, Mr Evans,' she answered, looking at the floor. She felt the tears coming to her eyes.

'Humph,' he said, but no more. He continued to look into the fire.'

'It iss hard to know. There iss always two sides. Yess,' he said as though to himself. Then he addressed the fire. 'Haf you had a think?'

'Had a think! But it iss what other people think.'

The old man looked up for the first time. 'No, Beti fach, it iss not that way at all. Not a bit like that.'

'When you were a young man, Mr Evans...?'

'Ay. A long time ago for sure.'

'When you were a young man you could have gone?'

'I won't say yes. I won't say no.'

'And been famous like your brothers?'

'I won't say *that*,' he said without looking up. 'You arr fishing Beti now, I can see.'

'And you did not go. Why iss that?' She was beyond herself, twisting and untwisting her hands.

'Peace now Beti fach. Peace. A grand word peace. Means nothing in a way; silly old word. I, a silly old man too.' He held up his hands in a gesture. 'It iss the way of things, Beti. Silly again you say? All right! But truth, Beti.'

He brought out his little broken clay and twirled a finger in the bowl. He did not look up.

'My brother – a famous man! No doubt, whateffer, I suppose, about *that*.' He stopped and looked hard at the fire. 'Comes home from America now and then – five years, ten years – no matter. Funny hat on his head – like a bow-lair gone squash. I go meet him at the junction. Famous man my brother! He takes a look up the old valley and the old hiraeth comes in his throat; words stuck halfway! He can smell the old air and the old wind blowing down it.'

83

The old man wagged his grey head as he spoke. The words came hard.

'He goes back, Beti. End of story – he goes back!'

His head went backwards and forwards.

'Beyond you and me, Beti. Some must go – and for why? Now all must go – and for why? Progress? May be! There is no pushing back the sun, Beti fach.'

He sat looking at the fire for some time.

'We old people – marrow all gone shrivel. Out of it we arr. The young wans know these days. Go here, go there for why? No breath to stop – off I must go...'

He moved his elbows like the piston of a steam engine and waved his hand at an imaginary crowd.

'Not stopping this station...'

He waved his hand to the platform in a final gesture. His arms went faster and faster as the express roared through. 'No time for you,' he shouted to the passengers he had left behind. Backwards and forwards went his arms.

'True Beti. Why for you laugh? All I say Beti,' and he was serious again. 'All I say iss – Nature she iss not an ex-press. No, no, Beti. Stopping at *all* stations she iss – or there iss a *nell* of a smash.'

He had finished his speech – one of the longest he had ever made. But the accompaniment to the parable, particularly the express train, had made him thirsty, and he emptied his glass at a gulp, fumbled for his stick and moved off to the door.

''Y negeneth i', he said as a last word. 'A lovely girl, you arr. Yess, yess! Lovely as the young spring herself.'

He reached a hand up for his eyes but his spectacles were in the way.

'There's an old fool for you,' he said, lashing his boots with his stick. He thrashed himself as though to drive out his foolishness. He slung his bag around him and then walked into the door. He fumbled for the latch with much cursing and then was off along the road without a word.

'Express train – no time to wait!' Beti laughed at the memory of it. But Ben was serious and Beti, after the laughter was done, became serious.

She wanted to get out of the house. In the farmyard was the old 'jenny-ring' that she and Llew had played on as children. Two long timbers were joined in the form of a cross, to which the horses were harnessed, there to go round and round endlessly in a journey that had no beginning and no end. The flints had been worn down by their hooves, and the rain, running in from the yard, went swilling round the gutter, washing the stones white.

It was the old method of power used for kibbling, pulping and cutting fodder, and much else. As children they had learned to let out the ratchet in the barn, thus unlocking it, and, pushing a timber each, it gathered momentum and went whirling round and round. They would take a flying leap on a timber end and be whirled through space. There were no games like that now.

And the old 'jenny-ring', like most else, was doomed. Mr Shufflebotham, who knew a lot about machines, had explained how a little petrol engine would do twice the work in half the time. Her father had listened to him and said nothing. But there was no petrol engine as yet. Somehow this old criss-cross of timber between the stacks brought up her home before her. She decided she would not go, come what may.

CHAPTER VII

Evan the Mill stood on the cold stone stairs of the police court and leaned his arms on the sill of the open window, watching the sun in its journey, dropping to the west. Then it fell behind a factory stack and was gone. But all up the valley where was his home, the light of it remained in the sky, like the red glow of burning gorse. All around was the lightless, fading sky. It was all very wonderful.

He felt better now. The chill spring wind tossed his hair about. It came up the stairs like a knife and took the flush off him. He heard men's footsteps clattering down the stone steps behind, but he did not turn his head. Then he saw them pass up the street, spread out like unequal runners in a race – the Official Receiver, the Registrar with his Clerk, two correspondents of the local newspapers, and the big man with the red bushy beard and checked trousers, who had represented the chief creditor.

The Official Receiver was lame and as he hurried to catch his train his leg kept giving way beneath him, causing him to lurch. He had a home, children, a wife; he laughed and joked, no doubt – he was a man like anyone else... yes, surely he was a man. How strange, how wonderful a thing that throb of life unanswerable like the wash of a wave.

Evan was already feeling better. The 'feel' of life always restored him, no matter what had happened. It began in that placid contemplation of the human scene, but it was soon to transcend it. If one had the courage to see, to become selfless, then almost as the dawn breaking, this other light would come, filling the beholder with a vague fear and wonder. There were no questions, then, and no answers: all was harmony, still and dropping and it seemed as though the very stars sang.

He felt himself going now, much as an epileptic might, and the events of the afternoon alone remained to hold him to himself.

One by one they were being shuttered off and on, as a kaleidoscope. The Registrar was the last to go up the street, humming a few bars of Bach, occasionally beating time to the crescendos with a free hand, his clerk following at a respectful distance burdened with two immense ledgers. The red-bearded man had gone beyond sight, and the two newspaper correspondents went, heads together like horses nodding. He could see them again at the ink-stained table, toying with the inkwells and shooting bits of blotting-paper with their thumbs.

'Not much in it,' the one had said.

The other had nodded.

87

And then again he could see the Official Receiver, eyes cold as steel, lean forward to the Registrar.

'It appears that this man was all along acquainted with...'

Or: 'I have asked him to submit a return of his earnings between the dates...'

It was all over now. They had walked into his life and now they were walking out of it.

There was a state of being whereby, while one was conscious of all that went on around, one was at the same time as at a great distance. One saw and understood, but one could not feel, could not identify oneself with oneself. That was what had happened that afternoon. In so far as one's worldly state went Evan had reached rock bottom. He had been adjudged a bankrupt. The Law had been invoked and it had functioned. The men who had just spread themselves up the street had sat as at an inquest on his material self. One could go no farther than *that*.

And yet at this last, ultimate, stage he felt no bitterness. There was now not one solitary person whom he blamed. This overwhelming sense of compassion that he felt, not for one man but for all men, not for one thing but for all things, the earth and all that was on the earth and in the earth, and the great clear stars, worked within him until he shook with the knowledge of it. And then, sudden as it came, it had gone, as strange and unrealisable as a dream. But that moment when he stood there on the stairs of the police court was to remain with him throughout life.

The police sergeant had come down the top stairs in a clatter and was making an elaborate show of shutting the great studded doors. It was a hint that the young man took.

The sergeant presented an expanse of blue serge as he fumbled with the lock, but he suddenly turned and faced him.

'How are you getting home?' he said, ruder than he wished.

'There's a bus, I think. It's the fair.'

'Oh, aye, it's the fair,' said the sergeant, reassured. He bent over the lock again. 'Can you manage?' he said, as though talking to the door.

The young man did not understand him.

'Is half a crown any use? Say no if you don't want,' said the sergeant, forcing his casualness.

The young man bit his lip. His eyes flooded with tears and he could not speak. Instead he shook his head. Then he stretched out his hand and clasped the sergeant's big fist. His heart was too full for words. This man, almost a complete stranger to him! He wrung it fervently and then hurried away up the street. 'Too much for him, poor fellow,' said the sergeant to himself, and shook his head. 'And he looks as though breath inna in him.'

He had gone into a 'coffee-house' for a cup of tea. The 'coffee-house' was really a 'temperance' where the country people had their 'special' on market days. He sat there while the talk drifted around, sat there at a table by the wall as one in a trance. If one could refuse to think, if one could shutter down the mind, how easy it would be. But the mind was too active, and it went leaping about like a fire, picking out this thing, picking out that, and throwing them up in fantastic image.

The worst thing of all in this public examination had been the private inquiry, as remorseless as a probe, into the very details of his own home. It was as if his home – all that was left to him – had been turned out like a drawer, with all its odds and ends littered about. The little private things, the sacred things had passed beyond him. They were something to be inquired into, answered, entered into an inventory. His mother's old age pension, how much he contributed to her keep, the little presents he had given her – the poor, foolish little things of life – had been turned out with a sure, deliberate hand. And his mother was dying!

Evan had finished his tea. There was a long while to wait for the bus. The moon had risen now, like a curd, clear and white. There was a frost about – the last frost of the winter. It gave that clear-cut whiteness that frost gives.

The bustle in the High Street had subsided; groups of people still stood about in twos and threes. Roysterers were lurching out of an old timbered tavern opposite, a guttering lamp over the door. A few booths were still plying their trade: naphtha flares flickered here and there lighting up a pale ring of faces watching this final dispatch of oddments. They stood there on the fringe of light with their up-turned faces with the white glazed look of the dead.

A black man was closing up his trellis table of quack medicine; boys from the ironmongers were clearing away the debris of harness, bill-hooks, thatching gloves and pulleys which had been allowed to overflow into the street. The chug-chug of a petrol engine gradually died away; straw glistened over the road and paper was caught up by the wind and tossed about. An unending procession of traps lurched out of an archway and sagged off at a trot. They were like wasps, careless and heedless, but with no doubt as to their direction, taking a line like a rod to their nests as instinct bade them. And so too, were the little ponies, breaking into a trot and tossing their heads with a whinny. They were going home.

Evan walked towards the fairground. It was the noise of it all, the droning whine of the organ, the high shrill note of the siren sending up a plume of steam into the sky, the noise and the laughter. It always moved him, this – to behold life from however far a distance, but to behold it. There was a strange bewildering thrill about it – this other life that he could not enter, which was even unreal to him, but which was there. One could absorb it, not the life but the *sense* of it, the feel of it.

He went on with hurried strides with his face to the sky, the spreading glow over the fair like a fire smouldering, and beyond it again the endless heavens, very clear and light with the stars out, crisp and brilliant.

'Sorry,' he said. At a crossing he had bumped into a girl with her baskets. One of them had fallen on to the street, emptying itself. A packet of rice had burst and strewed the gutter, and lemons went rolling down the road. He ran forward, picked them up, and went back, anxious.

'Beti...'

She hung her head.

'There's sorry I am,' he said.

He put the last lemon into her basket. There was nothing he could say, he was going to leave her.

'Never mind, Evan,' she said, 'accidents *do* happen.'

He had hold of the basket and he yielded it up to her.

'I'll be going now,' he said and took a step away.

She took hold of his arm.

'Evan,' she said, 'I am very sorry.'

'Oh, *that*,' he said, 'can't be helped.'

They were at a loss for words, standing there at the street corner.

'How's your mam?' she said at last.

He looked aside.

'Bad,' he answered.

She was sorry she had asked.

'I would come over, Evan, only... you know.'

'Beti fach...' he said. The words would not come. He hung his head. 'I know.' He shook his head sadly. 'Never mind.'

They walked on together to the fairground.

'You want to go there?' he said, in the same hopeless voice.

'No, only to have a *look*,' she answered. They were on the stone wall which ran alongside the river. Below them on the river's bank, like a bright glittering toy, was the fairground. The booths with their coloured awnings, their naphtha flares spitting, lined the river's edge: and beyond, the smaller booths as the way opened out on to the bigger events, the hobby horses with their coloured snouts prancing; the swings, the side-shows, the rifle ranges. And beside them all, in flood, and yellow with fresh earth, the Severn swirled and eddied.

'Wait,' she said, and caught him by the arm. They leaned back into the shadow. Her cousin had gone by in a noisy crowd. He had a 'teaser', a lead tube filled with water, which a show woman, her fat arms buried in a bath of dirty water, was selling as fast as she made them. It was like a tube of toothpaste and had to be squeezed down the neck. It was the usual approach as between men and women.

Llew had a teaser and was making great play with it. He was trailing a woman of the town, a bad lot, broad-bosomed with a swagger from her hips and a leer on a face childish and foolish as a doll's. He squirted the water down her bosom and then dodged among the crowd, and she, shaking her blouse, took off in pursuit. They had run up to the top end of the fairground just under the wall, a grass patch in which the caravans were jostled together within the wall's shadow.

From under the wheels the lurchers tethered there growled and snarled as the two ran backwards and forwards, dodging in and out with shouting and laughter. Then Llew, turning suddenly, waited for the woman. He stood there insolently, hands down. She went to hit him but he caught her in his arms and, as she struggled pushed her head back and kissed her on the mouth. She had been pushed back breathless against a caravan. Shaking herself free she slapped him across the face.

'That's for you,' she said. 'You keep your hands to yourself.'

She straightened her dress and shook the confetti out of her hair. Then she stalked back to the fair. Llew stood laughing. Then he walked back after her.

Beti looked very troubled. She could not pretend that she had not seen.

'It's only fun,' said Evan.

'Fun,' said Beti, her eyes going hard. 'Fun – ach y fi.'

Llew had joined the company again and they were all marching towards the hammer. He went with a saunter and a strut, just like a game-cock, arrogant to his toes. There was much arguing among the lads and tittering and laughter, until Llew caught up the heavy mallet. He threw out his chest and loosened his shoulders with a shake, and then took two or three paces to the peg. Then with a quick, violent heave he swung it over his head and brought it down crack on the peg: the mark went whirling up the slot until it struck the bell high above them. Again he did it, and yet again, always ringing the bell. And then catching the mallet with one hand and setting his feet in balance like a young bull taking his stand, he crashed it down. Again he rang the bell.

It was a knack – not strength, but timing, but he saw not the slightest reason to explain this point to the company. Instead, he stroked his hands as though wiping the dust off them – as though wiping away all memory of it. Then he was lost in the crowd which heaved and moved like flood water, with its head of froth, the pale yellow clouded crust of faces seen under the flares, which moved uneasily as one watched. Like flood water, it seemed that at any moment it would burst through the banks that held it in.

Before a goal post a crowd had gathered as the town's centre forward, tipsy and rocking, was taking shots. Down the lightless alley a showman stood, hands on hips as he waited. Very seldom the ball came as far as him because the man tripped over it as he stumbled, or kicked the air. And then, taunted by the laughter, some light coming to his fuddled head, he sent the ball in a low hard drive – past the showman, through the net to go bouncing into the river. The showman, seeing it whisked away, went splashing into the flood after it.

That was when they saw Llew again – running down the bank following the ball, and on the point of going in after it when the showman fished it out. He was now very near to them – would have to pass them as he came up the wall to return.

'Let's go,' said Beti.

Evan said nothing, but picked up one of her baskets. But he looked sideways at Beti.

'You're going back now?' he said, his voice low.

'Yes,' she said. 'The Rallt people will be waiting.'

'I'll carry it to the yard,' he said.

'No.' And she unloosened his hand gently from the handle. They stood there at the street corner, Beti looking at the ground.

'It isn't me, Evan,' she said, after a while.

'I know that, Beti,' he turned his head away from her.

Her heart went out to him at that moment.

'If you like, then,' she said, ashamed, and let go the basket.

'No, Beti.' He shook his head in his weariness. 'No,' he said again, 'it's not fair to you.'

'And would I mind?' she asked, the tears coming to her eyes.

'No, Beti,' he said again, his voice kinder. 'I'm not that sort.'

They could not take leave of one another. There seemed nothing to say. They stood there, eyes on the ground, each

95

with a hand on the basket. There was something more to say – and yet there was nothing.

'Beti,' he said at last. 'It's been just like you. Don't think I am not feeling it.'

'It's little enough I can do.'

'Beti, you – you've no idea,' he shook his head. 'No idea,' he said again. 'I touched rock bottom – right down into the depths.' He brought himself up sharply and there was a long silence.

He felt ashamed of his weakness so he laughed with forced gaiety.

'We are friends now, Beti ay?'

'Why, of course,' she said, raising her eyes and meeting his gaze, looking at him in the same straight, fearless way that he did.

'Then let's shake,' he said, as an idea came to him. He reached out his hand impulsively.

'There's no need,' she answered. 'But just to make sure.' She laughed to cheer him up, but when she held his hand all joy left her. As she grasped his hand she felt a fear, a dread down within her, far beyond the reaches of the mind: it came from within like a sudden chill gust, wrapping her round about, cold and comfortless as death itself. It was all over in a flash, that little spasm of fear that left her numb, as though the life had gone from out of her. It was not fear of him, as him, of that she was sure.

Nor did he say anymore, but turned and without a word went up the street with long strides. She stood and watched him for a while and then went to look for the trap.

CHAPTER VIII

Life had gone back to its old way as it was bound to do. The 'jentlemens' had gone; there would be no more of them until the grouse shooting in August.

The spring had gone its way and summer was coming. Summer, more so than spring, was the great time for the inn. For the spring could be violent enough. The winds came over the cup of mountains straight from the sea and more often than not there was an edge to them. But in the summer they were tempered; the inn lay deep in the trees like an old nest, the brook had dropped to a trickle.

It was a grand time for Llew. He was up much oftener, coming and going as one of the family. It was a day out for him from the dirty little town, and he had his own ways of enjoying himself. Twmi never asked any questions, but he took the fish offered him with an appraising eye.

Llew now carried no fishing rod, only a white canvas bag on his back, and it was always bulging and sodden with its hidden load. There was no fishing in this water clear as gin, with the stones all bare and white, and only the pools holding any water.

Sometimes Beti went with him, but most often not. She made excuses and he did not mind. A woman was in the way. There were many ways of getting those fish that the 'jentlemens' were never likely to see. The easiest way was to clod up a pool and bale the water out, which was a long job but a sure one.

Or again, he dropped a silk net around a turf clump and, after much prodding, the big trout which were under the bank darted out, nosing into it and causing it to twitch convulsively; with a heave they were yanked out onto the bank. There was the gridling too, the feeling for the fish, the soft sensual tickle along the belly until the hand passed up the head, and then the sudden thrust of the thumb through the gills, and out it came. But lime and dynamite alike he never touched. He had no place for the dead and dying.

When he stopped to think of Beti, he wondered. There had never been any reason to think of Beti. But she had gone away from him in some way and it made him worried. All he knew was that things were not the same. He was not going to ask her why, though: if she felt that way she could get on with it. But somehow the old place was not the same to him.

As he trudged along the road he became more and more irritable. Why had he to answer to her, anyhow? Perhaps it would be best to have it out with her. He had done nothing.

He went round through the back and entered the kitchen door. She was standing over the fire, holding a pan for a 'special' for some visitors who had just arrived. The dull red glow shone up into her face; she was very lovely in her childlike way, standing there in the half-light. She did not turn round.

'These any good to you?' he said, irritated, and pulling out the fish by the tails.

'There's a plate over there.'

'Will you look? They *arr* fish!'

'I can see,' she answered, half turning and then bending over the fire again. 'Very nice they arr.'

He flung them on the plate one by one.

'Sorry to trouble.'

'No trouble I'm *sure*.'

'There's funny,' he said bitterly.

'Nothing funny. You can see I am busy – or can't you?'

'What has gone wrong?' He was fuming.

'Nothing that I know.' She was not going to say any more.

He stood there on one foot, his pride telling him to go, and yet unable to go. It came to him as a shout – this knowledge of how much Beti meant to him. Without her nothing was the same – as though the flavour had gone out of things, had become flat and stale. It was just as if the sun had gone in and the day hung over dreary and hopeless. It made him angry to think so, angry with Beti when he remembered that she was the cause of it.

'Please yourself,' he said, sullen.

She did not answer. She was rocking the pan backwards

and forwards on the fire, giving it a tilt as it needed. Her arms were bare to the elbows and the firelight shone up them. He noticed for the first time how very small and tender were her hands. He had never thought of her hands before. He had never thought of Beti before – the way she tumbled her hair back and the way it fell into place about her neck; the poise of her head and the violent little way she had of standing.

The excitement of it all brought a catch to his throat and he felt his stomach move within him. The glow came upwards, flooding him. He took a step towards her, unknowing.

'Llew!' She held the pan before her and leaned back to the wall. Her eyes were very wide and frightened. She had gone as pale as death and she trembled as she stood. 'Well,' he said dropping his hands. 'Whose iss the fault then?'

'You had better go I think.' Her voice was empty. She had been hurt, he knew.

At the door he turned.

'I didn't mean...' he said sheepishly. 'No offence.'

'Best let it drop,' she answered without looking up.

He walked into the taproom, his feet heavy. Something told him that he had done it now. So simple a thing, like breaking a glass! He ought to be on the way home but he could not go. It was enough to be in the same house with her. Things would be bound to straighten themselves out in a bit. But all the time something told him that what was done was done, and was beyond repair. She had been slipping away from him – and now she had gone.

And yet he had done not one thing of which he could feel

ashamed. That was the hard part of it. He could not help himself and that was all there was to it. He could not enter this world of hers – only blunder in. But then why should he? How could he be other than he was? She would find out her mistake one of these days. If that was so, he told himself with magnanimity, he would allow her to come back as though nothing had happened. But all the time it seemed as though there was a great weight over him. He had never felt like it before.

The taproom was filling up. There was much noise and laughter, and his uncle was straddling about with trays and mugs.

He nodded to the old man in the family way; he did not want to face him. But there was no avoiding his uncle's raw, shadowed eye. He never quite knew what his uncle was thinking, though he was nearer to him than anyone in the world. And though he shuffled up to a bench against the wall, sitting as far away from the light as he could, he felt his uncle's glance, like a spike of light, picking him out. He scraped his feet and looked down at the floor.

The old man grunted and cocked a thumb in his direction.

'Daro. Jeremiah come to life.'

They all looked across at him.

'A cop?' said Dici.

Llew shook his head. He did not trouble to answer.

'Well. You will come unstuck one of these days. I tell you straight.'

Llew put his fingers to his nose.

'There iss wiser than you has,' said Dici, nettled.

'What iss that to you, ay?' Llew answered, bristling and clenching his fists.

The old man saw trouble brewing.

'Hey! You go and clean those glasses now behind. How many hands you think I haf?'

But the old man's eyes were twinkling.

Llew went off in a slouch. But he was glad to be alone. In another minute there would have been a row. He was sure that Dici was provoking him on purpose. The old man was kinder to him than usual, Llew thought. That was why, hands in the tin bath, he said to him as he passed to the cellar:

'Uncle Twm?'

'Yess, yess. Be quick.'

'There's funny Beti's gone.'

'Nothing to notice.' He cocked an eye in that way of his.

'Well... I am not coming any more.'

'Shut your eye man!' His uncle gave him a playful prod in the belly, causing him to grunt. Llew was feeling very sorry for himself and his uncle was the only one he could confide in. But they were not near enough for this.

'Can I stay for supper?'

'You behave then.' He jerked his thumb towards the taproom. 'None of your nonsenses now.'

'Me, of course! But I will keep a civil tongue, whateffer.'

'Diawch. That iss a mouthful for you,' Twm said as he passed on to the cellar.

When Llew entered again good humour reigned. Dici slapped him on the back affably ('No offence, no?') and Wili the Hut gave him a whiff-whiff.

102

'We arr friends now,' said Dici to the company. 'What iss wrong with us Welshmens is that we think once, yess but not twice. Twice thinking is best. You know what them little Jap mans do, ay? Break a plate now.'

'Mind that ploody mug then,' said Twmi, drily.

'Wales is all right whateffer.' It was a roadman from the steam roller who came from a good way off. He was a quiet man and he spoke as though his own words surprised him. Then he went on peeling an onion into his bandana handkerchief.

'Oh, tamn!' said Twmi. 'Another argument.'

'Best place in the world – to get out off,' broke in Wili the Hut ponderously. 'Yr hen wlad! Forty years time there iss no Wales. House empty; call next door. You wait: you see.'

'Now, now,' said Moses anxiously. 'Wales wass Wales before ever England wass England.'

'Wrong man,' shouted Dici with heat. 'Wales wass Wales when Wales wass England.'

'Where you think Tanygraig will be in a bit?' went on Wili, red as a turkey-cock. 'Where you think?'

'Bottom of the sea.' Dici spat into the fire. He had had enough of it.

'No jokes,' warned Wili. 'You know? No! Right you arr gwas. I tell. A new road come slap bang up the middle...'

'An down the sides,' sniffed Dici.

'I know see!' shouted Wili. 'You laugh the wrong side bye and bye.'

'Shutapp man,' said Twmi, fixing him with a raw eye.

'Job's comforter,' said Moses.

'You hear perhaps?' Wili appealed to the roadman.

'I haf *heard* but that iss all, I must say,' answered the stranger.

Wili leaned back in his chair and placed his fingers together placidly. He was the bringer of tidings. 'Chary-bonks like ploody bees in a swarm! You wait: you see.'

Twmi was halfway across the room. He stopped and fixed Wili with a glare, his eyes hard and shadowed, and cut short the man's brief triumph.

'Hi, gwas,' he said, pointing to the pint mug. 'Get on with it now. I say no more.'

These happenings came up sudden as squalls. There were many altercations at the Red Lion but only one argument. It was a time of change. The uneasiness worked its way down into the older people who were never to go. But this new wind from across the Border, this new way of life which no one could guess at, disturbed them. They took refuge before it, as they did now, and let their uneasiness spend itself in talk.

Llew had got up to go into the kitchen. He could not wait any longer. He had kept looking at the clock and deciding when it would best become his dignity to go. But he had cut his measurement short by a good half-hour.

They watched him go.

'Him now,' said Wili, who objected to losing a listener. 'That restless! Up and down like a jack in the box.'

Dici winked a very obvious wink. He waited until Twmi had made one of his journeys to the cellar and then leaned forward, shielding his mouth with his hands.

'The spring, see?'

'Oh,' said Wili.

'Stale news,' broke in Wati. 'Plain as plain can be.'

'Ah,' went on Dici thoughtfully, 'but he iss too *wild*. A March hare, you know. His big ears always sticking up and never flatten.'

'Well,' spoke Wati. 'Beti iss a girl of sense. Fery deep iss Beti.'

'Too deep,' answered Dici. 'Too deep for *him*, whateffer.'

'Let be,' said Wati with heat. 'He iss a man – or will be. What more you want, ay? If they wass all like Llew there iss no harm.'

'Oh,' said Wili leaning back as though in pain. He looked towards the kitchen door and lowered his voice. 'The harm done iss not undone. You know! He iss a beauty he iss.'

Llew in the kitchen saw no one but Gwenno knitting over the fire. She looked up with that intimate, impudent look a woman gives a man she is not sure about. It was a challenge too. Llew had a nice name.

'Where's Beti?'

'Gone to the choral,' she said and went on with her knitting. She would put him in his place.

'She never said.' He stood there anxious, hesitant.

'Must she ask *you* of all people?'

'Don't be funny, now.'

'It's you who iss funny. You *arr* funny now if you would only take a look.'

But he was not going to quarrel with Gwenno. He had no use for her.

'Mind your business then,' he answered rudely.

'You got a cheek.' She looked up at him derisively. 'And I know.'

105

'Know what?'

'Never mind *what*. I know.'

'You know a lot, you do.'

'And what's more,' she said, her red face whitening, 'it's not you who will get Beti. Take that wan, Mister Llew.'

'Daft you arr. I don't know what it iss all about.'

'No? You will. You wait; you see!'

He went back to the taproom and slammed the door. It was true that he did not know what it was all about. But he would wait. He would see it through now. He wanted to be alone – to think it all out. And then he did not want to be alone. Two strangers had come in and he was glad. They would take his mind off, as the familiar faces could not.

They were two men in worn navy blue suits, rubbed and shining, with white chokers round their necks, caps struck back on their heads, their faces scoured and white. They were two shonihois from the South, one could see at a glance, even if the little blue streaks of coal dust, worked under the skin like tiny veins, did not give them away.

The one man went over to look for the bar and the other took his seat beside 'rhen Shacob.

'Cardiff City – going down an' down,' he said confidentially.

Shacob went on moving his toothless gums. But the stranger was not deterred.

'Things is bad down South,' he said again in the same easy confidential tone.

But still Shacob did not answer. In a final effort the man spoke again.

'Jack Petersen – there's a boy for you!'

There was still no answer, and he was now vaguely alarmed. 'Hey, Ianto!' he called to his butty and cocked his head at the old man. 'Ploody waxworks, myn uffern i!'

Dici leaned across. He had not heard what was going on in the general hubbub. He tapped his ear knowingly.

'Hard of hearing he iss,' he said apologetically. The man's face lightened.

'Don't men-shun,' he answered waving his hand affably.

'You come a long way?' broke in Wati, making conversation.

'Down South,' he said briefly and then, to be more explicit. 'You know that murdah – how long, Ianto, aye two yeahs sure to be – when they found the girl on the tip. That's our 'ome,' he said with finality.

'Never?' Dici answered in astonishment.

'Aye aye, mun. Knew him well.' He wiped a hand backwards across his mouth. 'Little pugah he wass, too.'

They crowded round the men as if they had been monkeys. Their ways, their talk, their dress were all different. 'Down South' was another world.

'Arr you going farr?' asked Wati anxiously. He looked down at their feet. Their boots, patched and tied with string, were hanging on their feet.

'Farr enough,' he replied. 'What you say, Ianto? It's all done down there.' He cocked a finger over his shoulder and shook his head hopelessly. 'Thirty-four yeahs of it mun. Look at me now! Look at 'im.'

He did not want to say any more. They were men who did not parade their sorrows. He took a gulp at his beer and his face brightened.

'Plenty jobs in London. So they say.'

'You come a long way round,' broke in Twmi. He stood there a moment facing them, the same old changeless expression on his face.

'Wrong for you, mun,' said the old miner looking up from the fire. 'Up 'eah we got it,' and he tapped his head knowingly.

'We goin' to try the Mersey Tunnel,' broke in his mate, a thin, hatchet-faced man, with bright quick eyes.

'We wass only saying,' said Wili in his most ponderous way. 'We wass only saying as how Wales iss all done and finished for.'

'Done, you say?' The miner lifted his face, gone haggard, put his hands on his knees and spat into the fire. He was deep in thought.

'Damn it all mun, what you know?' he said, a light in his eye. 'You come down South and see.' He dropped his voice: and the light went out of his eye. 'We gone past been done for,' he said after a while. He put his hands to his head and looked at the floor. He had gone beyond words.

'The Rhondda...' He could say no more. 'One end to the other. Tonypandy, Ton Pentre, Treorchy... Worse than death; not as quick.'

But now it was Ianto's turn. He was a different type altogether.

'Four yeahs I been out. Laf that wan off! I go to the over-man. He got a down on me – I'm a communist, see? "What about it now boss?" He looks me up and down as though I was a bit of dirt. "Come back in the spring" he says. Diawl ario'd – up comes the lamp. "What you think I am gwas –

108

a ploody cuck-oo?" No more work for me. That done it.'

The older man, his head whitened, his eyes tired and hopeless, let him have his head. He was like the jackal after the lion.

'There wass Iddy Pryce now...' went on the younger man in his shrill high voice. 'A sort of relation of mine...'

'Shutapp, mun,' said his mate, roused from out of himself. 'Sort of relation! No relation at all.'

'Yess, yess, he iss,' went on the other in his shrill way. 'Ignorant he iss.' Then dropping his voice to a confidential whisper. 'My wife wass haf a kid by him, see?'

The company looked down their noses, and moved uneasily in their seats.

And Ianto, having disposed of the point, went scampering off.

'When the work-ahs get together, you wait! Ploody ruckshuns I tell you! I'm on the committee, see?' He nodded knowingly.

'What iss he?' asked Wili pointing to the older man who had sunk back into himself.

'He's labah,' he said apologetically. 'But he's *tamping* to the left fast.'

It was long past time and Twmi had only just noticed it. No bells were rung at the Red Lion. When Twmi remembered, he waved his hands upwards as though saying 'shoo'. One by one the company dribbled into the yard.

'You stay,' he said to the miners, his voice abrupt.

'What's on, mate?' asked the younger.

He brought them a pint of beer each and then returned with half a loaf and a skim cheese.

There were tears in the older man's eyes as he took them.

His mouth moved but no words came.

'Diolch yn fawr,' he faltered.

'Cot tamn it all,' said Twmi in a fury. 'You Welshmens aren't you – not ploody tramps!'

They looked one another straight in the eyes.

'Put it there, boss,' said the miner. He reached out his hand.

Twmi put the two pairs of boots that he had hunted up on the settle beside them as though doing a sleight of hand. The paper burst and they fell on the floor with a clatter. He began to curse.

When they had finished their supper he showed them the way to the loft.

Beti had not come in. Llew waited as long as he could and then got his bike out of the barn and rode off home.

CHAPTER IX

Twmi was at the window looking out on to the road. 'Diawch,' he said, as though to himself, 'the old man has had a skinful for sure.'

Then he turned and waddled across the taproom.

'Look out,' he shouted. 'He's coming. Hey, Beti,' he called out to her as she was passing through. 'You stop here now.'

'I am busy, Dad,' she said pouting.

'Busy?' he said with disgust. He turned to Dici who was alone on the settle. 'The only holy wan I got to offer!'

'And me!'

'Ay,' Twmi replied. 'You two, and where iss his flock; lost stolen or strayed with a ven-jance.'

Dici was 'church' and so, too, was Twmi though he never went; that was why he was making Beti a peace offering. In Wales you were either 'church' or chapel. There were many chapels, though one outreached all the others, but there was only one church. It was more than a denominational difference; it became almost a question of caste. Disestablishment had eased things as between the one and the other, but the gulf was as wide as the grave. And while the whole country was nonconformist there were strange little pockets where the older religion held on and in a way triumphed. This was true of the village.

It was the rector who was driving into the yard now, a most remarkable man whose fame had gone abroad. He used to drive into market in a tub behind a little brush-tailed pony, facing a basket of eggs and a hamper of garden produce, by which a frugal wife offset her husband's extravagances. The reverend gentleman occupied all the other side of the vehicle and although he contrived to sit as far as possible in the centre of the seat, the heaviest part of him, as it were, fell behind the axle so that the shafts, in consequence, were always set at an ambitious tilt, and the little pony looked as though it were just to be hoisted clear of the ground.

Round him he gathered his cape, green with age, and held together with frequent stitching. On the way back the little pony, knowing every yard of ground, ended up in a surprising burst of speed causing him to stand up. So he would go through the village, the same old cape trailing behind him in the wind, and a hand gently outstretched as though urging the tumult to desist, for all the world like a charioteer fresh from his triumphs in the Circus Maximus. This happened once a week.

But he always contrived to break the gallop at the Red Lion yard, where he stopped for a few minutes, the faint odour of whisky preceding him.

112

He was an immense man, in stature as in all things, with the heavy head of an old hound, and the same heavy, anxious eyes – light blue and strangely clear, as though they had outlasted their setting, for the face was worn and florid.

The son of a Welsh squire, the harp had been played in his father's house. He had seen the world. As a young man he had been sent as a missionary to the Patagonian Indians, but after his second dose of fever he wrote home to the authorities, giving it as his opinion that the Patagonian Indians were not worth civilising. He also explained, while God had certainly intended him to go, he was now convinced that He was just as emphatic on his return; that his conscience, which he had consulted at great length, was satisfied, and that he had signed on as a trimmer on a boat leaving Valparaiso and was returning at once.

But he did not leave the church. Though he never sought influence, there was always someone ready to invoke it on his behalf. He had been moved about from living to living like a chess-piece, until age had steadied him. And he was indeed a pillar of the Welsh church – of the British Church, as he always called it, thereby distinguishing it from the Italian Church which, he explained, was of a later foundation.

And he was the only man who could provoke Twmi to any sort of reverence, though he could not provoke him to attend as long as there was Beti to go in his stead. The church was three miles down the road, standing alone in the fields, a grey lichen-covered old pile with its pre-Norman open bell-cote, and its clean simple lines. The rood-screen was the cause of pilgrimage. It was dedicated to one of the early British saints.

LLYFRGELL COLEG MENAI LIBRARY

The rectory was across the brook adjoining the sister church, a distance of some two miles as the crow flew. But the old man did not fly, he walked, and this meant a distance of some three miles down the brookside to the nearest bridge – a matter of six miles out of his way. The parish council, who were chapel almost to a man, would not be troubled with erecting even a small trellis bridge, pointing out that no one but the rector would ever have need for it. Whether in protest, or because he could not be bothered to make the detour, he regularly went through the brook every Sunday. In summer it was a mere splash over his boots, but in winter the channel was bank high with storm water from the mountains. At such times he would carefully tuck his sermon in the band of his hat and wade through, hands above his head.

The only thing that ruffled him was to lose his spectacles in the pulpit. He would beat his pockets one by one, with a running commentary, quite audible, which was of a kind not usually heard in a place of worship.

He walked over to Beti and patted her on the head affectionately.

'What is this I hear Beti?' he asked in a voice which rolled around the room like thunder.

Beti's eyes widened in fear, and he saw it.

'A fine girl,' he said to Twmi affably. He looked at Beti, appraisingly, his face lightening. He had an artist's eye for beauty.

Beti was standing on one leg, blushing, embarrassed. She had not been so attentive as she might have been to church work lately. He was bound to know it, but she knew

114

he would not tell. It was not that she was afraid of – but she knew now that she could safely go.

'Haf you nothing to say to Mr Bryn-Rowland?' said Twmi, nettled. He knew what was coming to himself and took cover.

'What should she say?' replied the rector patting her on the shoulder. 'Beti and I understand one another, ay Beti?'

Then he shot out: 'How old are you Beti?'

'Eighteen Mr Bryn-Rowland – or will be next month.'

'The seventeenth,' broke in Twmi and looked across at Beti for confirmation. That was all he knew about his daughter and he was not sure of that.

'Ay,' said the rector. 'Eighteen!' He shook his old head once or twice and fumbled for his glass. 'Eighteen,' he repeated as though to himself. He had gone beyond them. Then he raised his head and looked at her, his eyes clouded with drink. But they were not the eyes of a drunken man. 'Take care of your life, Beti. Take care.'

He lifted his glass to his lips and wagged his head again.

'By Cod she will,' answered Twmi.

But the old man did not answer. He had gone off again.

'Off you go now,' said her father with a flourish, dismissing her.

'Twmi...' went on the old man reproachfully, heaving a sigh.

'No time!' replied Twmi, jumping on his words.

The parson reached for his glass with exaggerated care and brought it to his mouth.

'Hell for you,' he said briefly.

'Right you arr,' Twmi replied. 'Anywhere for peace.'

115

The parson waved his hand casually. 'Please yourself.' He was now maudlin.

'I'll be there,' said Twmi. 'When the roll is called up yon-dair, I'll be there.'

When the two got going it was immense. They were like two tritons among the minnows. But the old man was tired, had had too much, and Twmi had too fine a sense to profit by it.

'Not up yon-dair: down yon-dair,' said Dici chipping in like a bird, and cocking his finger over his shoulder.

'I wass sorry about last Sunday,' went on Dici.

The old man shook his head; he could not remember.

'Oh tamn,' went on Dici. 'I wass that wild. Pure mistake. I assh-ure you.'

It was all forgotten, but it was still very fresh with Dici. Not the least of the innovations that the old man had introduced was to allow the mountain farmers to bring their dogs into church. It was a real boon to these men who had often a walk of five or six miles over bog and moor, and the arrangement had worked perfectly.

But this last Sunday Dici's little corgi bitch had been attended by a prancing cavalcade of dogs of all shapes and sizes who had come bounding out from farms and smallholdings until, when Dici reached the church, it seemed he was the master of a pack of beagles. He had thrown stones and clods at them until he was tired, and at the church door he wisely decided that he would not take advantage of the concession given. But when a late-comer arrived and the door was opened the little bitch trotted to his feet with that knavish, ancient look, and behind her the whole of her escort.

The old man was at the lectern at the time, but he broke into the lesson and gravely walked down the steps, down the length of the church, to Dici's pew beside the font.

Discovering the cause of the commotion he delivered a brief homily on Nature and her inscrutable workings. They transcended all thought and all wisdom, he said, and before their mysteries the wisest man was dumb. He had no wish to disturb the act of creation in the Creator's own house, except that the dogs could just as well attend to their needs outside. So opening the great oak door he pointed the way out and helped the more attentive spirits into the darkness with the toe of his boot. Then he went back to the lectern and continued the lesson.

The old man shook his head again and Dici saw no reason to remind him of it.

'Tell Beti... to come and see me,' he said, raising his head.

Twmi was going to shout into the kitchen but the parson waved his hand irritably.

'Not now: not now,' he went on. 'A time for all things.' He staggered to his feet.

They could hear him stumbling about the yard feeling for his pony. Not for worlds would they have offered to help him, for no man dared do that.

Twmi listened to the pony clattering out of the yard before he took his seat. He was worried. A nod and a wink meant a lot to him. He sensed as much as he heard. And that the old parson knew something he was sure; but he was just as sure that it was safe in the old man's keeping. Beti had been out a great deal lately – but he would never ask her why or where. When she chose she would tell him.

But he was worried all the same.

CHAPTER X

Llew wondered what he was going to do with his life. It was not like him to worry, but the upset with Beti had put him off his balance.

He had made up his mind that he would not go to the Red Lion again – at least, not for a long time. It was a gesture on his part that he found very hard to keep up. The Red Lion had been a second home to him as long as he remembered. Not until now did he realise quite how much it meant. That was why he had gone back into himself – why he began to think about life.

He had left the 'intermediate' six months before, having failed the London Matric. three times, and the headmaster having held out little hope of him ever getting it. He had not even a Welsh matric. The way to Aberystwyth College was thus closed, and with it the jobs a Welsh degree carried – the teaching and the preaching, for neither of which he had any special desire. And unlike the lads who left the elementary school, he could not now be apprenticed to a trade. He was halfway up a ladder, and there he had to stay.

His father had been one of the Young Men of Wales. In his dark, bitter, fuming eyes, his long narrow face, his lean spindle body, one glimpsed the passion that was to devour him. He came at a time when the country was turning anxiously, as though in sleep. The young man, his soul aflame, had proclaimed the new birth. And as the pulpit went hand in hand with politics, he forgot the wedded bride for this new mistress, more provocative, more tantalising and with the infinite promise of greater reward. He neglected his God, but he served his country, and his pastorate in this little town had been the penalty of that neglect.

It was there that he met his wife – Twmi's sister – a farmer's daughter, with the soft, easy paganism of the earth, red and glowing as a sunset in her ripening beauty. The easy, placid sensuality of her overwhelmed him as a flood; he yielded himself up in the naked frenzy of his spirit – this other world infinitely dark and menacing, that he was to know. They had never met – they were as two people shouting at one another across an abyss.

He died of what in rural Wales they called galloping consumption when Llew was a year old. The mother brought up the boy. She never married again, though she could easily have done so, and with the family money left her and the small pension from the Church Benevolent Fund, she was just able to manage. But now that Llew had left school and was of an age to work this grant had been stopped, and this was a growing source of reproach to the lad.

119

This, and the breach with Beti, made him think about life – his life – for the first time. There were only two paths open to him, as he saw it – the army, or the City Police Force in a place like Birmingham or Manchester where there was a prospect of promotion. He set his face against both.

And yet he would have done anything to get away. He did not belong. That was why he was always heading for the Red Lion, which was Wales proper – an instinct as sure, as unanswerable, as makes the duckling in a brood head for water.

The little town stood there under its cloud of smoke which lifted and blew, towards the mountains, towards the coloured valley, like a signpost between two worlds. It belonged to neither. In the respite it had, it grew of itself, grew as a fungus grows, quick in its humidity. Industry had come there, the wheels had turned, the people had gone into the mills, had left the mills, when they fell derelict.

In its heyday, it had within itself aspired to greatness. The mills were throbbing, the new Severn fresh from the the mountain uplands, and before it was to expend its strength in the low-lying valleys, had been barricaded with weirs. Money flowed. On market-days, the butter women lined the kerb; all the week money and drink flowed in the ale-houses – there were scores, small and petulant like blisters in the streets.

Then the prosperity had suddenly gone, receded as a tide recedes, leaving this little town between two worlds neither land nor water, like a piece of flotsam, on the drying beach. It had gone back into itself, its people were 'townies'. They never belonged – belonged to anything but themselves.

On fair days and at the auctions, the people beyond them mingled – mingled, but never met; the hill farmer driving in his flock of Welsh mountain sheep, the mountain ponies, wild and unbroken, from the hard springing sour green pastures of the uplands; the Border farmer with his sleek, sweat-dropping Herefords, his Kerry-hills. They elbowed one another in the Smithfield, they were prey for the same dealers, but they were as remote, as unbridgeable in their distance, as the two poles.

That was the land the lad had grown in – Powys, once one of the three proud territorial divisions of the Cymru, named by them Powys, Paradwys Cymru – now frayed and broken in the east where the invader had come up the low-lying fertile valleys, come in possession, but not conquest.

Life – a portentous thought, and one that annoyed Llew! Far more important was to get away. And next in importance was to have some money by him. The sixpences and shillings his mother doled out to him were not enough even for his present requirements. A seat in the pictures among the 'class' – the small tradespeople who were the 'class' – was one and threepence: the rest, the rag-tag and bobtail, were herded in a pen to shout and whistle and stamp their feet at sixpence a head. He had no views as between the one and the other – they were all the same to him – but he had decided views on the difference between a one-and-threepenny seat and a sixpenny one.

And so 'life' now loomed up very ominously. He took stock of himself and knew that he could do nothing. But he was not in the least dismayed, for at the same time he was equally sure that he could do everything.

121

One of his best friends was secretary of the provincial eisteddfod. They would walk up and down the High Street discussing things, the fantastic world the County Library had opened up for them both – Anatole France and Tchehov, and the great god Tolstoi before whom they were both constrainedly silent, while boys ran backwards and forwards with penny slips shouting: 'Footba' results – footba' results'.

Llew would break off and listen. Even the unemployed went on a gala day to see Wolverhampton Wanderers. The world of fact was very different from this world of fiction. He had gone beyond them – these people who were neither Welsh nor English – but they had gone beyond him. He had never been to the Shrewsbury Flower Show.

His friend kept on talking, but he was not listening. He leaned his arms on the stone bridge. Even the Severn got away – Shrewsbury – Hereford – wherever it was.

'Well, have a shot, Llew,' he was saying, 'nothing to beat.'

Llew looked at him absently.

'And it's three quid. Three quids iss three quids.'

They were both Welshmen; they formed a colony on their own in this little town. At mention of three quids Llew came back to earth. He reached for the official programme his friend carried.

'How much time?' he asked.

'A week.'

'They are getting frisky,' he said. 'Short story! They'll be having a play next.'

'Pooh,' said the other man, 'move with the times. They are having Ibsen's *Pretenders* for the National.'

'No joke?' asked Llew anxiously. 'You mean I got nothing to beat?'

'You try,' answered his friend with a wink. Then he added: 'Three quids iss three quids. There's no joke *there*.'

He took the programme. If it had been upholstery or metal work it would have been all the same to him, except that he could do neither. But then he had never written a story in his life. He had always been top in English, but being top in English was not writing a story that would win three pounds at an eisteddfod.

Writing had seemed so remote, so foolish a thing that it had never entered his head, however many the schemes he had drawn up for his betterment. There were the local reporters who sat at a green baize table under a platform, with pencils sharpened at each end, people who caused a certain awe, it was true, but people whom he had never once considered joining. Nor did he now.

Below them was the fair ground, wet and desolate, a reach of clinkers on the river bank, with black puddles here and there where the rain had sluiced. It was an empty place now. Beyond the weir was the gasworks, fuming on the river bank, and beyond that again a skin yard.

'I'll try,' he said.

He had been afraid of making a fool of himself, that was all. It seemed a bit soft and sloppy.

'The Chair's a cert,' said his friend.

Llew was not listening. He had not even a remote interest in poetry.

'Yes?' he said, for something to say.

'There's a poet for you, man,' replied his companion warmly.

123

Llew looked at him in question.

'Evan Edwards – that keeps the mill at your uncle's,' he explained. 'Hope of Wales, that man iss.'

'Yes?' said Llew his eyes narrowing. There was that baleful light in them that people did not like.

'Know him?' said the other man.

'Yes and no,' answered Llew casually. 'I see him about.'

They dropped the subject and walked slowly back through the town.

The excitement worked in Llew. It was a new toy to him – a fresh release for his energies. Whether it was the three pounds or the thought of beating other people at their own game, he did not know, but the project, which he had nearly turned down with contempt, had now taken firm hold. He was like that in all things – there were no half-measures for him.

But it was not so easy to get started. That quick, instinctive self – the unanswerable self in him – had no place now. It was one thing to be oneself, but it was another thing to transfer oneself onto paper. The process choked him – the whole thing was unreal and foolish, he tried to tell himself, hurling the twentieth bit of paper across the room. He had always suspected as much, and now he knew it.

He worked in his father's study – 'Dad's room' – unaltered, unchanged, through the lad's life. The dark oak secretaire was still locked; within, all the rhetoric, the passion, the zeal of that young life, now mute and tongueless; a few scraps of paper scribbled over, under-lined, margined in red – little drawings of men streaming along the edges, when he had paused for the new thought, the burning phrase, which, caught and circumscribed, flew over the paper in a scrawl, as though impatient of the ink.

All done now; nothing that interested Llew, nothing that interested his mother, but for some strange streak of sentiment, reverence, perhaps, for his memory, had been kept.

Around about were all his books. Theological commentaries jostled one another along the shelves, political tracts, modern-day heresies. There was Locke and Spinoza, Hazlitt and William James, Cromwell's letters and speeches, a whole shelf of Carlyle. There were Welsh books, Dafydd ap Gwilym and Goronwy Owen, breasting the poets; many books on the old sources of Celtic literature, then so painstakingly unearthed: Renan's *Poetry of the Celtic Races*, and much else. It was as though the ghost of the mind, of the spirit, of the man who once inhabited the room, were walking within its walls.

Above the mantelpiece was a college photograph in a green frame, yellow moulded around the edges; a group of young men, posed and ponderous, in the quadrangle. One or two of them had become famous; the rest were forgotten. And there was his father, with that straight, staring look, as though looking beyond the camera, into truth itself. There were the hard-lined, searching eyes of genius.

Llew got up and looked straight at his father. Before, he had been a word, a memory, a legend. Now he saw him face to face. And he felt ashamed. He did not know why, but he felt ashamed. Something in his father's straight staring gaze, looking out at him from that old, mouldering print, moved him in a way that nothing else could have done.

125

He began again. He threw the half-finished story away in disgust – the voluptuous woman who moved from Paris to Monte Carlo and back to Paris like a shuttlecock, who sat sunning herself under palm trees and in orange groves, who sipped absinthe and whose collection of lovers, for ever being added to, caused even Llew to raise his eyebrows in wonder.

He had never thought of writing about Wales. It was like looking at one's own face. But he knew nothing else, and what he *knew* was at least real to him. He thought of a true story, and every detail came out clear, everything fell into place. A poacher had 'gone down' to Shrewsbury Gaol for setting night lines in a lake. The bench, the English colonels and majors – the local County – who abhorred poaching as they did the plague, really believed that the sentence fitted the crime.

It was not resentment, not bitterness that welled up like a flood; it transcended these. The furtive meetings, the word passed from mouth to mouth, the cloud no bigger than a man's hand that grew and grew until the sky was dark. They could not net the lake, they could not dynamite it, they could no longer poach it, with the example before them. But the lake *had* to be emptied.

It was Llew, stripling as he was, who outdid them all in cunning. They would go down to the Severn and net it for the penhwyad, as the pike was called. They would drop one or two in the lake and let things take their course. Llew had gone with them, trundling a milk churn down the bank, their faces blackened, their tempers desperate.

He could see the scene now – the black core of the clouds

and their lighted edges, and he praying that the moon would stay hidden. Then the sudden sheen on the water as it rode out into the clear sky, and how the willows came alight and the long bare fields glistened, as in a frost. He could hear the men splashing waist-high in the water, hear their low cursing, hear the sharp, metallic tinkle on the stones, and feel his breath catch at every strange sound beyond them.

He would tell how the lake, from being one of the best preserved in Wales, was desolate within two years, and how no re-stocking ever helped. He would finish on the high note of revenge, which was as real a feeling as any he knew. He would write that all up just as he felt it.

He did not care a rap about art, and all its implications. He trusted his instinct, and his instinct told him that what was true came off, and what was not true did not.

His mother called him down for supper.

'Going fine,' he said, glowing and ecstatic. He put his arms round her to humour her.

'Something new, then,' she said drily, teapot in hand.

'Going with a swim... like a trout upstream.'

In her heart she was worried about him, but he was her son, and she could not worry for long. There was that shouting, triumphant note about him that warmed her even against her own reason. She fought against it as she did now; she had never spoiled him.

'Making a mess up there,' she went on. 'Who is going to clean up for you, I should like to know?'

'I will,' he said grandly over his supper.

'Yes,' she replied, 'I know your "I will", my boy. It's been "I will" all your life.'

He went on eating in silence, the edge going off his enthusiasm.

'It's time you thought of something serious.'

Their relationship was on a hair-spring – a touch, and it had gone. There was no compromise then in this battle of wills, each as taut as a bowstring.

'That shorthand,' she said, 'never looked at! Three and sixpence I gave for the books from Johnnie Evans the Shop, and unopened to this day.'

'Pooh,' he said, moving his feet. 'Shorthand iss for clerks.'

'What did your Uncle David say?' she countered.

'Fat lot of good what he said.'

His uncle David, his father's brother, was a journalist in London who had made a reputation. He would have done something for the lad for his brother's sake, if he could, but he had only seen him once, and then as a child. And the most that he could advise at the distance was that he should learn shorthand.

His mother only quoted uncle David in extremities, for there was no love lost as between the two sides of the family. Uncle David was reserved for special occasions.

'All right,' he said, pushing his supper away from him, half-finished, 'if that's how you feel...'

'Oh, Llew,' she said, 'and it's spare-rib, that your auntie Alys sent special!'

It was his trump card, as he knew. That was a real issue – that he should refuse to eat. The rest was talk, but this was a reality. That got home to his mother as nothing else, for food was a rite to the Tudors, to his mother no less than Twmi.

He reached for his cap on the chiffonier and stuck it on his head vindictively.

'Headstrong as ever,' she said, watching him go. 'That old billiards, I suppose, with all that riff-raff.'

He went through the hall and slammed the door. Then he slammed the gate.

That, she knew, was in defiance of her. It was like holding down a young colt. But would she have it otherwise? She told herself that she would, but she knew in her heart that she would not.

CHAPTER XI

Summer had gone. The trees had wilted and thinned – the stacks, the roof of the inn, were there again through the trees. And then, as suddenly as the turning over of a page, it was autumn. For a few brief days the colours would hold, the deep bronze and gold of leaf, the tumult of colour piled up around the village. And then as suddenly that would go too. The hawthorn berries, blood red, hung like drops around about; the sloes with their soft moist bloom on them; the blackthorn with the dew on it, glistened in the first frost.

It was the time of the year that excited Evan most. He walked through the little shop, stripped and bare, and stood at the door. The earth had the hard crisp look that frost gives it.

He saw too much – though he was always telling himself that he did not see enough. He saw things separately and with a vivid sense that was wearing him out. Only seldom came that glimpse working through the body, and beyond the body in which the whole landscape would fuse and melt and become a whole.

Before him a hill, cropped and sour, green with the sheen of frost on it. The cub hunting had begun and the fox had gone to earth up there. Backwards and forwards the horses went, framed in the sky. It was a wonderful sight, a man on a horse with the sky behind. Sometimes the horses were hidden and the riders seemed to be moving through space with an effortless, easy motion. He saw the sunlight pick out the horses, saw the flecks of foam on them, the wonderful lines of a horse seen in movement, and his heart thrilled at the sight.

Now and again he could hear the thud, thud of the spades striking the hard earth, and as he went beyond sight and thought he felt the old horror that he always felt. So lovely a thing as a fox on so lovely a morning, to be tossed up to the dogs and torn to pieces in a slaver of blood.

He felt the old panic, the old fear well up. Once to slip off this ecstatic state he was down in the depths. For all his love of life Evan was afraid of it, with a fear he dared not utter nor even contemplate. It was enough that it was there.

'Evan... Evan!' His mother's voice came to him from upstairs like a croak.

'Coming, Mam,' he shouted. Then he took the little tea-pot of pap which was warming on the hob up to her. He knew that she was dying. If he began to think then there was no end to his thinking. But he took a tip from the district nurse who came every day to do her dressing – a job, something to be done with a bustle and a few cheery words which were always on tap. If one refused to feel, if one shut out feeling, life was something quite different.

When the old lady had finished she called out to him:

'Evan... come close.'

He moved up from the end of the bed and held her hand, thin as a claw, and patted it.

'How iss things downstairs?'

'Quite well, Mam.'

She was silent, but she had fixed him with her steel-blue eyes, still keen as a razor – all that remained of her it seemed.

'Enough to eat Evan?'

'There's silly, Mam,' he laughed.

'Take care, Evan my boy.' She wagged her head in that wise way of the dying.

He went downstairs again and took out from the till the old ledger, half filled with his father's handwriting, in which he was writing his poem. He had still some fifty lines to do. But the eisteddfod was a 'job' as so many of them were, and his impulse was primarily lyrical. The subject was 'Peace', for, while Europe was like a bear-garden, a great many people in Wales still believed earnestly in the cause of peace. That was why it had been given for the Chair; it was propaganda at the same time. His county in a National Peace Ballot had established an overwhelming lead over all others, not only in England but in Wales itself.

Evan had been tipped as a cert for the Chair; his reputation as a poet was growing. It meant nothing to his station or his material welfare, for in Wales, where everyone is a poet of some kind, poetry had no commercial significance at all. Ceiriog, the most sublime poet in the language, worked on the railway; Eifion Wyn was in the post office, and Hedd Wyn, to whom the National Chair, draped in black, was posthumously awarded (he had been killed in France a few days before) was a mountain shepherd.

And so Evan, who bid fair to rise among the very great ones, was writing in his father's old ledger because there was no other paper about. He had glimpsed Peace as the spirit of Christmas, the great-hearted joy of man with Peace on Earth, goodwill to all men. The 'goodwill to all men' which at one time of the year rose like a flood to submerge the backbiting, the jealousies, the smallnesses of man to man – that was what had caught alight in his imagination; that, and the line of a Welsh poet who was killed in the War, in his anthem to doomed youth, a line that unwound itself like an illuminated scroll and which he thought the most wonderful line in all poetry:

'Their flowers the tenderness of silent minds.'

He began to hunt for a thought as he walked to and fro across the bare shop, but no thoughts were to come to him that morning. Death – that was the final and ultimate thing – the great unasked-for, as he told himself, trying to laugh away the fear that was rising in him.

His mother had upset him, she had not meant to, but she had upset him, had set his mind going like a car with the brakes gone, plunging into an abyss. That was the final drop curtain – 'hence vain deluding joys: hence vain deluding joys' – the line ran through his head until he could have cried out in his torment. No one knew his fear, his dread, but himself. Beti could only guess at it.

He took the granary key from the wall and, as though it was something evil, pushed it in the till drawer. There it was out of sight. But he knew it was there. That was the awful significance of it – that it was there, that he would take it out, however much he told himself he would not. It was the one thing that was to happen, however much he told himself it would not happen. Nothing could help him – he could not help himself. But the test of courage was to know – to face things.

He took it out and unlocked the granary door. The old iron scales were covered with empty sacks and lumber. He shoved them off with his foot in his urgency. Then he took up the weights one by one and dropped them on the arm. Ten stone eight he had weighed before. Perhaps he had put on weight! For a moment he really believed that he had put on weight; he clutched at the thought. But he knew that he had *not* done so. Ah, but he had held his weight – yes, he had held his weight.

He fingered the weights and then dropped them on the arm. Then he stood on the platform; the arm remained down. However much he fumbled and shuffled, the arm remained down without the suggestion of a lift. Panic came to him. He caught hold of the framework and forced his feet on to the platform and the arm lifted: then he let go his hold and the arm dropped. He thought that he would go away without knowing, but he knew that he could not go away without knowing. Then he took off the weights one by one. At ten stone four the arm quivered. He slid the racket which marked out the ounces across – ten stone, three and three quarters.

He had lost more than four pounds in a fortnight! What did it matter – he was not the first person in the world to lose weight! He passed his hands over his jaws and felt the jaw bones sticking out. Fear and hope alternated like a see-saw. It was nothing: it was everything. Without Beti life would have been unendurable. But Beti could not reach him now. There was no place for her *there*.

He had forgotten the hunt. They had moved on to draw another covert and the noise of the hounds in full cry – 'the musical confusion of hounds' – brought him back to himself. He ran to the door and saw them spread out in line, in all their colour, like a paper streamer.

He could not see the fox, though it must be very close. And then as he stood there, something like a brown paper parcel thrown past him, went into the granary. He turned and saw the fox in a corner among the sacks, flecked with sweat, its thin muzzle out and curled in a snarl; standing there defiant, on legs thin as twigs, its brush drooped but its head up.

Over the brook into the yard came the pack, their heavy ancient heads nodding, their jaws a slaver of foam – up to where Evan stood, with a final exultant bay. He slammed to the door and turned the key. They leapt up over it and around him until he was splattered with sweat. But he remained there; standing back against the door, his arms outstretched.

135

The hunt was drawing up but one rider had outdistanced all the others. Beti hanging clothes at the bottom of the Red Lion garden, and dropping the basket at the sudden burst of tongue, right out of the village itself, had run to the hedge. And at the distance she knew him, riding hard and pushing his horse through the brook without searching for the ford.

The local hunt was a thing for everybody – for the farmers and the local 'sports' whosoever they might be, provided they were mounted. And Llew, whenever he could, borrowed a horse from a jobbing stables in the town, the owner of which was himself an old huntsman. Often enough its wind had gone, but any horse was better than no horse at all. But up here, as he knew every inch of ground for miles around, every glat and every gate, he had contrived to leave the rest of the hunt behind.

He slipped off his horse and strode through the yelping dogs, his eyes, usually light and vibrant, now cold and hard with that peculiar stone-grey look of the killer, a light as on a tarn when the sun is down and the light is within it. He peered through the netted window and then walked up to the door. A crowd had gathered; they were dribbling in twos and threes from all the houses in the village.

He strode up to Evan and thrust his face against his, eyes narrowing.

'What's the game, ay?' He clenched his fists involuntarily. Evan faced him with no word spoken. He had gone very white and still.

'Let him out,' said Llew between his teeth.

But Evan did not move; his arms were still upraised

across the door as though crucified on it. Then Llew caught him by the shoulder and with a quick jerk flung him away from it. He ran up the steps and tried the ring, first one way, then the other, and then rattled it. Then, standing back a pace, he put his shoulder to the door, but it did not move.

He turned and took a step forward, a baleful glint in his eye like a spark struck.

'Out with it,' he said.

Evan was standing there among the crowd.

'No, Llew,' he said shaking his head, 'enough for today.' He took the heavy key from his pocket and tossed it over their heads into the mill-race. It dropped in with a plop. 'Sorry,' he said, facing him.

Llew watched it fly over their heads in an arc – followed it till it reached the water. The tension broke like a snapped string.

'Now,' he said, dropping his head like a young bull. 'Now we'll see!' He dropped into a crouch and came forward. The crowd fell back instinctively, but Evan stood there.

It was Beti who ran between them. She had just come up, breathless, and pushed her way through the little group.

She stood there and faced Llew.

'Go away, Beti,' he said with a toss of the head.

Beti stood there.

'Brave you arr!' she said, her mouth hard in contempt. She had her father's spirit. Then she took a step backwards so that the men faced one another again. She waved her hand.

'A sick man is about your mark,' she said. Her tone cut Llew to the quick.

She waved him on again.

'For shame to stop.'

The rest of the hunt were riding up. Llew dropped his hands. In the bustle they were separated. The old Whip, a Border character, face like a sunset, was whipping in the hounds. He had known such things happen before, especially in Wales; it was the chapels. It was a good run finished – that was all.

'Come on,' he said digging his crop into Llew. 'Haud thee breath. Thee't a damned sight less need of it, though, than that thing thee't on.'

He waited until he saw Llew mounted and then walked his horse beside him.

'I rode him as a booy,' he said, 'but the only wind he 'ad was on a wik on grass. No mor'n a puff; if 'e as much as raise his yead he'd have to loose it go.'

The hunt trickled out of the village, they were off to the next covert.

Beti watched them go. She said no word to Evan; but she knew the village tongues would be busy. All her troubles were only just beginning.

CHAPTER XII

Llew could not forget that unhappy meeting in the mill-yard, try as he would. It rankled within him: a slow bitterness that was new to him began to work. That he was beaten and humiliated without so much as a blow struck – that was the cause of it all. He could not fight that way and he knew it. That was the bitter part of it – that he should be pulled up short like this. It was a sort of treachery to his own self. And he knew in his heart that he stood no chance against this man however much he might blackguard him. There would have to be another way, but – there was no other way; as it was it was only beating the air – there was nothing to hit at.

And he felt that old savage resentment his uncle felt well up within him. He and Evan had looked at one another across a chasm as wide as the grave. They had no place for one another: they were men of different worlds.

He had never hated anyone in this way before. It went very deep – far, far beyond the reaches of the mind. And his own helplessness in face of such poor odds moved him to frenzy.

He had gone off for the day. His mother asked no questions – he could go if he wanted. There was no doing anything with him these days: he had to have his own head.

She did not believe all she heard of him, but he was 'getting his name up' fine. There was no doing anything about it, she told herself. This easy paganism – that things must work themselves out – was a part of her. And those little trollops, with all they had on their backs, were all after him. It was no good blaming the lad.

The street she looked out on was not the main street of the town, but it was the spine. It was England and Wales: it was town and country. Up it went the coal-women from the slums of the town, their little trolleys rattling on their loose axles, heads bent down, shawls around them, hands on the shaft and the body doubled, pushing their boxes straight in front of them unpainted, blown with coal-dust – on to the siding they went for their coal.

And here, too, was the 'fair' on fair days – still was the 'fair', in spite of the Smithfield. There were the dealers, loud and noisy, gaitered, in check caps, coloured kerchiefs round their necks, hands in pockets, very loud and arrogant.

And this was where Llew's mother looked out on now, watching them troop by to the eisteddfod – not the national: but a semi-national – the Powys Provincial Eisteddfod. This time they had come down from the mountains, from Wales, as though in a gush. The brakes and charabancs and traps had been 'put up'; the people moved ceaselessly through the town, but not of it, as unsubstantial as wraiths, for all the pageantry and colour.

They were going on to the Pavilion, had been going on all day. All the morning had been the 'Prelims', all the afternoon the adjudications of the lesser works; and the evening meeting, as a wave gathering and crested, would be a burst, a tumult, of song.

But she was not interested; the clamour and violence reminded her of her husband, of the unbridgeable gulf there had been between them. It would break into the quiet of herself; she would have to yield too much in the going. She wanted to be herself with no calls on herself; she wanted to be alone.

Then the door opened, anxiously, and a head peered in.

She arranged her dress, let fall the curtain; she was sitting there like some Gioconda in the falling twilight.

'Are you there, Mrs Morgan?'

'Come in, Mrs Trotter.'

Mrs Trotter was Welsh, married to an Englishman – sour and sedate, a 'death-hunter', who went round touting insurances among the rich and the poor, and those who were neither rich nor poor. The marriage had gone wrong; she hadn't held him – this callow little man with his straw hat and his fair, waxed moustache. He was trying to be 'big', drunk at the Unicorn, got in with a loose lot and let his business flounder. And then in the mixing of the elements he had found no solace in this hard-faced, malignant woman, whom the years had destroyed. They called him 'Perce-is-he-in?' and his wanderings were known; he had two children on the Parish.

She had gone back into herself, she was sour and malignant; her head was always bobbing about in an upstairs room; scandal had become rite, something religious, sacramental. She could not rest without it, in some way it was necessary to her. That was why the mother pulled her dress about her, covered herself, as though in protection. Everything would be noticed, absorbed and be spouted out when and how it pleased. She was like a crow with her dark, waving head – a crow full of evil portent.

'Come in, Mrs Trotter.'

The woman took a chair.

'There's proud you arr! Well, so should I.'

'Proud?' said the mother looking at her in the gathering darkness.

'Now, now, you *arr* proud. Don't say no.'

'It's all double Dutch to me,' she said stolidly.

'But Llew! He iss a wan!'

She wagged her finger at the mother roguishly.

'Joking you arr,' she said. It was too much to hope that she was carrying tidings to the lad's own home. 'And fancy you not there!'

The mother was at her wits' end, she could keep it up no longer, but she would give nothing away.

'Too much trouble,' she said casually.

'Wa-at?' said Mrs Trotter, her voice going up in a shriek. 'Aren't you glad, then?'

'Oh, yes.' She paused. 'Who wouldn't be?'

'And three pounds. Just fancy... three pounds!'

'Three pounds?' said the mother, as though she had been struck. And then she forgot herself. 'Whatever for?' She knew the moment she had said it that it was all over.

Mrs Trotter took her triumph in silence. There was no need for words.

'Well, well!' she said with mock solicitude. 'That iss too bad.' She wagged her head in the half-light backwards and forwards. 'His mother and all!'

There was no more to be said, it was enough for one day. She would have volunteered details, but she dared not.

'I'll be going now,' she said, all of a bustle, with a final peer around the room. 'That's a nice antimacassar,' she added as a last thought. 'Real silk, I suppose,' she fingered it as she passed. 'No... cashmere. But it *looks* like silk. Perce brought me a beautiful silk one from Southport on the last Oddfellows outing – must have cost a mint of money, he's always bringing me presents, though.

'I thought I'd just pop in,' she added, as a final word. She was out through the door and down the street, leaving the mother there in the twilight, gathering her pride about her, her mouth gone grim and her eyes hard.

She didn't care tuppence for Mrs Percy Trotter, or what she thought, but the nastiness of it all had assailed her like a foul breath. It had broken into her serenity, the easy-flowing peace within her. But what rankled most was the thought that her son had not told her, had ignored her. To think that this woman, of all people, had to tell her about her own son!

She heard the low whine of the 'Mail' from far off, and

143

then the confused clatter of it as it ran into the station. Then she sat back and waited.

She had got some sausages cooking for him in the kitchen – the home-made sausages that he loved. They were done to a turn. In spite of herself, she got up to look at them. She said that she would not go – but she went.

Then the gate clicked and he came in, very like a gust, his lively young face tanned by the wind, his eyes alight.

'Look, Mam... all for you!'

He laid the mountain trout out one by one, bright and silvery and clean-run as the mountain streams themselves: the sheen of gold on their bellies – yellow as pollen, and the dark, livid red spots: violent and lovely in shape, their brilliant colours not yet clouded by death.

'There's a place for them,' she said, her mouth hard. 'Look at the mess you arr making.'

He bent down and picked up the grass and rushes that had come out with them. Then he suddenly stopped, in the act of stooping.

'What's wrong?' he said, stiffening.

'You ask me *that*?'

They stood facing one another. There were many things that might have been wrong.

'And Mrs Percy Trotter to tell me – *she* of all people!

Llew's eyes widened. He knew now. He had meant to wait to be told and then treat it casually. That was why he had gone out for the day – to show how little he cared. He could always pretend then that he had never really bothered, and he had prepared the way by abusing the eisteddfod, and all that it stood for, during the past week.

As no one had mentioned it at the station – and he felt quite sure that the whole town must have known if he had won – he had become reconciled to losing. He would say nothing about it and very few people would know any the better, thanks to the bardic pseudonyms which were the custom.

But he was not casual now, he was like a turkey cock.

'Pooh!' he said with a wave of the hand. 'That's nothing.'

'It's about time,' rejoined his mother, 'little as it iss.' She knew there would be no holding him now.

'Little as it iss!' he fumed. 'I like that! You watch me,' he said, wagging his finger, 'you just watch!'

'Go and get your supper, now. It's going cold.' It was the only way of stopping him. She wanted to make light of it for her own sake. It would never do to let him know that she was proud of him.

When he began to talk again, she just said: '*Will* you get on? It will be night and no clearing away.'

He was already turning over in his mind how he would send a marked copy of the local paper, which printed all the adjudications, to his uncle David.

He was finishing when he said with affected casualness: 'Beti not been in?'

His mother looked across at him with narrowed eyes: Llew bent over his plate.

'I only asked,' he said irritably. 'No harm done, I suppose?'

'Funny,' said the mother slowly. 'She iss sure to be down. What have you done to her?'

'Oh, me... it would be me!' he snorted.

'Who else?'

As they were talking there was a hand on the door and Beti came in. It was a family rite: her father would be sure to ask when she got home.

She went over and kissed the mother and then sat opposite her. Llew did not get up.

'Congrats,' she said, without looking at him.

'One for you!' said Llew bitterly.

'Llew!' shouted his mother. 'If you dare! Never mind him, Beti fach, rude that he iss.'

'It's all right, Auntie Meg,' said Beti, her voice trembling.

The two women exchanged such odds and ends of gossip as they had.

'I must be going now.' Beti had got up.

'Llew,' said the mother, 'see Beti back to the hall.'

'Too tired,' he said casually.

'You hear what I say!' she flamed. 'This minute, now!'

'Never mind, Auntie Meg, really...'

'Llew!' shouted the mother, taut.

He shuffled to the passage for his cap and opened the door. The two went out into the street. They walked to the top of the road in silence.

'You can go now,' said Beti, not looking at him. 'You haf done your bit,' she added bitterly.

Llew walked along in silence; his misery was too real for words. It lay on him like a load.

'Who got the Chair?' he said, not looking up.

'Evan.'

She answered in the same casual way. But the word

'Evan' struck him like a lash. She did not say 'Evan the Mill', but just 'Evan'. He read a wealth of meaning in it.

He said nothing. She knew what the effort cost him. Then she looked at him sideways and glimpsed his agony.

They had reached the Pavilion. It lay there low and squat in the darkness. A converted airship hangar, bought cheap, its great curved roof showed up through the beech trees, waving white and brilliant in the night. A shaft of light came out through the great sliding door like a knife cutting into the darkness. It lay there squat and dark and brooding in the cleared-away field, with the sodden cinder path running across the half-turned loam.

'Beti,' he said, his voice very low and charged beyond him.

She wanted to cry out against it. His very voice possessed her. And it seemed as if his own world, some infinitely dark, brooding, savage world, had come about her and encompassed her. She had been wafted up into it with a terrible joy, and was unafraid.

And then, like the wind gathering in a howl, came the slow, unearthly cadences of a hymn; it began, slow, inevitable, gathering strength just as the wind; as wild and pitiless as the wind. It had no place, like the wind. It began and it ended, but it gave nothing. It went in a whine, in fury, overhead, to the unreachable places. The human voice that had gone into it had become lost; the hymn had absorbed it, had taken it as the earth takes in its own growth. The hymn was beyond the choir, beyond them, beyond the sweat-smelling, rustling multitude; beyond them all. It was like some dark, clouded flame, leaping up in its sombre beauty, remote and pure.

147

'Let me go,' Beti cried in terror beyond herself. Her eyes were wild and frightened.

He stood there, his face gone empty and ageless. He had gone beyond her, it was Llew – and it was not Llew.

As though waking from sleep, as though waking from a dream that had been real and was now breaking, she ran across the cinder path to the Pavilion.

Llew was still standing there by the gate.

CHAPTER XIII

The wood climbed halfway up the hill, dark and brooding. As though cut off with a knife it ended. Over the fields, bright with rain, the sunset filtered like mist. Around Llew was the subdued, faltering music of the evening, the crack-crack of a woodpecker in the old elm above, the chirping of the small birds lifting their voices in a cheeky phantasmal chorus, the larks bubbling overhead.

Down the valley the sunset had gone in a glitter, picking out the fields, the hedges, the few roads: the valley lay there beneath him like an old patched quilt, grim and threadbare, its colours half held. And there too was the little town he had just left, labouring there under its load of smoke, which hung down low about it. It looked like a heap of refuse left to smoulder.

It was a mad thing to do – that Llew knew. There was a time for all things – even in poaching. But he could not help himself. He had been chafing at the bit for so long that now in very desperation he sought to free himself. And this was the only way he knew. It was thought that got him down: likewise it was the act, instinctive and within the blood, that set him up again.

His uncle David had not yet written. He dared not think that he would not write. But now, with the prospect of release, life within the little town became unendurable. He actually felt the weight of it, heavy as a load, on his spirit. He turned to look at it again, smouldering there below him, and spat out his contempt. It looked separate now, under its lifting load of smoke, with the green uplands reaching up around it; something put there, something that had been done – not something that was.

As to Beti – what was he to make of it all? He could not make anything of it, and that was why he dared not think. The sense of his own helplessness provoked him beyond himself. If there had been no holding him before there was to be none now.

And yet everything he did was aimed at her. But the more he tried to show her what a fine fellow he was the less he succeeded. Even the eisteddfod prize had gone flat. Just as though it were nothing at all to go in and win on the first time out. And then the feeling – the certainty – came to him, in his bitterness, that were Evan to fail it would count for more with Beti than if he, Llew, were to win. What was one to do against *that*? It was hopeless!

A cock pheasant had broken into his reverie – a cock pheasant, screeching with its peculiar imperious hulla-baloo, rose in its commotion out of the wood, its brilliant plumage fired in the sunlight. Through the creaking branches it went in its effort to free itself, and then, lifting on the breeze, droned away out of sight. Then the blackbirds began to screech – that sharp high screech of terror – a jay joined in with his raucous note and a little owlet, suddenly startled from sleep, tossed out into the light and went fluttering round and round.

'Diawl. A fox!'

Llew knew there was no time to lose. As between the two poachers who were to go padding noiselessly through the darkness, the fox was the first. He scampered from his cover, crouching low with the easy animal crouch, clambered over the fence, and was within the wood. It was another world there within: the soft lithe trunks standing shadowless, end on end, limitless and vague in this strange twilight. Above there was no sky but a roof that rustled and creaked ominously. Below, the sodden carpet of pine needles, moist with wet earth. And everywhere alleys dim and lightless and the sharp acrid scent of resin.

He held on to the air-gun grimly. For a rustling pheasant there was nothing to touch a good air-gun. It was the poacher's weapon, it made no noise. You got a sight on the roosting pheasant, like a dark nest up above in the branches, and then there was the tiny crack. It would come down, all of a flutter, dropping from branch to branch. Then there was the quick snatch and a turn of the neck.

He had walked for half an hour through the wood's dripping silences, anxious, expectant, finger on trigger, and then, through a break towards the wood's end, there was a sudden glimpse of the sky, and the dropping sunlight spread around like blown powder.

There was a pheasant on the edge of the wood. He took careful aim and pressed the trigger. It came tumbling down into the field and then went squawking off – a runner!

And then as he stood, there was a report so near it was as if the sound had hit him. Over his head went the stream of shot, the whistling ping of it as it cut its way through the branches, sending a shower of pine needles and leaves over him. Again another shot, another shower, and then the noise and the shouting.

'Diawch... we'll have him now. Quick, quick! Through there, man, through there.'

In answer to the sharp, excited Welsh voice came the homely Border tongue:

'Bide a minute now! I inna roamin' into six shot for thee or thee betters.'

Llew knew them without seeing them, knew Mathias, the keeper, dry, beetle-browed with his dripping moustache, coarse as a mane, furtive, secret; knew old Ned Jarman, with his front of corduroy, an old rogue, fat as a water-butt, straddling as an ape, with the wicked rogue eyes of the roamer.

And he could hear the wire in the fence rattle as the keeper crossed into the wood; he could hear the breech snap to as the man reloaded his gun.

He dared not run as yet.

Within in the wood, with its dancing shadows, Mathias was beside himself with fright.

He began to bellow:

'Who... who iss there?'

There was no answer, but the peculiar deadening echo of his voice trailing off through the still trees.

152

'If you arr there, you must come out now, indeed, this min-nit!'

He waited for an answer, but there was none. Then he shouted almost coyly, as though it were some spectral game of blind man's buff.

'I *see* you!'

Llew, some insistent, unanswerable demon bidding him, shouted from the depths:

'Peep-bo!'

Up came Mathias' gun. From where the voice came he let first the right, and then the left, barrel.

The charge went very near Llew: he saw the bark rip off the tree next his. So close was the shot he thought he had been hit. Instinctively he rubbed his coat sleeve, his thighs, to feel. A sudden sense of danger came to him. Half-crawling, he bolted off through the wood while the keeper was re-loading. And after a while, panting and breathless, he leaned against a tree. He had gone very white around the gills, and that shutter had come down over the eyes, making them hard.

Slowly he crept forward, alert and braced, ears attuned to the innumerable rustlings in the wood. He knew the bury they were ferreting; he knew the keeper would go back there.

Then he heard the sound of voices: the keeper and his companion.

'You'm back,' hailed old Jarman. 'You'm best leave well alone. Them folk dunna like that sort o' welcome.'

'Diawch!' the other shouted in exasperation. 'I know the little pugair. I know: I know!'

'Well, if you'm know, you'm been a long time findin' out. And this 'uns killed below.' Jarman pointed to the hole. 'We'm best put in the liner and find 'un. It'll soon be dark.'

'I know him,' shouted the other in his frenzy. 'And it's lucky for him his hass isn't sprinkled... yes, indeed to Cod.'

'And that inna your fault,' grunted the other. 'You'm bite off more'n you can chew and you shot a man in cold blood.'

'I wass only frightening him,' said the keeper.

'Aye: maybe. But it's the sort o' fright you wunna like yourself.'

'Phut!' said the other. 'I shot up.'

'You'm shot pretty low, by the sound, whatsomever,' answered Jarman.

'The little pugair,' shouted the other viciously. 'There's more in pickle for him yet. By Cod, and he goes down for this.'

'Am you getting the ferret out or no?' bawled Jarman.

But the other went on: 'Oh, leave the tamn thing. It was who I see. And who I see? It was a lad, I say. And what lad? All right! Shooting feesants out of season, one; shooting game without game licence, two; carrying gun without gun licence, three; on the estate, four...'

'Leave 'im be; leave 'im be. You'm might ha' got a charge youmself.' Jarman was a wag, a local 'character' made pious by his professional status – that of rabbit-catcher – but wearing authority hardly.

'Shoot me you say! Ha, ha, ha, I go in one side; he go out like bolt rabbit the other. And who wass he, ay? Llew Morgan. I put ten gold sov-rains on it now for you. The good-for-nothin' lout he iss. Where iss my wandering boy tonight? Shooting feesants on the estate!'

'He's young and windy,' said the other, and then, dismissing it all, shouted: 'Am you getting the liner out or no?'

'Haf you tried paunching a rabbit?' said the keeper, returning to business.

The old man took out a clasp knife and paunched a rabbit, putting the steaming guts on a windward hole.

'That wunna fetch 'un out,' said the old man derisively. 'He's sweeter meat down there, I reckon.'

Fussing about, the keeper ran from hole to hole, listening. He had his head down to the ground, listening to the mute drumming in the bowels of the earth, the faint drumming of the slaughter in the depths of the warren.

And then, posturing and turning, he suddenly presented a side of corduroy to the lad, his buttocks stuck up like a mushroom over the bury.

Very carefully Llew lifted his gun. It was a good ninety yards away, and at ninety yards there was no danger. The pellet would bounce off his trousers.

He pressed the trigger. The head emerged, the two arms went waving aloft. And then, holding his trousers, the keeper began a mad scamper across the fields, old Jarman following him. Away through the gorse he went, in furious speed, never a word spoken, the old rabbit-catcher lumbering and bellowing in his rear. He began running in and out of the clumps of gorse, gambolling like a spring lamb, still with both hands holding tightly the seat of his trousers. With both hands he began to beat a tattoo on his hindquarters.

'Be Cod I'm shot: be Cod I'm dead. Diawch ario'd, this iss the end of me, straight!'

Jarman drew level with him, panting and blowing, waddling along like an old bear.

'Bide a minnit, man; bide a minnit. You'm a'right,' he got out between his breaths.

'Be Cod and I'm dead,' the other wailed.

'You'm too much alive,' said the old man. 'Where'm you feel it?'

'Oh, I'm killed, as sure as Cod.'

'You inna killed that end,' said the old man stoically. 'Haud on.' He unhitched the braces and cast an approving eye around.

'Iss there plood, man? Any plood?' wailed the keeper.

'Never a bit,' answered the other, musing. 'Not a scratch, for all thee trouble.'

'Do something, in the name of Cod,' shouted Mathias.

The old man searched around for a dock leaf, plucked it and then, very painstakingly, rubbed it on the affected part.

'Mind out,' he said. 'There's ladies a-comin'.'

The keeper hitched up his trousers hurriedly.

'This iss not a laughing matter,' he said. 'This iss murder by the inten-shun, if not the deed. This iss fery, fery, fery serious.'

The old man bowed his head.

'And whoeffer, or whateffer, fired that shot iss charged with manslaughter. There now!'

'But you'm not dead,' said the old man, puzzled.

'I am not, ay? Then why not, ay? Whose thanks iss that? It iss thanks be to Cod, it iss then.'

156

'And them corduroys,' said old Jarman admiringly. 'Them inna ready-made, I'll warrant.'

'No jokes, please,' said the keeper through his teeth. 'There iss a time for all things. You arr witness, remember. Come on.'

They hurried back to the bury, collecting their gear. The keeper was still rubbing his haunches ruefully.

Arguing and expostulating, they made off; the keeper's voice, high and excitable, came across to Llew in broken sequences. He watched them go, old Jarman straddling along with his two sacks of ferrets, the keeper with his gun, the liver bitch padding along in the rear.

He waited until it was dark before he set off. The town lay before him in the valley: he caught the sparkle of its lights and the copper glow over it, and above the great vault of the sky, very still and quiet in its space. He had a feeling within him that trouble was brewing.

He hid his gun on the way down and went on whistling. But at the end of the street he met the sergeant of the town police with the keeper.

'Am I wrong now, then?' said the keeper. 'Where's the little pugair blown from then?'

'Haud on: haud on,' said the sergeant ponderously. 'Where you been?' he said to the youth.

Llew had stopped whistling. He looked at them impudently.

'Bird nesting,' he answered. It was early autumn.

'None of that,' said the sergeant.

'None of what?'

'None of your nonsenses. Where you been?'

'Never mind.'

'Nefer mind!' shouted the keeper. 'By Cod it iss nefer mind and me with plood-poisoning on me any min-nit. To the station, sergeant, and no waste of time.'

'You give an account of yourself, me lad,' went on the sergeant.

'Search me,' said Llew, holding open the flaps of his coat.

'The knavish little pugair,' went on the keeper in his venom.

'What you want?' said Llew. 'Anything on me?'

'A ploody lot!' shouted the keeper.

'Shut your mouth.'

'By Cod...'

Llew put his fists up. 'Come on!' he said.

The sergeant ran between them, puffing.

'You li-arr,' shouted the keeper.

Llew had gone very white around the gills.

'You wait...' said Llew nodding.

The sergeant ran his hands around his pockets and shook his head.

'A good thing for you,' he said.

'Don't men-shun,' Llew sneered. 'Anything else?'

'Pug-air off,' said the keeper, beside himself.

Llew turned in his stride and knotted his fists.

'You wait!' he said again. He nodded his head like a young bull. He had the same glare in the eye.

'Get along with you,' said the sergeant, glad it was all over. 'Off you go.'

Llew went on down the street whistling and kicking a stone before him. It was only later he remembered that it had nearly put paid to all hopes he had of his uncle David.

CHAPTER XIV

Whatever happened to Beti, whatever tumult her young life was in, life at the Red Lion went on just the same. If it was breaking up – this old life – then it would go slowly. It would fall away a bit at a time like the old castles that dotted the country around – flaking off with wind and weather but still there, and with some of the character of the men that built them; grim and arrogant though a thousand years had gone. That was what the English could do, who had marched in. And they said that Wales, which was there then and had remained throughout the conquest, was going – that in a few years yr hen wlad would be no more. And her father stood there like a bulwark. He did not *think* like Evan, he did not aspire like Llew: he was.

The last to go had been Seth Rowlands. He would be back by the next harvest he told them – but he had gone. A relation by marriage had a milk walk in Bethnal Green,

London, and he had taken to the road as was his way. He had sent a postcard to them, with the picture of a college on it, saying that he was 'passing through Oxford'. It was addressed to Twmi but it was meant for everyone. The old man wedged it behind a piece of brass harness over the hearth and those who read it wagged their heads just the same as though Seth were there.

Twmi had become more and more daring – that is to say he now made no pretence of humouring authority. He established the fact that his house could open when and how he wished. That was his answer to this uncertain wind that came from the east. And his wife, who knew that the loss of the licence would mean the loss of everything, had become worse than ever.

To Beti they were her father and mother and that was all there was to it: but they were two different people, strangers to one another, a thought that had never before come to her. She understood her mother and she did not understand her father: but she would have done anything for him all the same. In a way they did understand one another.

It had been a hectic Saturday night. It gave promise of being a still more hectic Sunday.

The 'jentlemens' had gone; the grouse shooting was over. Twmi kept a record of the 'bags' on a piece of cardboard cut out of a boot box and carefully ruled across, which he hung over the cellar stairs. Now that it was all over he brought out the record of the 'season' and read it aloud to the company: 'Thursday, 25th. Two grouse, one blackcock ("blind at birth"), one hare ("trodden on")', and he would go on improvising quips throughout the reading.

At the height of the revelry the parson had come in, as was his wont. The fun had begun again. Dici had told a story of the Methodist minister, with many incidentals. Although the village was largely 'church' there was a chapel, a huge hummock of a thing, like a barn, with the word PENIEL let into its cement front in pebbles.

And the minister, Isaac Jenkyns, an old man like the parson, was in his way just as remarkable. Always with his head cocked like a robin, as though waiting for the celestial voice, a long white beard, tea-stained and ragged, and mild blue, anxious eyes, not one word of reproach had ever been levelled at him. He had been a poet as a young man: he was still a poet, though he never wrote poetry now. He knew very little of what was going on around him: he believed everyone. No one had ever heard him use a harsh word or come to a harsh judgement. He was a laughing-stock, even among his own people, though the laughter was kind: it could not be otherwise.

Dici was telling the story of how old Jenkyns had been invited to preach at the Big Meetings at Llandrindod Wells. It was a tribute to his lifetime of labour and was also an attempt to bring him up a bit nationally. The old man would live and die in his own village, though he was a great preacher and when he got on the hwyl – the sing-song note of ecstasy which is the test of a sermon – he made the chapel rock.

And so Mr Jenkyns went with his little black leather gladstone, through the junction set in the fields, to preach at the Big Meeting. It was one of his best sermons but the old man found, on arriving, that it would not go into

English. He had two glasses of chalybeate at the springs and then walked several times around the lake searching for the English, of which he had very little.

Dici told the story with gusto, one eye on the parson, spread across the settle in a flood, but who never, by nod or wink, showed that he was listening. He never referred to nonconformity in any shape or form; it was something that had happened. But he waved his hand to Dici intimating that he could proceed if he wished.

So Dici went on. It appeared that they did not want to send the old man back – it was nearly a day's journey – without something to show for his pains. Would he give the children's address? The chapel was crowded: the children had walked down to the front pews as was their custom. The old man, pushing the pulpit Bible away from him and leaning over the rails, held up his hands in the old way of his.

'Leetle children... what I say to you? I know. I KNOW!' He wagged his finger knowingly and his old eyes sparkled. 'JONAH!' It came out like the clap of a bell. He leaned back and threw his head in the air. There was a long wait, the old man with his beaming eyes, holding fast on to his secret. Then he leaned forward and in an awesome whisper went on, 'Jonah! Three days and three nights in the pelly of the whale!'

He wagged his finger from one end of the row to the other. 'Three days... and three nights. There's a little pugair for you, yess?' His voice went up on a note of triumph.

The old parson never laughed, never even looked up. Twmi only nodded to show that he had heard. But it set some of the others off and the chapel people, who would have laughed if they could, looked down their noses discomfited.

'A fine preacher though,' said Moses, musing. 'He can let it rip, I tell you. None better.'

'None better?' said Dici on his mettle. He looked over to the settle with a proprietary nod. The old parson had sunk back into himself, a way he had when he had taken too much. If provoked, he would raise his great head in a mild stare like an old bull browsing.

'No personalities,' said Moses, worried. 'Please!' He lifted his hand calling on Dici to desist.

But Dici went on, judging his audience:

'What iss a sermon, ay? Something spontantanous.'

Wili the Hut, who was also 'church', concurred with a wise nod.

'For spontan-tantiety there iss only wan man in Wales: in England come to that.'

'Ay,' said Wili, 'no smells of the lamp for *him*.'

Moses sniffed contemptuously.

'I bet you then!' said Dici in challenge. The argument had gone too far now.

'Excuse me, sirr...' But the old man never raised his head. Dici touched him lightly on the shoulder and he raised his bloodshot eyes and slowly surveyed the room.

'We were saying, sirr, as how you can preach on anything.'

The old man wrinkled his forehead. He was annoyed at being disturbed.

'What's anything?' said Moses. 'Be fair now.'

'I was saying, sirr... I was saying to these jentlemens,' he cocked his thumb contemptuously behind him, 'that, give you a text, sirr, and off you go, sirr, like a trout up stream, sirr.'

'Text?' said the old man, like a bear at bay. He fumbled for his spectacles and staggered to his feet.

'Not now, sirr. Tomorrow.' He patted the parson on the back and gently forced him back to his seat. The old man glared round the room, his blue eyes glinting, and then sank back into his doze.

'There's two pounds on it,' said Dici gleefully, pulling out his pigskin purse and giving them to Twmi to hold. 'A man iss as goot as his money.'

That was how the bet came to be made. The text was to be handed up to the pulpit in a sealed envelope during the morning service and just prior to the sermon. It was the best bit of sport there had been for a long time.

That was why, on this Sunday morning, Twmi had gone, searching for his hard collar which hung on a peg behind the taproom door. He wore it only for church and auctions. Beti had to go round him several times with a brush, taking the fluff off his best navy blue suit, while he reached and twisted his neck in the encumbrance like a hen with the gapes.

Beti, her prayer-book in her hand, walked with him along the road, proud in her heart. It suddenly struck her that, although he was her father, he was almost a stranger to her. It was like an adventure – to be out with him like this. For all his weight he carried himself with a swagger, and his top hat was set at a rakish tilt. Again she wondered what her father might have done, might have been. Like Llew, whatever clothes he was wearing, he always gave them a certain grace, gave life to them. He could have held his own anywhere if he wanted to: had the 'manner' as all the Tudors had.

The little church was very full, for word of it had gone round. It was not often there was something like this to look forward to.

There was a hush as the old man came out of the vestry and strode across to the lectern, his tattered surplice spread out behind him. He made one or two attempts to take it up with his free hand and then let it go: he knew that it would follow him. He went through the first part of the service with his usual formal take-it or leave-it way. He showed not the least concern, beyond looking over the church and finding it, with a grunt of approval, to be more than moderately full.

When he came to announce his text the silence was awful. But he fumbled about the pulpit for a long time, making great show of the preliminaries. Then he raised a finger and beckoned to Twmi. It was the first indication that he was aware of the congregation – aware of them except in so far as they were something that filled the church. Twmi went up to the pulpit rails and fumbled in his pocket. The old man reached out a hand casually while Twmi was fumbling.

And then Twmi handed it up to him – the sealed envelope he had been given. He nodded affably to Twmi and tore the top off the envelope. He looked first one side of the paper and then the other and then pushed his spectacles up on his forehead. He gave Twmi a nasty look but said nothing. He glanced casually around the congregation and then, screwing the paper up into a ball, dropped it at his feet. It was a blank sheet.

'The text,' he said, 'is…'

He wetted his fingers and turned over the pages of the Bible. He went backwards and forwards several times before he found it, and the commentary that accompanied his search was heard from one end of the church to the other.

'The Book of Kings,' he said, his voice rising on a note of hope. 'The First Book of Kings… the eighteenth chapter, and the forty-third verse. "And he went up, and looked, and said: There is nothing".'

He began his sermon – one of the most remarkable sermons that had ever been heard in that part of Wales.

He ran briefly through the story of the creation, and then gave a vivid account of the wanderings of Noah in the ark with minute details as to the countries over which the ark passed, which, although submerged, were yet individual. Here black men; there yellow men and, still farther afield, the redskins and the immense prairies with their yellow corn waving under the still waters and almost brushing the keel, until eventually he came to rest with the ark on Mount Ararat and gave a minute description of the flora and fauna on the unsubmerged crest.

Here, as the list was running out, he brought in several local herbs such as Robin-run-the-hedge and others, with a detailed account of their medicinal properties and, as he got to the end of these, in the full flood of eloquence, invented some remarkable ones of his own, such as whiff-of-cowslip and dandelion's daughter, investing them with cures so wonderful as to cause his audience to gasp in wonder.

And then, having drawn this covert, he was off again in full cry, coming to the seed of Abraham which kept him going for the best part of an hour without a pause. He rattled off the sons Zimran and Jokshan and Ishbak, and the sons' sons as if they had been his own, touching up one or two of the more interesting names with several anecdotes, from what source no one knew. Cleopatra, he explained, had jilted Abimelech for Ephron the Hittite, thus incurring the jealousy of her half-sister, the Queen of Sheba, and so bringing on the tribes of Israel the trials and tribulations which had scattered them to the four winds. That was why there were Jews all over the place, he said.

He then faltered a little but came out strongly on Elisha and the bears, explaining the various kinds of bear, the brown bear and the tree bear, the Himalayan bear and even the polar bear, with much useful information as to their food and habits and methods of breeding and much else. He was taking flight to the passage of the Israelites over the Red Sea when fatigue and thirst brought him to a stop. He had been speaking for three hours and nineteen minutes without so much as a note, and with scarcely a pause.

When they got back the Sunday dinner was ruined. It was a sirloin done on the spit, but the outside was caked and burnt and the very 'quick' of the meat as Twmi called it – the blood-red centre of it – was gone. It worked on the father and mother in different ways and Beti sat there silent between them. To her mother it was a meal spoilt – the worst thing that could happen: to her father it was not a meal at all. He pushed the plate away from him, half-done.

'And your old committee,' his wife said with a sniff. Her

face was very white and strained. 'You will go to the well wance too much: yes you will. You mark my words.'

'Haf be!' shouted Twmi across the table. His eyes had gone narrow and there was a glint in them.

The committee was a Sunday night institution, as sacred to Twmi as the Sabbath itself. There was Sunday closing in Wales and the committee had been formed, not so much to combat it, as to transcend it. It was both church and chapel: the odour of sanctity clung to it in a way, and redeemed it. It was drinking, it was true, but it was not week-day drinking. It was hard to explain the difference, but it was a very real difference. The churchwardens, the deacons, came as they were – frock coats, top-hats, and umbrellas – and met to discuss local gossip, to tell funny stories. It was true that there was a great deal of drink, but that was incidental. No one worried very much about it. Twmi, who was always in the chair, certainly did not, and if any of the others did they were always prepared to waive a point, as the circumstances were altogether special.

'Haf be! haf be!' he said, dangerous. This sort of talk was sacrilege.

'And wan more time you want,' went on his wife in her shrill voice. 'Wan more: Peepy-Tom says to you as plain as plain can be.'

'Woman!' he roared. He got to his feet and caught hold of the table with both hands until the legs creaked.

'Dad!' shouted Beti, frightened. She had never seen him like this before. He was as if one possessed. And then, as suddenly, the rage left him. He let go the table, and straddled off without another word for his Sunday sleep.

He would sleep for two hours in the front room, a handkerchief over his face.

But in the evening he unlatched the front door, put an armful of logs on the fire and sprinkled a bit of sand on the flags. Then he pulled the long table away from the wall and set a bench on either side of it.

One by one the elders dropped in and took their accustomed places. They laid their top hats on the table before them and swept the tails of their frock coats over the bench as they took their seats. Some of them came through the yard.

Moses was the last to arrive, panting.

'It's a bit funny,' he said.

They all looked up at him.

'Who you think on the bridge as I came past?' He paused, as the bringer of tidings. 'Peepy-Tom *and* Sergeant Pugh!'

'*And* Sergeant Pugh?' said Twmi, raising an eyebrow.

'Sergeant is a sport,' broke in Dici.

The country sergeant was a large, florid man, with greying hair which stuck up from his head. He had kind blue eyes which made people laugh to look at them. The delight of his life was fishing, but he never caught any fish. He had great hopes of a steel minnow from London which he kept in his tunic pocket and looked at many times a day.

'They wass give me a nasty look, whateffer,' said Moses, who was not happy.

Twmi got up and slipped the latch on the front door.

They went on telling stories but Moses had taken the edge off things, and the first sign of life was when Dici and

Dan Meredith got into violent argument about the difference between a collision and an explosion – an argument that would have come to blows had not Twmi intervened.

'Silence,' he said. 'Cod damn it...' and banged the table, with the mallet he had brought up from the cellar, until the rafters rang.

'Chair: chair!' chirped the others.

Twmi swung the mallet round in his hands and then tested its weight. He glared at the two men in turn and in another minute he would have given them a tap on the head to show them their places.

'It's this way,' he said ponderously, giving judgement. 'In a colle-shun there you arr!' he brought his great hands together in a clap; then he flung them open, 'In an explo-shun... where arr you?'

He had no sooner finished than there came a hammering at the back door. He cocked his head with that ancient look of his.

'Quick pooys,' he said. He caught hold of the top hat nearest him and placed it over a mug. They all did the same. He waved his hand briefly and they all bowed their heads.

When the police came in Twmi was well under way. He had rolled his head backwards and his eyes were half-shut in bliss. He prayed and he prayed. It was in the old tradition and he let it go. The heads before him nodded an accompaniment, here a heave, there a sigh, a groan. And, extemporaneous effort as it was, Twmi got caught up in his own fervour. He went on and on. The tears were trickling down Dici's nose on to the table: Moses was wagging his head like an old horse and heaving up such sighs as if his heart would break.

'O annwyl Dduw bach. Tyrfa y diafol allan o galonnau y sataniad sydd yn byw yn ein plith… ac y rhai hyn sydd yn meddwi ac yn tyngu a rhegi ac heb ddim myned yn agos i gapel… ond yn gwneuthur pob math o ddrygioni. O Dduw – dyro i mi dy glust a gwrandawa ar fy ngweddi…'

One large drop like a crystal hung on the sergeant's nose. He was trying to get his sleeve to it and then, surrendering, reached for his red bandana handkerchief. Peepy-Tom was shuffling his head and sniffing.

Twmi went on and on. They were all in tears now. And then, as a hush after a storm, his voice dropped to a whisper. Like a frail barque, having battled with storm and tempest, it now rode into the harbour's quiet. He began the opening bars of a hymn, which rounded off a prayer. It spread to them all like a low echo. The sergeant's *basso profundo* came like a blast from the doorway. He was letting it go.

It had begun and now it ended. It was all over. Twmi, the sweat heavy on his forehead, turned an anxious face to the visitors.

The sergeant came over and wrung his hand in fervour. Twmi affected to look pained.

'Oh tamn!' the sergeant said. 'There's sorry I am to disturb.' He wrung his hand again, 'Pure mistake I assh-ure you.'

Twmi patted him kindly on the back. He had forgiven him. Then he led the sergeant away.

As they were passing through the back bar Twmi gave him a nudge.

'Just wan,' said the sergeant.

'That man waiting out there!' he added while Twmi was drawing the beer. He cocked his thumb to the yard and gave a significant nod.

'Yess; yess,' said Twmi in sympathy. 'Got eyes in his hass, that wan.'

He turned off the tap and came over with the mug.

'And here,' he said, dropping his voice to a whisper and jerking his thumb backwards, 'Those would not be thinking twice about a drop... Sunday or no Sunday.'

'Ay. Ploody gluttons,' answered the sergeant viciously, and wiping a hand backwards across his mouth in expectation.

'Yn gampus!' said the sergeant in frank admiration as he took a gulp. 'You got that top note all right.'

'Not pad,' answered Twmi modestly. 'No practtees though.'

The sergeant finished his drink in great secrecy and laid the glass down gently. Then Twmi led him to the door and let him out into the yard.

CHAPTER XV

Uncle David had turned up trumps. Nevertheless Llew made his leave-takings with bad grace. He would have just gone off without a word but his mother kept him down to it. So he went the rounds very cocksure of himself, and the supercilious note in his farewells cut short much good advice that would have been piled on him. He did not want it. He told the worthies as much by a toss of the head and a certain insolent cocking of the eye.

He had wanted to go – and he was going; that was all there was to it. So they wagged their heads after he had left them; after all they were glad he was going, too. Only Llew – because he was Llew – made no bones about it.

His three-ply trunk – fresh from the 'Emporium' – was locked down in the little hall. He had spent two penny packets of labels on it so that the ends, top and sides bore the word PADDINGTON in block capitals. He was taking no chances.

He was an outsider – he did not belong – and he resented the people of the town taking any interest in him. He had always pictured his last night as something like this.

He ransacked his mind. Was there anyone in the town who had any real call on him – something more than the dumb show of leave-taking? There was not one. Yes – there was one, and he felt a sudden pang as he remembered. The old man was nobody and yet to Llew he was very real. He went out of the house for the second time, in search of him.

Old Jarman was waddling over to the hutches when he heard a shout. He pivoted round, brandishing the skewered liver like a lowered lance.

'Oh. You it be.' There was a warmth in the old man's tone that came out beyond the words as Llew approached him. 'You'm scare one out a one's wits... little as I have.'

Llew stretched out his hand sheepishly.

'Good-bye, Ned.' The old man lifted the hand and then dropped it.

'You'm bringing strange news, nemma God.'

'I'm off tomorrow. On the "express".'

'Never now!'

'I am. Off to London.'

'Lunnon! Nemma God! And what's in Lunnon that's ketched thy eye all at once? It's a mighty long way away.'

'Never mind. I came to say good-bye.'

He felt very ashamed about it all.

'Well, I never,' said the old man turning it over slowly in his mind. 'Hey. Hauld on! You inna goin' like that. Come you on in. Them ferrets can wait.'

He led the way into his cottage, low and close-smelling.

'Florrie, Florrie,' he called. 'Damn it, where is the 'ooman?'

His wife had been mixing pig-wash in the yard. She came in, wiping her hands on her apron; old and bent, with light lively eyes in a face lined and bleached like an old apple.

'This young varmint be off,' he said, jerking his finger. 'Off to Lunnon.'

'Well, fancy!' she said, beaming.

'Aye. Goin' to be a gentleman,' he said. 'He wonna know us after a bit.'

'Now, Ned. None of that,' said Llew, hurt.

'Dear me,' said the wife, sentimental. 'An' I knew him *that* high. I putt him in a clothes-basket on washin' days; when his mother wanna looking. Aye – he was a one! Had a temper worse than thee Ned – and that's enough for a wik o' Sundays. He wonna remember when I washed up there.'

'Leave be: leave be,' said Ned. He had no place for sentiment. 'But we inna sendin' him off without someat.'

He went off to the back and when he returned shook out the net he was carrying. It was a silk partridge net of his own making. 'There thee art,' he said casually, tossing it over to him.

'Mind they dunna ketch thee tho'. Them's sure to be smart in Lunnon.'

Llew fingered the net lovingly. He knew how much it had cost the old man in time and money.

'Tell me how thee'st get on with it,' went on the old man in the same casual way. 'Thee't find it a'right in a bit.'

Llew promised that he would. He assured the old man that he would play havoc with the London partridges.

175

Jarman moved off to a cupboard under the stairs, grunting and groaning in the darkness. He struck his head against the rafters and began to blaspheme.

'This auld house inna bigger than a decent 'utch,' he said. 'There inna much o' me auld yead left. There now – ' he brought out a bottle, gently rocking it, then held it to the light, then very gently puffed on it, blowing away the dust

'They anna *this* in Lunnon, I warrant.'

'It's tee-tee, Ned? You know I'm a Rechabite.'

'A reckobite! Be God and thee't not the first that's smelt the wrong end o' a cork! This wonna hurt: dandelion bloom. Five year auld.'

He poured out a glass slowly, the dark yellow liquid trickling out with a gurgle.

'Thee taste that. It'll warm the cockles o' thee 'eart all right.'

'And it's tee-total, Ned?'

'Phut. It's only pissabeds. Thee't a man now.'

The two sat down together, the lad drinking gingerly; Ned filled up his glass.

The wine brought a glow to Llew's stomach. The last few days had been anxious ones for him, had moved him off his own centre. And this stuff restored order in chaos. It was very good.

'You mun have a drop o' birch, too.'

'No, no,' said the boy, anxious.

'What's birch?' said the old man. 'It dunna hurt.'

The boy began again. And why not? He had never tasted anything like this before. It made you feel better after you had drunk it, not made you belch like pop. The world was glowing, and rosy, and very right.

'An' to think,' said Ned, 'as how it were more good luck than judgement thee inna picking ookum.' He paused at the contemplation of it, of the bewildering twists of life.

'Oh, that! The swine!' Llew spoke with mounting bitterness.

'Aye,' said Ned placidly, 'he canna sleep o' nights for watchin' hisself. But that inna to say he nearly had *thee*.'

'It would take a better man than *him*,' said the boy. But the gamekeeper began to take shape in his imagination, gathering shape like a picture in smoke.

'He had it in pickle for thee all right.'

'Did he?' said the lad menacingly.

'Oh, aye. Once he'd stopped rubbing his hass. He'd have got thee sent down all right, trust him. Oh, but theest ought to ha' seed it. Oh dear: oh dear me...' He laughed at the remembrance, laughed until the tears trickled down his face. 'The way he went over that field! "Be Cod – it's murder, blue murder," he shouts. "Hauld on, hauld on," I says. "By Christ, it's blue, all right," I says, havin' a look. "I shall die," he says. "Well, what odds?" I says. "Thee't die hass up like a nero." Oh dear me! I canna help laughin'.'

But the lad had gone very white and silent.

'Going to do for me, was he?' he said strangely.

'He was that.' And then as Jarman looked across at him he added. 'Well – what o' that? Throw it over thee shoulder.'

The old man was disturbed. Somewhere within his slow-thinking brain he was worried and alarmed.

'You know what he said? Called me a liar.'

'He shunna ha' done that. Too bad.'

'A liar!'

'Ah well. Dunna let that worry thee. Thee stick to the truth and it ull get thee in a right auld pickle sooner or later.'

He was temporising. The lad's mood worried him.

'He shall see – shall our Mister Mathias...' said Llew through his teeth, the wine in his head, all restraint gone. There was nothing in the world now but the keeper: nothing but the insult. It burned through him like acid.

'Oh deary me! Thee't like all thy kind – only worse with that red head o' thine. Thee't as hot-hassed as a wasp. Let him be. He inna worth a breath o' thine, I say.'

'A breath!' shouted the lad quivering. 'Liar, am I? All right.' He got up to go.

'Now look,' said Ned. He had waddled to the door and flung out his huge arms across it. He knew now; he was in earnest and his little eyes winked menacingly, serious. He wagged his finger, once, twice. 'Thee dare not lay hands on that man – thee't be killed. Be a good booy now; be a good booy – for old Ned's sake and go 'ome.'

Llew was beside himself. He was very white and quiet; but his eyes had gone hard and baneful. There was no stopping him now.

'Ned – let me go.' His voice was very quiet and still. 'Perhaps you'll fetch the sergeant,' he sneered; 'and you one of the old-timers; took on all comers. And says "Go home" as if I was a lurcher.'

'All right: have it thee own way,' said Ned. There was something inevitable about it, and he yielded. He could not

178

argue against himself. He was too near the earth and the ways of the blood. It was no use.

'Thee't not a chance,' he shouted after him. 'Not a chance.'

He wished he was young again in the old far-away days of his glory. He crooked his left elbow and put his left knee out in the old-time stance of the old knuckle-fighters. He had been a match for anyone on the Border then; had fought the champion of Staffordshire over fifty-seven rounds and was still standing when the police broke up the ring. He would have gone and taken on the lad's quarrel without as much as a thought, because he liked him, liked him in that knowledgeless companionship of the earth. But he was an old man now and he could do nothing. It made him annoyed. But he put on his cap and straddled up the gas-lit street after Llew's hurrying figure.

Llew was making for the King's Head. He could not help himself now: he was past all thought or reason. His spirit leapt up within him like a single consuming flame. The thought of the insult – so long ago forgotten – almost choked him. The cool night air with the chill of winter in it, swept around him, around his head, flushed and hot with the wine.

But within he had gone ice-cold. The weight of the insult seemed to press on him like a load, crying for relief.

He went along quickly, in his long stalking stride, never once asking himself the reason; there was no reason. He did not know what he was to do – only in some vague uncertain way did he know that he was to justify himself, that life, to him, under the load he was carrying, was killing him.

At the King's Head he paused. The air of it came out

stale and acid; within was the gas-lit taproom and the noise and banter. It was a place that he feared, a place apart and beyond him. There were men there and it was the man's world, distant a few years, but as remote as the stars.

He would not go in on sufferance and he would not be laughed at. Mathias he would settle, but not the easy tolerance of this world beyond him, the eye-lifting questioning, the joke and the wink and the loud laugh. He was a lad, and he dared not meet them; they held their position by a right older than he knew, but a right he guessed at. It was that thought that kept him in the dark alley-way, passing and re-passing the lighted door.

Then he went in. He knew he would find his man there. It was his particular place of call – this pub that was not quite a hotel nor yet a beer-house, the place not of the tradespeople, but of the farmers and keepers and small sporting folk thereabout. He went in with his head down, fearing to think, anxious to get it over without fuss.

And the keeper was there at the bar, his liver bitch beside him, deep in talk with some of his own kidney.

Without a word the boy walked up behind him and plucked his sleeve.

'Just a minute.'

The man turned round, staring insolently. 'What do you want with me? Be quick about it.'

The other men had heard. They made a great show of toying with their glasses.

'You can come outside then.' Llew got the words out with a gulp. He felt easier now; it was all over and done with.

The keeper started back as though he had been hit. His eyes narrowed malignantly. A sudden hate transformed him. Then he remembered his audience.

'Outside be Cod! It's cold enough in here. What iss it? These jentlemen won't mind, I'm sure.'

'I'll tell you that outside,' said the boy, his face hard and white.

'No, indeed you won't. You'll tell me here or — off. So there!'

'Oh, yes!' said the boy, his stomach moving, his strength returning. 'And supposing I don't — off?'

'Then you stay here and be tamned, for what I care.'

He turned his back on him. The boy caught him by the shoulder and swung him round. The keeper pushed him off heavily. The crowd in the taproom gathered round in a circle.

'What you want, ay? A kick in the backside, ay? By Cod I have patience, but not too much.'

'You will kick, ay? And scratch too, ay?' said the boy in bitter mimicry, his eyes cold and grey as stone. 'But you will fight too, ay?'

It was a threat, a command. He carried all before him in his mounting frenzy.

'Be off with you, I say now.' The keeper glared at the lad through narrowed eyes. His courage was that of the coward cornered, vindictive, malignant: 'Be off, you hear. I don't thrash pups, and good for you.'

'You don't, ay?' Llew put up his fists, his body slipping into the poised animal crouch, sprung as steel.

Two or three of the men ran between them.

'Harry!' shouted the keeper to the potman. 'Throw the little — out. What have I come here for, ay?'

'Throw him out!' said the boy through his teeth. 'Throw the little — out, Harry. That's right. *You* try! And call your ploody dog too!'

'Do you hear, Harry. By Cod...' The men hustled the boy back.

'*Sow!*' he said, his voice very low, the word coming like a breath.

'Now, now,' said one of the men. 'What's it all about? Leave hold of the boy, I say.'

He was a miller from beyond the town, one of the local sports, in check suit, dandy bowler and leggings. His favourite phrase was 'a bit o' sport'. All life was 'a bit o' sport' – badgering, clay pigeon shooting, cock-fighting; he was always there.

The sympathy had gone out to the boy. These men, in their rough and ready way, were genuine enough. Courage was a real thing to them.

'Out with it now...'

'Ask him!' said the boy, quiet again, jerking a finger at the keeper. 'He knows. Only by Cod he won't split,' he said in mimicry.

The men began to laugh. They were enjoying themselves secretly, the secret delight in a quarrel.

'What's it all about, Math?' asked the miller, self-elected judge.

'You ask me now: I like that. The little whelp wants his hass kicked.'

'Oh yes,' sneered the lad. 'And who's going to do it? Now

you – all of you,' he said, turning to them, 'Give him a chance; be sports.'

The men laughed outright. He had turned the tables upside down. His impudence had caught them unawares.

'You're going to: you're going to have the chance of your life. Here – or outside.'

The men were flabbergasted. The boy had carried them along with his impudence.

'Well he inna chicken-hearted whatever. Give un his due,' said an old farmer, moving his pipe across his teeth and spitting in emphasis.

And the miller said. 'No more chin-wagging. Out with it: now or never. We'm been patient.'

'There's nothing to say,' went on the lad. 'Once he tried to get me down. That's his job. But he never saw me, see: that's dirty that is, very dirty. But look at him – he's lower than a snake's bottom.'

'Ho, ho, ho. Now then; no personalities, please, please.'

'And he called me a liar after I was cleared. Called me a liar!'

'Oh, dear, dear. That inna right. What about that, Math?'

'He said he'd get me,' went on the boy. 'This iss his chance; I'm off to London tomorrow.'

'Go on me booy: go on.'

'He can say he's sorry,' said the boy. 'If he doesn't... I'll knock his ploody teeth back – and that's straight.'

'Wait a minnit; wait a minnit,' said the miller, throwing

up his hands. 'Not so fast; not so fast. Do I understand this is right? Your turn now Math. Out with it.'

The keeper stood there scowling, face twisted with hate and fear, the fear of the cornered. He wanted no more than to get out of it as best he could.

'I never called him a liar now.'

'Liar.'

'Hauld on; hauld on. Keep thee mouth shut.'

'Liar!' shouted the boy again. 'You can ask the sergeant.'

'What about that, Math?' They were provoking a quarrel for 'a bit o' sport'.

'That he iss a liar to say that...'

'Now we are agreed,' said the miller, business-like. 'Liar: liar.' He moved his big hand from left to right. 'There canna be two liars anyway.' He was warming up to it. 'What you say?' He turned to the boy.

'Nothing.'

'How nothin'?'

'I said I say nothing,' said the boy quietly. 'I'll wait outside.'

'Nemma God. Now we know where we are. And you, Math?'

'I will kick him down the street if he dares to lay hands on me.'

'If he dare? You'm heard him.'

'All right. I haf said too. It will not be on my hands.'

'Call him out,' said the boy. 'Into the yard – that's all.'

The keeper hung back. 'He iss a bit of wind: that's all. You had best be getting him home.'

'Listen,' said the boy. 'Here's my fare. Two pounds and

one over. It's all I got. Hold on to it – there. Now ask him to cover it: and you can all stand by and see fair play.'

'That *is* the best of all ways,' said the miller. It had been what he was waiting for. The old farmer nodded approvingly. The others began to mumble among themselves.

'And I'll lay an even quid,' said Bound the Garage. 'Ginger for pluck all right.'

'I'll have it,' another shouted. 'It's easy. He canna last a round: good lad as he is.'

They began talking among themselves, the hum and buzz floating over the two who stood facing one another. It was going to be 'a bit o' sport' all right.

'Some of Iago Powell's bif steak we want; will in a bit.'

'Up in the warehouse booys. There's room for all up there.'

They carried up chairs. Two hurricane lamps had come up from the cellar. 'Not a word, mind. There'll be a fine auld to-do if it gets round.'

'You'm ref,' someone shouted at the miller. 'Queensberry rules and all fair all round. Let's be sports anyhow.'

'And now seconds,' said the miller. 'Who'm you want, me booy? Take your choice. There's a lot with you.'

'I don't care,' and then, as his eyes wandered to the door, 'old Jarman.'

The old man had waddled in, his big head bent forward like an old bull, grand, impassive, taking in his surroundings.

'And nobody better. The old man's seen the best o' em. You'm in his corner,' shouted the miller. 'Come on, Ned.'

The old man wagged his head. 'It inna my doin'. I done my best,' he said.

185

LLYFRGELL COLEG MENAI LIBRARY

'Don't you want to, Ned?' said the boy hurt.

'Come along wid you,' he said roughly, 'and get thee shirt off: thee't have thee yead off in a bit.'

They went up the old dust-blown stairs that creaked beneath them, following the voices and the glimpse of lamps right up to the top storey, above the housetops, with its broken beams and falling plaster, its half-shuttered windows and its grime. The rats scuttled off in the rafters at the invasion, the breaking up of the years' silence.

Old Jarman held his nose as the sour air assailed him.

'It inna very sweet,' he said wheezing. 'The bats wonna hang up here.' He pushed the lad into a chair and peeled off his shirt; he was himself again.

'Now hauld him off; keep dabbing at him.' He flicked his great fist in and out to give emphasis. 'Dunna mix it; nemma God, dunna mix it.' He lowered his large head and dropped his voice to a whisper. 'Dunna thee mix it in the name o' God, or on you'm back you'll be – like that.' He clapped his huge hands in a crack.

Llew, startled, jumped up out of his seat.

'Easy now, easy,' said old Jarman relenting. 'An' dunna hauld on – you'm not goin' to push twelve stone about. He's too heavy for thee there. Futwork: futwork. Run the auld — around a bit. He inna no fairy. He'll blow – give him time. And old Ned's watching thee. Dunna thee worry, me booy.'

He slapped the boy's back and plucked at the muscles, ran his hands down his legs as though he were a racehorse. And the lad nervous and quivering on his mettle, nerves on edge, his feet pawing at the floor, was a racehorse.

The lamps were hung on the rafters. They threw out a pale yellow fitful gloom into the dark spaces of the old warehouse. The men crowded round: the miller stood there, watch in hand, importance in every gesture.

'Give 'em room now booys: fair play all round. Stand back agin the wall. Now,' he said, 'am you two ready? When I ring the bell start; when I ring the bell stop.' He held up the little brass bell from the bar counter. 'No wrastlin', no dirty work. Fair's fair. I wonna say any more. Come out where I am.'

They came off their chairs, out from the shadows, and stood there facing one another, Llew lean and lithe as a panther, poised on his toes, his eyes alight and his shock of red hair over his pale drawn face like a nimbus; the keeper dour and sturdy with a man's bulk and shoulder, malignant in his darkness, in his sour, down-drooping eyes, narrowed in hate.

They stood there, man and lad, with the breadth, not of age but of race – the 'little dark people' and the full loose-limbed Celt – between them; a knowledgeless enmity which neither of them knew. They stood there, toe to toe like the powers of light and darkness, watching one another with the instinctive watch of animals. The man's was the provoked courage of the baited, of the turned on, unyielding and passive, with no life in it, but life-defying in its stillness, its oriental depthlessness. But the lad had the exultant, leaping courage of his race, flame-like and pure. It was the adventure, the battle that brought joy to his nostrils.

'Am you ready – you two?' The miller held up the bell. Then he brought down his arm and the two rushed together. All fear left Llew as he came forth; all thought and anxiety went. It was life itself, the fight. It could have gone on for ever. Everything moved into place; became a perfect part of things – that rich undreamt-of feeling flooded him as with a glow. That he would be beaten, that he would triumph: these were the unthought-of-things. It was the fight that mattered.

And the keeper came out swinging his arms like a flail, his eyes fixed and scowling. The lad, poised there, met him. He took it all on his arms and gave ground step by step. They were wild blows and he counted on them. He kept his left arm up and he slid back on his feet, right back into the line of men. He could not meet the man's weight and he knew it. He backed out into the room again, the man after him.

The men were shouting and yelling.

'Let him have it, booy. Do summat.'

But still Llew went back, round and round, watching for them and taking them on his arms. He had to watch those fists as they came pounding at him. Round and round they went, like two animals circling. The keeper stood back a moment, blown with his clouts, his fists working. Then he made a sudden rush. But Llew, as with instinct, had seen it. He side-stepped him as he came in and then belted him, once, twice, as he passed, half-turning him round. Then he rushed in and crossed him with his right, clean on the jaw and rushed out again, circling round beyond range.

It was the first real blow of the fight. The keeper, shaken, came on head down. But Llew, on his toes, was ready for him. Once, twice, he flicked out his long left hand, sending the man's head back with a jerk. They landed fair and square between the eyes but they did not stop him. He swung a blow that caught the lad in the ribs causing him to grunt on the impact.

'Hauld 'im off: hauld 'im off,' shouted Jarman.

Again the man caught him, and yet again. Llew, winded, held on. His feet dragged after him, his breath came again with infinite pain. He shook himself free and moved off out of distance. But his head began to nod as a poplar in the wind.

'Time,' shouted the miller. The little bell clanked. The men went to their chairs.

Old Jarman flapped a towel over Llew: his life came back.

'Nemma God! He nearly had thee. Watch them swings I say,' panted the old man. 'One of 'em's enough. Move around, and bide thee time. He unna breath for prayers by the look of him: he canna last. Keep thee left in his face: dunna let up. That'll moither him. Get thee body into it though. He wonna want many.'

The old man sluiced him from a jug and slapped him with his great hands until he winced.

'Easy does it: easy does it,' he shouted as the boy left the chair.

But Llew was now alight. All thought and desire had left him: his limbs moved with a soft easy richness as though melting around him. He moved and pranced round in a lovely easy motion as though poised in the air. And he had taken up the tempo of the fight, that effortless flowing tide which moved with slow motion beyond the blow on blow,

189

the rush and clout and counter. It played on him like the wind on a full sheet, every breath of it caught and held. On a bit: off a bit, in a ringing, unthought-of rhythm.

The keeper had done with rushes. He stood there glowering and defiant, his dark eyes glowing, pivoting around on his right leg, his fists doubled up before him: like a great bear, harassed and defiant, before the dogs.

And then in a flash Llew's head went down on his shoulder and his left arm shot out like the strike of a snake. Crash on the mouth it landed, drawing blood. The keeper spat and spluttered and moved his mouth from side to side and then brought the back of his hand across the trickle. Round and round went Llew, weaving the air with his hands, his body sprung and taut and poised on his toes. Again he shot out the left and then drew off from the vicious swinging counter that would have dropped him.

The crowd was in an uproar.

'Go it booy...'

'Thee'st got him going, now...'

But old Jarman, his great head bobbing anxiously: 'Bide thee time now. Ease off, ease off.'

Llew drew away out of distance. Through the clamour old Jarman's roar came to him. He had wanted to go in and finish it on the impulse.

So they circled around again, their eyes glaring, as if held. And then, with old cunning, Llew rose on his feet and flicked out his left arm in a feint. The keeper was waiting for it: he swung his arm right in a counter in one tremendous lunge, meeting only the air. He remained there for one split second like a reaper in the act of throwing, his right arm about his own neck, half blinding him, his left stuck out taut and useless. Llew, his left leg bent up like a show horse, went forward with a stamp. Foot and fist crashed together, all the weight of his young body in his up-going right. It sank in under the man's breastbone; he heaved back under the impact and then fell like a dropped ox, on his knee.

'One... two... three... four... five...' called out the miller.

Then the little bell clanged. It had saved him. They heaved him on to his chair frantically. Llew began to pace the floor, all fire.

Old Jarman rushed forward and clasped him, lifting him to the chair.

'Keep thee yead: nemma God keep thee yead. It inna over yet. Thee'll want that breath.'

The old man's face was aglow as he busied over the lad.

'That'll hauld him. But take thee time. Hauld theeself right back now and do it nicely. Oh, what a clout,' he said forgetting himself. '*What* a clout – as nice as iver I see'd.'

'Mind he dunna get dirty,' whispered the old man in parting. 'Hauld theeself out. Dunna spoil theeself now. How's thee hands ?'

Llew held them up. 'They'll do.' He patted him on the back. 'Auld Ned's behind thee. Dunna worry, me booy.' He calmed him as he would a chafing horse.

The men were out again, the same circling round, the same stolid, revengeful stance of the keeper. He was holding himself back, and Llew, sensing it, was wary. He was content to hover around, picking his blows when he could.

191

And then, all of a sudden, the keeper had rushed him. He staggered back under the impact, his young frame creaking, but he did not fall. Instead he held on as he was pushed backwards, working his arms around the keeper's in the clinch and so stifling the blows. Grunt after grunt the man gave as he tried to free himself, tried to lunge into the boy with his tied arms.

And then, as they twisted and turned, the boy lifted clean off his feet in the man's desperate vigour, the keeper, in the scrimmage, brought his knee up. It caught Llew in the groin, paralysing him. Consciousness slipped and came, and then slipped again like a dancing star. He watched the blurred lights heave and dance and then quietly subside and straighten themselves. He saw the people again, heard old Jarman shouting. But the pain cut through him like a knife. He would not, he dared not, let go and fall. And no one knew what had happened, not even Jarman.

And then, with the man's breath on him, heads together, he whispered in Welsh, whispered with infinite menace:

'Diawl...'

He loosened his right hand and brought it up viciously across the man's face, tearing it. Then he brought his head down on the man's nose with a crack and heaved himself free.

Restraint gone, he stood there toe to toe, slugging in his savagery. A cloud in his head numbed and half blinded him. He shook himself like a dog and plunged after the retreating figure before him. His very violence forced the man back. Right and left he swung his arms in frenzy. He had landed by luck, the man's head went back with a crack and his arms dropped.

192

'Stop it: stop it,' they shouted.

'Leave be: leave be. He's bate...'

But Llew neither heard nor saw. In one quivering single instant in the dull clouded haze before him, he saw only a head rocking and the eyes up. He brought his fist back and put all his young life into it, teeth bared, nostrils snorting. Crash went his right in one wild, sweeping hook. It landed flush on the man's jaw, toppling him backwards; he fell like a log, never moving.

Llew staggered back, blood on his face, his legs weary and leaden and his head all of a hum.

He felt Jarman clasp him and then the sharp acid trickle of cold water on his bruised mouth. The room turned and swayed in an awful motion. The shouting and the uproar were beyond him, as though at the end of a long dark passage. He was all in.

Jarman bent him double, forcing his head into the bucket, then slapped him hard across the face. He put a hand up feebly to save his mouth.

'Where am I?' he asked dully.

'On thee feet me booy, and that's summat. Thee't be better in a minnit. Keep thee breath to blow thee supper.'

'He's good for a young 'un. By God he is an' all,' said the miller coming over. 'What sent him off... ?'

'It's down here,' said Llew in pain.

'Dunna worry,' said old Jarman. 'Them'll last thee a few years yet awhile.'

'Come on,' said the miller. 'Cover him up. He's goin' to have somethin' as ull help him up a bit.'

They had all gone in a body down the stairs.

'Here,' said the miller. 'Give him this – and by God he deserves it.'

The brandy burnt Llew's throat and then sent the blood flowing again. His neck was very stiff and his limbs ached, but he was much better.

'An' a bit o' plaster for his mouth,' said old Jarman.

'There now thee't dolled up right and proper. Thee't in a bad way for courtin' – upstairs an' down.'

Llew had remembered. It came to him as a shock. He looked at the clock; it was already half-past seven. He felt very sorry now. But he would brave it out. But it was too bad of him – on this last night of his at home. He owed it Beti, he thought with sudden generousness, no matter what.

He bade Jarman good-bye, the old man pretending to be casual about it. But the lad was after his own heart, and he would have done anything for him. The old man made light of it all as they shook hands for the second time that night. Then Llew went home for his bike in the passage and headed for Tanygraig and the Red Lion.

CHAPTER XVI

The long ride through the night air had cleared Llew's head. He still felt the glow within him – the exuberant retching of his stomach, but his head was clear now after a few miles. But there was no stopping him: he stemmed down reason. He was going to the Red Lion to say good-bye, but he was really going to show off before Beti.

It was time she knew what a man he was. She should know. He had fiddled about too long, and perhaps he had lost her – fiddled about because the exact niceties of her little world were beyond him, and he was afraid of putting his foot down. And this was Beti – the grown-up Beti. But it was not her world that mattered – it was his. He could not understand her now, but then he had no need to; it was her place to understand him.

He jumped off the bike at Craig-y-Pistyll his forehead wet with sweat, and the clear air came to him off the moors. He smelt that air. It was always the same; it had a body to it, rich as cream. Above him the gorse reached up the mountainside; the bracken, wilted and brown, rustled in the wind, its crinkled stems sounding hollow and distant. The road bent round the mountain like hairpin, a ledge on its face. There was a drop of many hundred feet into a gullet of a valley, down which a torrent tumbled, a reach upwards of many hundred feet to the summit, with its pale crust showing up against the moon-flooded sky.

This was really the thin insubstantial line between England and Wales – the real Wales. He always felt it as he passed the old bent bridge over the ravine, with its rails of piping and its moss-encrusted posts. He always felt a load lift from him and all his senses become awake. That was why he sniffed the air, because he actually felt it; it was as real to him as anything was real. He threw his head back and his chest went out in his exultation. He did not know when he would see this old familiar place again – not for many years, perhaps. But he did not feel sorry. He had never thought about it, so he could not feel sorry. It was.

He ran his bike against the turf rim of the road and walked into the bracken. He stood there, the self gone out of him, his face gone mute and ageless. Then he bent down and felt for the moss at his feet – felt for it with the hand of a lover. He fingered a bracken stem, passing his hand down it and feeling the rough touch of it, and then in his excitement he broke it off and crushed it in his hand into ripe splintered spears.

In a moment of ecstasy he bent down and pressed his face into the earth and got the smell of it. His nostrils were wide and his face transfigured. He threw up his arms to the sky like a man in prayer. Then, as suddenly, he came back to himself and went in search of his bike. He had made his leave-taking: it was hail and farewell in one.

When he got to the Red Lion the house was full. Twmi was sweating with his exertions.

'When you off?' he said to the lad, with a nod.

'Tomorrow.'

'Good riddance,' said Twmi blandly. He winked to the company. 'Young pugair will have London by the yeahs in a month.'

'Now, now,' said Dici, breaking in. 'Llew has it up there!' He tapped his head. 'I back Llew any day.'

'Ay,' said Twmi, 'I back him too – both ways. There and back.'

'Never you mind, Llew,' went on Dici.

Llew did not mind. His uncle's chaff was something understood between them.

'Have a look for Seth,' went on Dici. 'Bound to see him, man – Bethnal Green is the place. Grand place, sure to be.'

'Ay,' said Moses, ruminating, 'he was always a one for the green fields, Seth was. Trust him to smell out a bit o' green.

He will be finding a blade or two in the clinkers when he gets down below.'

'By Christ he hass no place on Heaven with the like of you there,' snorted Dici, who was 'church'. 'It will be Sunday all the week.'

'Peace, boys – peace, boys,' said Wili, unctuously and holding up his hands.

That was how trouble always started.

Llew took a seat near the light. He was annoyed they had not seen the sticking-plaster.

'What you done now?' said Dici all at once.

Then the old man waddled over and lifted his chin up.

'Cod tamn!' said Twmi. 'You got what's coming now, haf you? Serve you right!'

Llew dismissed them with a wave of the hand.

'They carried *him* out!'

The men crowded round.

'Be a sport, Llew bach. Come on!'

'Mathias,' said Llew, and left it at that.

'Shutapp man!' Twmi snorted, roused beyond himself.

'They carried him out, I tell you. What you think I am, ay? See that!' He showed his bared knuckles. 'That's what he got.'

'Iesu mawr!' said Dici, aghast.

Like his uncle, Llew, stripling as he was, dominated the company. He rode rough-shod over them. But then the Tudors were an old family, born for leadership wherever they were. But for his uncle he had no word. It was not that he feared him or respected him. It was simply that his uncle was himself, grown older.

'Hey, you!' shouted Twmi, bringing the drama to a close.

He cocked his head towards the kitchen. 'Go to your auntie now and get some fresh.'

Llew went off to the kitchen without a word. He knew that Beti would be there. All the way along the road he had pondered on what he would say; now he knew he would say nothing.

His auntie was there, crocheting under the light. Beti sat opposite her, also crocheting. She dropped her eyes as he came in. She sat there under the lamp very mute and silent as though she had gone back into herself. She felt him, and closed up like a sea anemone.

'Uncle says I'm to have some fresh,' Llew said briefly. He pointed to his mouth and his face twisted in emphasis. 'What for I don't know,' he added casually.

'Llew! What *haf* you done?' exclaimed his aunt, pushing his face to the light.

'Fell down,' he said. It was for Beti's benefit.

'Fighting, more like,' said the woman, bustling around. 'Nice thing, too!'

'How you know?' Llew asked, looking over to Beti. Her head was bent over the table.

'How I *know*? I wish I was wrong for wance!'

'Well you arr not,' said Llew. 'No need to hide it.'

'No need indeed...' The woman wrinkled her nose in contempt. 'And no plaster in the house that I know of.' She went bustling out of the room. The only thing that interested her was to find the plaster. It was something to be done.

Beti and he were left alone.

'Sorry...' he said after a while.

She looked up for the first time. He felt uneasy under her steady stare.

'For what?'

'For causing the trouble.'

Llew had hoped to be a hero or a martyr. He struck an attitude that would have done for either. But instead Beti

199

took no notice. Something was between them and there was no breaking it down.

'Don't you think we'd better haf it out?' he said, after a while.

'If you like.'

'When?'

'When you like.'

'There's anxious!' he said bitterly. 'When you like!'

'When you like iss when you like,' said Beti again.

They could hear the woman bustling about above them. She was on her way down.

'When I come back,' said Llew briefly. 'I am going for the salmon.'

'Llew!'

She had almost shouted at him.

'Why not?' he asked, amazed.

'You must be mad!' she said in contempt.

'Mind your business!'

'Llew!' she said again. She got up and faced him. 'You off tomorrow!'

'Well?'

'Just suppose – suppose you arr caught?'

'Me caught! I like that. There's going to be some fun to-night, I tell you.'

'You arr a fool, Llew,' she said in the same even voice. 'You arr just a fool.'

'When I come back,' he said in a final breath as he heard his aunt on the stairs.

'Llew, please...'

But his aunt had come in and with a great to-do cut off

two strips of plaster and then put them cross-ways on the cut.

'Lot of good to you it iss,' she sniffed. 'Nice thing to go to London with, I'm sure!'

He did not trouble to answer her. In such things he took his cue from Twmi. They were things to be endured.

When he got back into the taproom he guessed they had been talking about him. They fell silent as he entered.

'What about it?' he said cocking his head to the brook. There was no holding him.

'Too late,' said Dici. 'They gone down three days since.'

'I bet you!'

'One or two, maybe,' said Dici giving ground. 'A few old cock fish that gone wrong. Ach y fi! Like old bits of wood.'

'Right you arr, Llew bach. Count on me, gwas. A bit of sport is a bit of sport any day.' It was Wati, who had just come in.

Wati's river, over the watershed, ran to the sea in a few miles and the sewin which flooded the estuary went up it in a cloud of silver. But the sewin was only the small brother of the salmon. Here in the brook were the real thing – the twenty and thirty pounders which had come up two hundred miles of river to spend themselves in the spawning grounds at the brook's source.

'Here's wan,' said Wati again, giving himself a dig in the stomach.

Three or four other men joined in.

'Only the gaffs now, boss.'

'Silly pugairs!' said Twmi in contempt. 'What you hope for, ay? You will be getting more in a sixpenny tin twice times over.'

201

He went off and got the gaffs, nevertheless.

'Not very sharp,' he said taking the beer corks off the points and rubbing his finger over them. 'They haf been pulling out trees with these wans.' He gave a flourish. He was enjoying himself.

The men were reaching up the great chimney for the soot. They wiped their hands on the soft sides of it and then rubbed them over their faces. In a few minutes the transformation was complete. They looked like nigger minstrels with only the red moist line of their lips and their eyes showing.

'How many you want?' said Llew at the door.

'Get along with you!' Twmi shoved them out into the yard. 'You keep a watch out now, I tell you! They arr up the brook two pairs at a time. Anything in knickerbockers – first time for it!'

'Ay, them bloomer things that comes over the knee. You effer see a watcher in trousers?' Wati spat in his contempt.

Outside Llew, looking up to the sky said:

'Too much moon.'

The moon, pale as an ice disc, went sailing over them, the sky empty save for a few clouds that hung about like fleeces.

'Ay – but there's better coming,' said Wati pointing to the distance, where a dark cloud lay like a smudge across the heavens.

'Only the lamp, Llew,' said one of the men.

'Afraid?' Llew sneered.

He took the acetylene lamp from his bike. It would throw a bright hard spike across the brook to bring the salmon up, and it could be shuttered off at will. But it was not the best way, though it was the safest. The old way was to soak some sacks in paraffin and tar and hold them, flaming, on the end of a pole over the water. But they threw a fitful gleam, like gorse blazing, over all the countryside and watchers miles down the river could see it. But Llew was beyond all thought. He went into a barn to search for the sacks.

They went laughing down the road, their voices lowered and carrying the gaffs upright before them like shepherds' crooks.

Then they dropped over the hedge and went off across a meadow to a dipping pool fenced around with stakes. The pool itself was edged around with a crust of bank worn under by the water: the turf dropped off in flakes at the slightest touch and they had to be careful. Where the sheep went in it shelved off into the water on a gravel bottom, but here it was too shallow.

They sat down and watched the moon, smoking with their hands cupped.

'Well, Llew...' began Wati. The little man was at a loss for words. All that he felt he could not say. 'The last night...'

'Ay.'

'Pity.'

Llew did not want to think. The moonlight lay across the fields like a hoar frost, very white and clean. Sometimes a cow coughed from somewhere beyond them and the owls in the wood across the brook were awake. These and the swilling gurgle of the brook beside them, the low swish of the wind in the trees, were the only sounds in the whole of their world. Around about, in line against the sky, were mountains.

'Pity,' said Wati again. 'We haf had some good times.'

They fell silent. There was nothing more to say.

'You seen Beti?' said Wati after a while.

'When I go back.'

'Pity'

'How – pity?' said Llew roused from out of himself.

'You gone the wrong way about it, Llew.'

'Oh, him!' Llew leaned over and spat into the water.

'Not much cop,' said Wati consolingly. 'Diawch! But women arr funny things, man.'

Llew did not bother to answer. He felt his spirit leaving him. But Wati went on in mounting anger.

'Like fishes they iss. Take an old spent gnat, now, after you haf tried all the book. Funny; fery funny.' He shook his head in his despair and kicked his feet into the turf.

'Haf be,' said Llew warningly.

'No offence. But, oh tamn, if they would only haf sense!'

The moon rode into the clouds and the landscape fell away quietly, inevitably. With it the men's senses quickened. They felt their own presences now that they could not see. With quick hands they got the sacking alight and held it out like a torch over the dark water. The light fell around in a golden pool. Bits of the sacking, burnt incandescent, fell off and floated into the water. The men stood there, braced, gaffs in hand. They were watching the circle of light that flamed over the dark water, lighting up its surface.

For a long time they stood there. Nothing had happened.

'No goot,' said Wati who held the pole. 'They gone down all right.'

'A bit longer,' Llew answered. He had rubbed the point

sharp with a stone and leaned over the bank, his body sprung.

Then he shouted: 'Watch for you!'

A shadow, indistinct in the swift running current, was backing into the circle of light. They felt it rather than saw it. It floated into it like a half-sunk log.

'Tamn, he's a pig wan,' whispered Wati. He gave the pole a twist sending the sparks out.

The salmon, bemused and wandering, beat its way out of the glare and circled round. As it passed in an arc Llew, leaning over the bank, got his gaff over its back. With a turn of the wrist he struck it home good and true into the soft flesh of the belly. The water was whipped into foam with the splashing.

'Steady Llew!' shouted Wati. He handed the pole to one of the men and reached over the bank. Then he bent down and felt for the gills. With a heave they had it on land. Llew knelt on the head as it struggled in convulsive flaps; it sent him up in the air and Wati ran for a stone to finish it.

'Nearly thirty pound,' he said casually as he watched it flounder. 'And out in a ploody wink.'

The little man rubbed the scales off his hands.

'There's more about, I'm thinking,' said Llew.

'Whist!' shouted one of the men.

They all stood upright.

Someone was coming. They felt it first through their feet – the drumming of feet on the earth. They stood there and waited.

'First time,' said Wati knotting his fists. 'Sooner the better.'

Now they could hear the dull thud of the feet, but they could not see. They were hemmed in by the brook which was in flood.

'All right, Llew?' said Wati. That was his only thought. 'Stand close, boys.'

Llew felt for a handkerchief and wrapped it round his bruised fist.

'Sticks iss no good,' he said briefly. 'First come first served.' He crouched down, waiting.

They could see the men now, three or four of them, moving as shadows before them.

'Who iss there?' came a voice. There was no answer.

'I know that wan,' whispered Wati.

'Jentlemen, stand still.'

'A put up,' said Wati in disgust. 'You know him?'

Llew was not sure.

'Wili the Hut,' said Wati.

'Don't let on then, keep it up.'

'Caught red-handed,' went on the voice. 'Nice state of things. What iss that with you?'

'He jumped out,' shouted Wati. 'We arr putting him back this minnit.'

'Put him back, then.'

'He can't swim,' said Llew, 'he forgot how.'

'None of your nonsenses,' roared the voice.

'Yess sir.'

The men had come up, they had handkerchiefs over their faces. Llew edged around them.

'What's the game, ay?' said the voice.

Suddenly Llew bent down and crooked an arm round the

man's thigh. He gave a heave and sent him headlong into the brook. He fell face forward with a splash.

'Help – help!' he wailed.

'Drown, you pugair!' said Llew in disgust.

But Wati had run down the bank with a pole and reached it out to him. Wili had clambered on to the bank, dripping. He was wringing out his trousers, his teeth chattering.

'Iesu mawr!' said Wati. 'He nearly went.'

'Sorry,' said Llew going up to him. 'Pure mistake.'

Wili was cursing in his shivers.

'Get him back,' said Wati, 'he will catch his death.'

'How was I to know?' said Llew innocently. They were laughing until the tears came. 'There's a fright you gave us, man.'

'Tamn you,' said Wili, through his teeth as he squelched along the bank.

They made him run about the field to get his circulation, and Wati followed him with a gaff to keep him at it. The others were doubled up with laughter, holding their bellies until they were bent in two. It was a daft night.

Then they walked back to the inn, shouting and laughing. Wati had stuck a gaff haft through the gills of the fish and tried to carry it in a stagger, but its tail flapped on the ground, so they lashed it on to a pole.

They weighed it in an outhouse. It was just over twenty-seven pounds, an old kelt with the big thin head and spiked jaw. Still, it was the biggest they had had for years.

'Give it to the cat,' said Wati, giving it a prod with his foot. 'If it had been a hen fish we'd haf had the roe.'

'Let's go back.' Llew was ripe for anything.

'No we haf had enough for tonight.'

Wati plucked his sleeve and whispered.

'Go and see Beti now. You do as I tell.'

'When I please,' said Llew, on his dignity.

'No good at all, man.'

'Who – me?' flared Llew.

'No, no,' said Wati irritably. 'You are going the wrong way altogether.'

'We will see,' said Llew with a savage nod as they walked back to the house.

'Ay, we will see all right!' Then he added under his breath, 'That is all we will.'

'Silly hass, you arr,' said Twmi to the lad as he came in. 'Get his death he will!'

They had got Wili's clothes off and put them to dry around the hearth. He was sitting in a suit of Twmi's which hung around him like a shroud.

'Whose fault?' said Llew. 'He shouldn't go playing with fire.'

'Fire be tamned,' said Twmi. 'He looks like burning – poor little pugair!'

'Gone too far,' said Dici shaking his head.

Llew was in bad grace.

'You learn some sense,' said Twmi, wagging his finger. 'You get more than you bargain in London.'

'Haf be,' broke in Wati. 'Llew wass not meaning any-thing, wass you Llew?'

But Llew was sulking. The high spirit had left him like a breath gone out. He was annoyed with them all – they were all in league against him, he felt sure. Most of all he was annoyed with Beti. All his gathering annoyance centred on her. He would give her a bit of his mind.

Wati saw him get up to go.

'Haf wan first?' he said as he plucked him by the sleeve. He knew Llew did not drink, but at that moment he felt that he should. He saw that nasty glint in the eye which was Llew right enough, but a very different Llew from the lad he could be. Llew at his best and at his worst showed in the eyes, more expressive than speech and over which he had no control.

Llew shook his arm free.

'Llew...!'

'Mind your business!'

And this was to his best friend. Wati sighed and shook his head.

In the kitchen Beti was alone. The lamplight fell on her dark head, giving it a glint. Her hair, so neatly parted, fell around her neck in a tumble, and however demure she sat this suggestion of wildness always clung to her. She did her best to subdue it, but to no purpose – the little unlooked for things always gave her away. That was all Llew ever remembered of her and all that he understood. The sad, bewildered searching of her eyes, so dark and round and lustrous, were part of a Beti he did not know, nor want to know.

'Where's your mam?' he said gruffly.

'Gone out.' She did not look up.

His aunt seldom went out, she was one of the appurtenances of the house like the mice and the cats.

'Nothing special?'

'No... nothing special.'

Llew fell silent. He did not know how to begin. He shuffled his feet anxiously and twisted and untwisted the handkerchief on his hand. This was so unreal a thing, this talking with Beti. He felt that it had to be done and he was going to do it. But why, he did not know. That he was going away and would not see Beti for a long time – that he could understand. He knew that was bound to happen. It was the same as leaving Wales. But there was no need for a lot of talk. For Beti was still there and Wales was still there – and as they were there so they were a part of him. If that was *all* things would have been easy. But that was not all, and he was bewildered and lost. He could no longer act out of himself – and therefore he had to be false to himself. He could only bluster and he had a premonition that blustering would not do; things had gone too far for that now.

'Beti...'

'Well?'

'Let's go out.'

'You know I can't, there's no one in the house.'

She went silent again. And then, as though speaking to herself said: 'Say what you've got to say.'

Llew took the challenge.

'Well... what's the game?' That was all he could say.

'No game... that I know of.'

'Don't be funny, Beti.'

'Don't *you* be funny either.'

'Haf I done anything?'

Beti looked up at him.

'No... not that I know.'

'Well... what's the game, then?'

'I don't understand.'

'You've got somebody else?' asked Llew.

'I am not saying.'

'Yes, you haf.'

'Well... you seem to know.'

'Funny you arr!' said Llew bitterly. He had come to a full stop. There was nothing more to say.

'You seem to know,' said Beti again.

'Yes... I *do* know,' Llew answered threateningly.

'Then why ask?'

'Say no more,' said Llew. His mouth shut in a line. His face had gone hard and still.

'Anything I done?' he said after a while. No words came to him.

She looked up at him, facing him.

'No.'

'You know me.' That was all he could say.

'Well... ?'

'Then what's the game?'

'You had better go,' she said. 'There's no use staying.'

'Oh yes?' he sneered.

'Please...'

'Oh, yes?'

'Please, Llew!' she got up and opened the door.

He stood there back to the fire, his eyes hard and relentless.

'Shut the door,' he said. It was a command. She obeyed him as she had to. 'Now listen...'

She bowed her head, afraid to look at him.

'I got a word to say.'

'Go on.' Her voice came in a whisper. Her head had drooped.

'Who you think I am?'

'Go on,' she said again. She could not hear her own voice.

'You think I don't know, ay?'

She did not answer. There was nothing she could say. Then some voice within her spoke.

'It does not matter. It iss all the same.'

'Nothing to say, then?'

'No.'

'Gone as far as that, has it?'

She drooped her head.

'Two can play at that game...'

He stepped forward and caught her in his arms. She bent before him like a twig, her face still and mute. He brushed a hand up through her hair and then felt for her lips. He held her there in the crook of his arm as in a vice. She struggled to free herself and then fell limp. That heavy sensual glow clung around him like a nimbus. But it was more than that. Right at the quick of her – that unreachable place far, far beyond the mind – she felt it. That was the final, unanswerable knocking. And there was no answer to him. She felt her body melt around her and her spirit take flight without, streaming away from her as a breath; a hard resolute knot within her had eased and loosened in the moist gathering cloud that spread like a slow fire in her bowels. In that dark, timeless clouded world there was only Llew.

She cried out against it and her own voice saved her.

'Llew,' she cried through her tears. 'Go! Go away...'

Her eyes were very wide and frightened. He always knew when she was frightened.

'Oh, Llew, go...' She stumbled to the door and unlatched it 'Go!' she shouted in her terror.

'I'll come back,' said Llew. 'You hear? I'll find you... yes, in hell itself.'

His face was twisted beyond itself and his eyes had that stone-like look. His ears stuck out from his head and his eyebrows had gone up in a slant. He had that ageless, evil look that could cross Twmi's face as a cloud the sky. And here it was – fixed and timeless.

'Go,' she said at the door. She was spent with it all. She held on to the door which swung with her, that was all she could do.

Llew walked out without looking at her.

In the bar, Wati said: 'Give him wan, Twmi, he deserves it.' Twmi stopped before him, that raw eye fixed in a spike. 'A pad start,' he grumbled. He shuffled off into the inner bar and came back with a tumbler of whisky.

'Present from your uncle,' he said as he slapped it down before him.

Llew drank it down at a gulp. It warmed him down to his feet.

'The young pugair knows how,' said Twmi with a wink.

'Wan for me.' Wati was feeling for his old purse. Llew knew that it was all that he had, but he knew that Wati would be cut to the quick if he refused.

Llew tossed that one back.

'Any more?' he asked, looking round the company.

'Hey,' shouted Twmi. 'You get your bike.'

Llew stood up and shook himself.

'Good-bye,' he said as he reached out his hand.

'Be goot,' said his uncle, dropping it. He did not like these formalities.

'Trust Llew,' said Wati.

'Ay... trust him!' answered the old man.

The lad went round the company one by one. They patted him on the back.

'Watch Llew,' said Wati admiringly. 'A great man he will be.'

'Ay,' said Twmi. 'To himself!'

'You watch, then,' said Wati. 'What I say, I say.' Wati went out with Llew into the yard.

'Good-bye, Wati.'

'Got enough carbide?' said Wati, busying himself about the lamp. It was something for him to think about. Then he looked up into the sky.

'A good moon whateffer.'

The mountains stood out around them. They were like a crust up against the sky, a thin line of silver marking them off.

'Good-bye,' said Llew again, in the saddle as he dragged his legs on the ground.

'I will be sending that fly on,' said Wati. 'Soon as you give the address. Extra spee-shall.' He turned his head aside. Then he spat on to the ground. The little man waved his hand up in the air without looking.

Llew stepped on the pedals and rode out of the yard.

CHAPTER XVII

It was all over now. The formalities, the grim ceremonial had to be gone through. Evan lifted up his head and knew that he would go through with it. What did it matter, this parade of righteousness – some of it was genuine, some of it was not. But the parade of death followed death; it was as inevitable as death itself. These things must happen – why, no one knew. But they must happen.

And death was so small, so secretive a thing. It was just a furtive snatching at life – what life there was.

One day his mother, her face thin as a chisel, had asked for the *Sunday Companion*. In the morning when he went into her room the paper was on the floor, spread out in its pages, and she lay there, thin nose above the counterpane, and face white and glazed.

'Mam,' he said.

But he did not expect an answer. There was no answer.

And now they were carrying her down the stairs. They were awkward stairs, with a bend, and Ben the Post, who was one of the bearers, had struck his top hat against a beam. It had come down over his ears. He was the shortest of the four and the weight came down on him. He began to curse under his breath, curse his gammy leg. Evan stood there watching them. Ben the Post had been one of her sweethearts in the old days. She had been a beauty. It was something the old postman had never forgotten. And there he was, wheezing on the bend of the stairs and patting his gammy leg and looking behind him to see what the others were doing.

At Peniel Mr Jenkyns conducted the service, as he was bound to do. He was the only real friend Evan had.

He stood there in the pulpit and reached for his tea-stained beard once or twice. Then he threw up his arms: '*O death, where is thy sting? O grave, where is thy vick-tory?*'

'Ay,' he went on, 'vick-tory.' He cocked his thumb to the graveyard. 'A small thing the grave. He trampled his feet on the pulpit floor, like a ram stamping. 'All over,' he said. 'Thy vick-tory...' He flung his arms upwards again and his voice went up in the hwyl. 'The old earth to which we return... you and me. *Thy vick-tory...* no, no, it iss not like that. We come from nowhere... yess: and we go to nowhere... yess? Who says? Where we come from... where we go? The clods that Dai Shovel heaves in? No more? Maybe... maybe not?'

He wagged his head backwards and forwards.

'Martha Edwards,' he said, pointing to the coffin, '... a beautiful woman... lovely in her life... No word to say against her. Her home... that was all. To do her best where the great God put her!'

Evan in the front row bowed his head. It had called up his mother to him as nothing else.

It was soon all over. Moses tilted his hat to keep the chill wind from his head. Evan saw everything. It was all unreal to him – and yet it was real. He took one last look at the coffin – lying there on its bed of clay.

The wreaths were spread about the bier, some of them already wilted; a poor bit of garish splendour, there between the straight standing slabs.

The old man had watched him from the porch, but now he walked out, his beard forked with the wind. He caught Evan by the arm and led him away.

'That's enough,' he said simply.

Evan turned and looked at him with tired shadowed eyes. Only his friend knew the extent of his suffering, for only he knew Evan.

'Quick work,' said Evan in the bitterness of his heart. His mouth was hard and lined and his face bloodless. He jerked his thumb to the grave. Over by the vestry Dai Shovel was waiting with his spade. He wanted to finish before dark.

'You had best be going,' said the old man. 'Not goot for you to stay, Evan.'

'I was only thinking,' said Evan, probing his misery.

'No goot for you to *think*, Evan bach.'

'No,' said Evan in a harsh breath. 'The Lord gives and the Lord takes away. That do?' he said bitterly.

'Evan...?'

Evan shook his arm free and leaned over the grave.

217

Ay, but to die, and go we know not where;
To lie in cold obstruction and to rot;

said Evan, in a voice as hollow as the grave itself.

'Think that wan out,' he said in mounting bitterness.

He picked up an armful of wreaths and flung them into the grave.

'Evan! Evan!' shouted the minister. 'My poor boy!' He caught him by the arm and led him away by force. They never spoke until they were down the road.

'We will haf a cup of tea, ay? You and me,' went on the old man, prattling away like a child. 'I make it. Fery goot hand I am, too.'

Evan was not taken in by it. But the sight of his old friend babbling away and cutting antics, doing everything but stand on his head, brought him back to himself.

They let themselves in through the shop, empty and desolate, and went in search of a lamp.

'There now,' said the old man, bustling about. 'In a wink, in a twink, tea for you and me to drink.' He rubbed his hands together chirping away like a bird.

There was a kettle on the side of the hob.

'And some bread and butter now,' went on the old man without stopping.

Evan faced him. They stood there in the long silence without a word.

The old man's eyes gradually widened.

'For how long?' said the minister, aghast. Evan dropped his head.

'Dear me,' said the old man, shaking his head. 'We arr better than that. Yess, yess. We arr better than *that*.'

218

'I never asked,' Evan replied.

'I bring some beef-tea down this min-nit. My wife make some only yesterday.'

Evan caught him by the arm, but the old man hurried out like a gust, forgetting his hat in his haste.

'Wa-at?' replied the minister. 'You to starve and under my fery eyes! Let me loose,' he said, beating his fists in his frenzy.

When he returned Evan was seated in the old chair by the fire, his head in his hands. The old man was unloading the basket, laying the things on the table one by one.

'My wife... something awful!' He threw up his hands. 'Why I not take you home? Why I not do this, why I not do that. Spare bed ready. I don't know wa-at...'

'No, no,' said Evan.

'Yess, yess. You come home all right. No question about that. But we must haf a talk... later, later!' He waved his hand casually. 'Things must be gone into.'

They ate the meal in silence. The old man never once looked up, but he knew by the way Evan was eating that he had had no food for days.

'All right?' he said at the end. 'Better now?'

Evan did not answer. He drew his chair up to the fire. The old man sat on one of the eisteddfodic chairs as on a throne. There were three of them in the room, carved out of plain oak with hard oak seats.

The old man began to pull his beard nervously.

'It iss not goot, Evan...'

Evan looked up at him.

'No goot at all.' The old man shook his head, his thoughts wandering.

219

'You must go away.' He shot out his hands to indicate distance. 'Right away.'

'Where?' broke in Evan drily.

'Away! Away iss away.'

'Where is away, then?'

The old man's head wagged.

'That is the quest-yan.'

'Yes,' said Evan, 'a big one.'

'Nowhere to go?'

'Nowhere!'

'Come, come! We must not lose heart.'

'No,' said Evan.

'We must ecks-plore.'

'Yes.'

'Your uncle?'

'No good,' said Evan.

His uncle was a draper in North London. They despised one another.

'Got a motor car?' said the old man.

'Got two motor cars.'

'Neffer!'

'Yess, yess. Haf three by and by.' His bitterness burned into his talk.

'We must think, my boy,' went on the old man. 'A job is a job.'

'Yes,' said Evan. 'Funny, you to say.'

'All fery well,' said the old man. 'Look at me! Forty years ago life was wan thing: forty years after, life another. Haf you heard me complain? Say... haf you?'

Evan bowed his head.

'I know Evan, my boy, I know! To meet life on its own terms... that is the great thing.'

The old man wagged his head again like a nodding horse. He had gone back into himself.

'I will try,' said Evan.

The old man lifted his head.

'No other way. You write to your uncle. Tell him *facts*.'

Mr Jenkyns felt easier.

'A poor 'orld for po-ets!' he said. He shook his head. 'But there it iss.'

'Something else...' said Evan.

'Yess, yess. No time to lose.'

'Funny,' said Evan. 'It plays tricks.'

'Go on.'

'You know about me and... Beti?'

'And Beti?'

'You know then?'

'First I hear.' The old man's eyes opened wide.

'No more to say.' Evan bent his head.

'The real thing?' asked the old man.

'Real enough.'

'Pity.'

'Why pity?'

'Dear me. Things iss fery hard. What you do now, Evan?'

'That's what I ask.'

'You go away and forget?'

'Oh, yes,' said Evan. 'Love iss a joke. Sorry.'

The old man got up and put his arms on his shoulder.

'You think *I* say that, my boy?'

Evan shook his head in his hopelessness.

'I know,' went on the old man. 'I can guess.' He wagged his head again. 'You go away...'

'Perhaps.'

'Pity! Pity!'

'Only pity?' said Evan in challenge.

'You haf my blessing,' said the old man.

'No matter what?'

'No matter what? Phut!' he said, shooting up his hands. 'Life iss too big for *that*.'

'And yet,' said Evan, 'pity?'

'No matter. Only my way.'

'A funny way,' said Evan drily.

'No, no. You see wan way. I see two. I see three... four... five.'

'There iss only one way,' said Evan bitterly, 'with or without.'

The old man leaned forward in his chair and put a hand on Evan's knees. His eyes were clouded, distant.

'Then... without, my boy.'

He kept his eyes on Evan's face in challenge.

'Easy said.' Evan could hardly hear his own voice. It was like the sentence of death. The last shred of hope had gone.

'The last straw,' he said. 'Nothing left now.'

The old man did not speak. He had to leave him to his misery.

'The Christian way?' Evan sneered.

'The only way,' replied the old man. 'What we suffer, we suffer. But we must take it on ourselves, my boy. That iss the way of Christ... the little voice of Nazareth that hass brought the light to this old 'orld. Fery simple... oh, yess, fery simple. Truth iss fery simple... like ABC.'

222

'Go on,' said Evan in a groan.

'No need for more. Beti... a lovely girl. The light iss on her face... the inside light, Evan, like a lamp in the dark. Oh, yess, watch for the light...'

He raised his old head upwards and wagged it in his ecstasy.

'If you ask her, she go. Go where? Home gone... all gone. Iss it fair, Evan? Tell me that.'

'No.' He got up and walked the room and then stood looking at the wall. It seemed an eternity.

When he came back his face was haggard and drawn. There was only life in the eyes. It was beyond belief. He was numbed to the heart.

'Nothing left now,' he said. He sat down on a chair and dropped his head in his hands.

'No,' answered the old man, his voice as from a distance. 'Only God...'

'God! "He moves in a mysterious way His wonders to perform!" ' Evan bowed his head to his knees. 'Yes – he does all right.'

'God,' said the old man steadily.

'Blast Him!' Evan drew himself up in his frenzy. The rage choked him. No words came; he gibbered helplessly, his fists clenching, his body atremble. And then, as suddenly, the rage left him, left him as a storm lifting, leaving the quiet more real. He dropped back into his chair and wept the silent scalded tears of his bitterness. His heart heaved with the sobs as though breaking.

And the old man stood there, his eyes clouded, his white head raised, his face aglow with the mild, white light of ecstasy. He raised his hand outstretched above him. He began in Welsh.

'Let us pray...' His head quivered as with the ague and no words came. Then his voice came quiet and low: 'O God, the Great One who movest in the light beyond the great stars. Dear Jesus, thou friend of the lowly, dear Jesus, light of the world. This poor lad... let him lift up his eyes and see now in his great darkness. A small thing I ask, I, one of thy poor servants who ever walk humbly before thee and whose poor life is thine now and always. Do it for me, God... Isaac Jenkyns, C.M. church, Tanygraig... wicked that I am to ask him who laid the foundations of the earth... yea and stretched thy line upon it, that time when the morning stars sang together and all the sons of God shouted for joy. Yess, yess. Let the great light shine in him, O God, and let him say with thy servant Job, who denied thee in his agony: "I had heard of thee by the hearing of the ear; but now mine eye seeth thee": Thank you God... Amen.'

Evan got up in the long breath-drawn silence, his face fixed and quiet. He reached behind the door for his coat, bare and patched, and fastened it across his neck with a safety-pin.

'I will go now,' he said at the door.

The old man did not answer.

224

CHAPTER XVIII

Evan hurried along the road to the old church where they always met. He was late and he felt a pang at the thought of keeping her waiting. The chill east wind went through his poor coat like spears, and he put his hands cross-ways before him to keep him warm. The Red Lion windows shone out with a warm soft glow. The old tin sign, with the rampant lion on it, rattled and creaked in the wind. From inside the house came the roar of revelry and laughter. It was her home. Every stick and stone of it he knew, every cornice – knew as only a lover can know it. It was no longer a house.

He would stand for hours at an upstairs window looking across to it, in the hope that he would catch a glimpse of Beti running on little feet to put the clothes out in the garden. And then, with empty basket, she would disappear behind a stone cornice, and a light went out. Their meetings were only half real; the wonder of it dulled the edge of thought. They were to be raked up from the memory piece by piece, but they moved away beyond him like some wonderful luminous cloud; they were as fleeting and as insubstantial as a cloud. This other life he lived was as a dream; reality had no place in it.

He laughed bitterly as he went along, his mind beginning to work again. Reality had a place in everything. It was the only count.

The peace, the surety that had come to him in his home – the *knowledge* which transcended thought, came back to him like an in-filling breath.

The night was very lovely. How or why was it lovely? He did not know. It had, of itself, gone empty; he felt it go from him, the last rememberable things: the wind in the beech trees, the long-drawn swish and then the rattle of the dead leaves – an unending chorus beginning beyond him, ending beyond him, as it went on its journey up the valley. And that had gone. He was there – but he could not see, could not feel. The whole world was bright and empty and starlit as the dawn itself. It *was* the dawn – the dawn of the world! There was all life for him in those few brief moments, snatched from time – no, within time, and yet beyond time.

There had been no stars as these: there *were* no stars as these. In their fearful light he beheld all time. He could look and was unafraid. There was no bitterness now, nor joy, nor sorrow. He saw life as from a great distance. He felt his own self stream out of him. In that awful joy that surged up in him there was neither past nor present, good nor evil. There was no time: there was no space. There was a joy from out of life, but beyond life – from all life ever created. *When the morning stars sang together*. That was it. Now he *knew* Job. It was all there, as he could never utter.

> And now men cannot look on the light when it
> is bright in the skies, when the wind hath
> passed, and cleansed them.

A tipsy voice came careering along the road. He stood back in the hedge as the man passed. It was the old parson, Bryn-Rowland, on his way back from the inn, singing a song in English:

> Oh, de Ribber of Jordan is deep and wide,
>   One mo' ribber to cross.
> I don't know how to get on de other side,
>   One mo' ribber to cross.

The old man fumbled for a glat in the hedge and let himself down the bank. Then he began to wade through the brook, knee-deep.

> Oh, you got Jesus, hold him fast,
>   One mo' ribber to cross.

'Hup, hup... Cod damn and blast!'

He was reaching the other side when he slipped on a stone and fell back on his haunches in a splash, Evan ran forward but the old man was up again, cursing solidly as he let the water out of his trousers. He saw him moving across the meadow in the moonlight, the flow of language receding with him.

And then, from the far distance, less a voice than a sound, came:

Oh, Jordan's Ribber am chilly an' cold,
One mo' ribber to cross,
It chills de body, but not de soul,
One mo' ribber to cross...

It had served to break Evan's reverie. He was no longer the same – the remembrance of it was left him. It was like a fire gone low, the warmth coming from the embers, but no fire. He had gone back to himself. And with the return to himself came all the old doubts and worries. When he came to the church he saw Beti in a bend of the wall. He saw her there in silhouette and ran forward to meet her, the old triumphant feeling that he always felt with her rising up in him.

'Fy nghariad...'

She put her arms about his neck.

'There's long you haf been.' But it was not a reproach. 'But neffer mind,' she said brightening. 'We got half an hour.'

'Half an hour...'

He looked down at the ground.

'Why, Evan...'

'Half an hour. All we got!' his voice sounded like the grave.

'Till next time,' she said cheering him.

'Next time...?' he said in the same hollow voice. He raised his face to her.

'Evan...?' She caught hold of his coat and clung to him. He stood there, his face mute and silent.

'Evan...?' she said again.

'All done.' That was all he could say.

'Evan...?' Her voice, half sob, half cry, cut him to the heart.

He had been sure of himself in that walk into the wind. He had renounced all that was left him. What he would say, how he would say it – that remained. That still quiet glimpse of things – where was it now? He fought against the old tumult.

He caught her by the shoulders and turned her face up to him.

'Beti!'

'Go on...'

'What iss the end of it all?'

There was no word from her.

'Yes... but *what*?' he said in a shout. His agony brought him to a stop.

'There iss no end for *me*,' she said and added bitterly. 'I don't look for ends. Sorry!' She bowed her head.

'It iss not that,' he said.

Beti did not answer. Her silence moved him as nothing else. He felt himself break within him.

'We must think things out.'

'*Think*! I see.' She tilted her face up to the sky. It had gone very white and quiet.

'*Beti*...!'

'Haf your think,' she said, 'and be quick.'

'Oh, Beti,' he said beside himself, 'don't you see?'

'Not yet,' she said, her voice distant. Her face was still tilted away from him.

'There iss no hope,' he said. 'Not for us...'

'Go on,' she said in the same empty voice.

'I must go away.'

'Yess,' she said, 'you need a change.'

'Beti! It iss not that way at all.'

'No,' she said, '*pure* mistake.'

'Beti, let us face facts.'

'Oh,' she said, '*facts* now.'

'There arr facts, Beti.'

'Yes,' she answered, silent. She still had her face tilted to the distance. She stood there beside him in the moonlight. He dared not look at her. Instead he spoke as though into the ground.

'There iss no hope for us...'

Beti said, bitterly: 'That all?'

'Listen,' he said. 'You think it easy for me?'

'Very easy,' she answered. 'You go away: I stay behind. What more easy?'

'Beti!'

'Say what iss on your mind,' she said. 'I am ready.'

'Only this, Beti,' he answered. He tried to keep his voice from faltering. 'There iss nothing left me. Nothing at all. All gone and done with.' He threw up his hands in a hopeless gesture. 'Why worry? Oh yes, I will *try*...' He shook his head hopelessly.

'You know my trying,' he said after a while. 'You know what's come of it.'

'Well?' she said, her eyebrows lifting. She turned and looked at him for the first time.

'If I fail, I fail. Quite simple! I can take it. No need to worry.'

'Well?'

'What right,' he said facing her, 'to ask *you*?'

She looked up at him in her sudden fearless way, her eyes wide. She did not know what was coming: she could only wait. Then she turned her head away again.

'What right...?' His voice dropped low in his tenderness. 'What hope we got?'

'Hope of what?' she asked, very mute and still. The words struck her like blows.

'Hope...' he went on with a forlorn gesture. He could not explain. Instead he waved his hand upwards in his despair.

'You got nothing to look to,' he added.

'I see,' said Beti in bitter reproach. 'A good time?' Her voice, like her father's, scorched like a flame.

'That iss not my way at all,' she broke in, during the long silence.

'I know,' he said, and bowed his head.

'Yes,' she added. 'You *do* know that.'

'And *I* to take you away! How can I?' he implored. He raised his head.

'And that all?' she asked in her relief. Life came tumbling back to her.

'Beti! Beti! Stay and think, I beg now. What hope you got? What hope at all?'

231

'Twice times a million,' she said counting her fingers.

There was no reaching her now.

'Stay and think,' he implored. 'No joke.'

'Very like,' she laughed. She had found herself now. He caught her in his arms.

'Oh, Beti, you think I leave you...'

'Please yourself!' She tossed her head back.

It was bound to come to this. He had had a presentiment of it all along. But he could not make that final effort – it was beyond him. He could not out-reach his destiny, not as he lived and breathed.

'Arr you sure, Beti?' he asked, unbelieving.

'Oh... only joking,' she said with a nervous little laugh. 'Silly!'

He looked down at her, so frail and wisp-like with her wide anxious eyes, clear and steadfast, her face so white and still.

'Oh, God,' said Evan shaking his head. 'I done my best... I done my best. The wrong iss with me.'

'Wrong?' said Beti, her spirit rising.

'Yess, Beti fach, wrong. It iss my job to stop you, but how...' He bowed his head and groaned.

She lifted his head and held it between her hands.

'Look up, Evan,' she said in a voice strange and distant.

He was bewildered by it, by her cloudless face, white and serene in the moonlight. The light fell around her as in an aura.

She reached for his hand and pressed it to her breast.

'It iss all here,' she said.

He could not speak. His lips moved but no words came.

It seemed to him that in that one tremulous moment, so soon to go, was all eternity. The joy surged up in him, up in his throat, like a song.

He gathered her up in his arms and with infinite tenderness pushed back the hair from her face and then lightly kissed her on the lips.

'Fy nghariad...' he said in a voice heaved out of his heart.

CHAPTER XIX

Evan held up the letter between his forefinger and thumb. Within it was a crisp ten-pound note. He knew how much it had cost his uncle to send it; he read through the letter again.

His uncle was as God made him. He was both right and wrong. In any case it did not matter very much. His uncle had said a bellyful – but he had sent ten pounds! The rest of the letter was all about the ten pounds.

Evan wanted to laugh about it all, but all the time he knew what was before him.

The old minister had said: 'You go, Evan! So far: fery goot. You take Beti: so far not so goot. You take up a flower by the roots. Yess, yess, by the roots. Haf a care, Evan. Do the right thing, my boy. Make things easy... straight and above board like.'

'It iss straight,' he said with the courage of despair.

'Yess,' said the old man wagging his head like an old dog, 'straight for you: straight for Beti, ay? Haf a think, my boy. I know; I know. Life is only you two. But life iss not only you two. Much more to it than that! Go and see him... there's a lad.'

Evan crumpled the letter in his pocket. One thing more to be done. He locked up the shop and walked across to the Red Lion.

Twmi was at the door as he entered.

'What you want?' he said rudely.

Evan looked him straight in the face. He was buoyed up with a courage beyond him.

'A word...' he said.

Twmi looked him up and down.

'Come in,' he said. He slammed the door after him. Then he led him into one of the back parlours.

Twmi sat down in a chair, filling it. He spread his hands over his knees.

'At your service,' he said, his voice empty.

'Mister Tudor...'

'Go on,' said Twmi. The straight staring eyes of the old man, bare as a gimlet, upset him. He coughed into his hand nervously.

'It iss serious,' said Evan.

'I hope so.' Twmi's answer was as dry as dust.

'Fery serious...'

'Get a start then,' said Twmi, placing his hands together.

'We arr not friends, Mister Tudor,' said Evan, at a loss for words.

'I neffer said.' Twmi lifted his hands casually.

'You keep all that against me.'

'No,' said Twmi. 'Your father... nothing to do with you. Besides... he was wan to look after himself.'

'And I come in for it.'

'Not at all,' said Twmi. 'Mistake on your part. I judge a man as a man... no more, no less.'

'Straight?' said Evan fixing him.

'Straight!' Twmi's eyes narrowed. 'What you mean... straight?'

'No offence, Mister Tudor. Sorry...'

'I am waiting,' said Twmi. 'Some day you will begin!' He put his hands in his breeches pockets and leaned back in the chair, his head raised to the ceiling.

'I take what's coming,' said Evan, summing up his courage. 'Nothing to do with me! No? I ask you?'

'Get a start,' said Twmi, closing his mouth with a snap.

'All right,' said Evan. 'I will.'

'That iss better,' said Twmi. 'Now we know.'

'About Beti...' said Evan in a plunge.

Twmi brought his eyes down from the ceiling with a jerk.

'Beti? Go on, my boy.'

'Nothing more to say...' said Evan holding him with his eyes.

'Indeed? A ploody lot more to say...'

'All right,' said Evan taking the challenge. 'I love Beti.'

'Goot for you,' said the old man. 'Any more?'

'Not much.'

'Get it done, then.'

'Only that Beti loves me.'

'Wa-at?' The old man rose to his feet. 'You!' he said, with narrowed derisive eyes.

'Yes,' said Evan. 'That's how it iss.'

'I see,' said Twmi. He sat back in his chair, his face gone mute and ageless. 'Anything else?'

Evan felt the contempt in his voice.

'A lot more,' said Evan. 'I am going away.'

'What a pity!'

'And Beti is coming with me.'.

'Arr you asking,' said the old man, 'or saying? Which is which?'

'Asking...'

'I see! Anything else?'

'Nothing else.'

The old man put his palms together.

'Feel proud of yourself?' His mouth had gone hard and his face drooped, his eyes turned up like marbles, the colour of stone.

'That iss not the point.'

'No? What iss, if I may ask?'

Evan did not answer. But he met the old man eye to eye.

Twmi raised his finger.

'Answer me this... how she live? No concern of mine, ay? Say so!'

He got up from the chair, his voice, like his eyes, cold as steel.

'I will try.' Evan floundered under that cold, inquisitive stare.

'Try! Don't talk daft, man.'

'I *will* try.'

'Shutapp!' said Twmi in contempt. 'Try... what a ploody hope! That all she got to look forward to?'

'Mister Tudor...'

'Get on with it,' he said with a jerk of the head.

'All right,' said Evan stiffening. 'Beti iss going.'

'Goot for you,' said Twmi. 'You done your stuff well and proper. When... may I ask?'

'That depends.'

'Yess,' he said grimly. 'It does and all.'

He put his head through the door and shouted. Beti came in, her eyes lowered. She came in very soft and birdlike, a quiet static beauty encompassing her as a cloud. Her eyes were soft and misted; they searched out the room.

The two men stood facing one another across a little table.

'What's this?' said Twmi with a jerk of his head.

'Oh, dad!'

'Speak plain,' he said, 'never mind "Oh, dad".' The old man in his quiet strength filled the room. Beti, who knew him so well, was frightened to the depths of her soul. It was the blood that spoke. But as she stood there courage came to her. It was something outside and beyond her.

In that breathless, dropping silence she raised her head and faced him.

'You know all,' she said.

'Do I?' The old man's stone-cold eyes never lifted.

'All there iss to know, Dad – we come to ask you.'

'There's goot of you!' It was beyond a sneer.

She faced him, met him straight in the eyes.

'There iss no way out, Dad.'

'Who said?'

'I say.'

238

'Which iss which in this?' he said. 'You or... him?' he jerked his thumb with contempt.

'Me,' Beti replied. 'It's my doing.'

'Wa-at?' His face was working. But this was real as between them. Evan was forgotten – a shadow beyond them.

'Yess,' said Beti.

'I see.' He had gone very quiet. He sank back into his chair and tapped the ends of his fingers.

'Anything more?' he added casually.

'Beti,' shouted Evan. 'Let me say.' The sight of Beti there, so frail and small, wrenched his heart. And yet he had no place in it, he knew. He had the actual sense of interfering as between them.

'Mister Tudor...'

The old man cocked his head, his cold eyes raised, the hard sardonic curl of his lips lifting. He raised his hand casually. He sat there like an oracle. Evan went on.

'You must not blame Beti. Indeed now. Beti thinks the world of you...'

'Get on with it,' said the old man with a fine contempt.

'What hass happened, hass happened...'

'Happened?' said Twmi raising an eyebrow, his face dark as night.

'No – not that, Mister Tudor.' Then he went on. 'Who am I to ask? Who am I to take? It hass come to me... that iss all.' Evan bowed his head, the words failing him.

'Speak sense,' said Twmi, not moving. 'Wrong time for sermons.'

'No more to say,' went on Evan floundering. 'God only knows, I am not worth it.'

239

'Ay,' said Twmi, 'quite likely.'

'Dad!'

'Haf be.'

'I would go away. Indeed I would,' Evan went on in a sing-song, his voice rising in ecstasy. 'My life iss nothing. I quite know tha-at. But Beti – we let her suffer to death: we break her poor heart.'

'You try it, gwas,' said Twmi. 'I take the risk.'

'Right, Mister Tudor...'

Evan stood up and nodded viciously. His body was numb around him, the whole world gone – only this single pure flame of his resolve.

'I give Beti up if she says. Will you...?'

He had flung out the challenge at the old man sitting there, before him. Twmi filled the room – but he seemed to fill the whole world – his own dark, knowledgeless world was like the night itself – all encompassing. Evan feared it to his soul.

'Phut, man!' said Twmi, spitting out his contempt. 'And you knowing the answer! You've got her warmed up to it.'

'Ask then,' shouted Evan in the triumph of his defeat.

'No,' said Twmi, 'not that way at all.' His voice came low, charged and beyond him, dark and brooding.

'Game to you.' The old man waved his hand upwards in mock flourish. 'Beti can go. You hear, Beti?' He turned round to search for her. Beti bowed her head.

'Oh, dad,' she cried out, 'be fair, dad!'

'Beti can go,' he said in the same low voice. 'You will be all right,' he nodded at Evan, his eyebrows raised. 'If Beti makes her bed she will lie in it. She hass got guts, you see

240

– those things inside.' His voice searched out Evan like an asp. He paused. Then he went on. 'Beti knows…'

He leaned back in his chair and turned his head up to the ceiling and then slowly curled his tongue around his lips.

'Hard on Beti,' he added.

They were there, all three in the room and no word spoken. The life had gone out of Evan, the strange, overwhelming terror of life, had numbed him. In that knowledgeless pit there was no light. And then, with the sight of Beti before him – all that was left him, all that life meant to him – his spirit quickened and the one single flame within flickered into life. She stood there so very still and resolute. She was so far beyond him that he dared not guess at her. He could not let that go. He felt strength pass into him.

Beti stood there, her fingers clasped, her great eyes clouded with tears and her sprung body all atremble. She would never cry before her father.

'No hurry,' said Twmi, lifting his hands casually. He got up out of the chair. The meeting was at an end.

'Go back to help your mam.' He nodded to his daughter. Beti went.

Then he went to let Evan out of the front door.

CHAPTER XX

Twmi had brought the table away from the wall and went sprinkling sand around the room. He threw it casually but with a final flourish, a flick of the wrist. Some of those who sat around drew up their feet instinctively.

But not one of them could glimpse what the old man thought, what he felt. On this day, as on any other, he was Twmi. They all sought him out by nod or glance – but he just went on with the sand.

It had come at last – as it was bound to. Rumour had come and gone. It was like bindweed: however much it was scotched there was always more. In time rumour had given way to a few half-hearted facts. But no one really thought the new road would come. They had convinced themselves that it could not come – and therefore it was not coming.

But it was to come. And this day was bound to come.

Twmi went for a chair. He had pulled his own armchair

half out of one of the sitting-rooms, but he stopped in the passage. He took it back. Instead he went for one from the kitchen and set it at the head of the table.

The taproom was crowded. There were some there who had never been there before. These Twmi greeted with a nod and a sardonic lift of the eye. 'Hey, Twmi,' shouted Dan Meredith, shuffling his feet anxiously. 'Give us a line. Be a sport, now.'

Twmi paused in the preparations.

'A line?' he said.

'Ay, be a sport, Twm.'

'A line is what you want, too. Round your neck or on your hass. All the same.'

'Come on, Twm!'

'You got your papers?'

Dan felt in his inside pocket. 'Lot of good, that,' he said with a sniff.

'What you think I am?' said Twmi. 'Moses on the Mount?'

'What we do?' shouted another.

'How the hell do I know?' said Twm.

'We got it fair?'

'Oh, ay,' said Twm, 'fery like. You do him and he do you. Fair enough!'

They crowded to the window, waiting.

'Twm, now,' said Dan, 'who he think we arr?'

The car drew up into the yard. They were all at the windows watching.

'Give him room,' said Twmi. He went to open the door. The man came in, tall and dry with a white bald head like an egg top. The county surveyor followed, carrying the leather portfolio, a little man with a round anxious face and a snub red nose like a raspberry.

'Well, gentlemen...' the official took his seat. 'I take it you all know the business.' He looked round the company with assumed affability. There was no answer. He made a show of spreading his papers. Before him was a large ordnance map that drooped over the end of the table.

'I think it is as well to explain,' he said, 'that the Ministry, while recognising all just claims, are empowered under sub-section...'

'Wa-at?' said Shacob, circling his trumpet round. It had been too much for him.

'From the Ministry,' nudged Dan.

'Neffer!' said Shacob, unconvinced.

'Hush!' said Dan.

'Funny preacher, to me. We got better.'

The official raised his eyes at the interruption. Then he went on explaining the Ministry of Transport regulations.

'So, gentlemen,' he said. 'The road goes. Neither you nor I stop it. That is understood.'

He looked up for assent, but none was forthcoming.

In the long silence Dan shouted out: 'Why Tanygraig? Plenty more places.'

It was the first hint of trouble and the official was prepared for it.

He spread out the map and pushed his spectacles up over his forehead. Then he made a diagonal slash with a pencil butt.

'Very simple, gentlemen...'

'Ay,' shouted Dan, 'simple iss the word. Who for, though?'

The county surveyor stood up with his hands raised.

'Gentlemen...' he shouted.

There was silence again.

The official went on: 'For the benefit of that gentleman,' he said indicating Dan, 'and such others of you who are in doubt, it may be necessary to make some explanation.' He coughed drily into his hand. 'This is to be an arterial road.'

'Wa-at?' Shacob leaned forward.

'Artificial road,' whispered Dan, 'I couldn't hear proper.'

'It is proposed to link up with a big new road from the Midlands, already under construction, at – at...'

'Cwmpenllydan,' said the county surveyor.

'Yes, at... that place. And from there to the coast the road carries the double traffic, thus causing a considerable saving. Along here – ' he indicated the proposed road, 'will go the traffic from the north, Manchester, Liverpool, Birkenhead. I think that adequately sums it up.'

He turned to the county surveyor, who nodded.

'So far fery goot,' shouted Dan, who was the articulate voice of the company. 'And Tanygraig go smash bang through Birkenhead, what you say then, ay?'

'The point does not arise,' said the official.

'For why?'

'Gentlemen, we are wasting time,' he said, sniffing. He had not the least idea how to proceed. It was his first experience of Wales.

The others wagged their heads encouragingly.

'Give him a hearing, mister. Fair's fair.'

'Gentlemen,' went on the official, exasperated. 'It is no

earthly use talking like this. The road is decided on. Facts are facts. Here is the brook, here is the village – a bottleneck. Some incursion into private property must be made. I quite understand your sentiment...'

'Sentiment!' shouted Dan threateningly. 'You watch your words, boss.'

'... but that some hundreds of thousands of less fortunate people want to visit your country – that is no occasion for shame, surely? – not to speak of the money they bring in...'

'Into where? Tanygraig?' shouted Dan. 'Laugh that wan off!' he said, turning to the company, 'you all be rich in a week.'

'Tell me, sirr,' shouted a man, 'Will there be any old chary-bonks?'

'Well!' said the official, throwing up his hands in a gesture of disgust. 'How on earth should I know?'

'Chary-bonks!' shouted Dan, beside himself, 'how you think they go – swim?'

'Really,' said the official, 'I can't waste any more time. This is pure obstruction on your part.' He turned to the county surveyor and reached out the papers from the portfolio.

'Jacob Morris, Wernddu,' he called.

Dan gave him a nudge and the old man tottered up to the table, his chaps moving and his stick waggling before him.

'You are Jacob Morris?'

'Wa-at?'

'Jacob Morris.'

The old man fumbled for his trumpet and fixed it at the speaker.

'JACOB MORRIS,' he roared.

The old man nodded his head like a goat. The company began to titter.

'Siarad Cymraeg?' said old Shacob.

'What?' shouted the official. He flung down his pencil with a thud and turned to the county surveyor hopelessly.

'He wants to know if you speak Welsh,' said the surveyor.

'No!' yelled the official at the old man before him.

Shacob shook his head dismally. The company was now in an uproar.

'Tamn it all; his language, man!' shouted Dan. 'What you expect in Wales – Chinese, or what?'

'You try.' The official turned to the surveyor and folded his arms grimly. He had gone very white about the gills.

'Shacob,' said the county surveyor in Welsh. 'You must give up a little bit of your garden – not much. Fifty feet by twelve. Very little bit. Now tell the gentleman how much you want for it.'

'Fifty pounds down,' said Shacob in English.

'What!' The official fell back as if he had been struck. 'Is this a game?' he asked grimly.

'He wants to know if it's a game,' translated the surveyor.

'Game?' answered the old man, wagging his head. 'Garden!'

The county surveyor could hardly control himself. He set his face straight and held back the laughter.

'Ask him how he gets fifty pounds,' said the official with a savage nod.

The county surveyor spoke again. The old man stood there like an owl, blinking, and then broke forth in a tumult.

This time the county surveyor could not hold back his laughter; but he let it go in one solitary puff and then rearranged his face.

'He says,' he went on, 'that it is Sharpes Express.'

'Sharpes Express...?' The official passed a hand over his head.

'Best in all the 'orld,' said old Shacob in English. 'Fery goot potato.'

'And he says,' went on the county surveyor, giving a literal translation, 'that they won't grow in tar macadam.'

'Enough of this,' said the official. He bent down and wrote out a chit and fluttered it before the old man.

'Two pounds ten...' he said.

Old Shacob broke into Welsh again.

'What does he say?' asked the official.

'He says that will do, and thank you very much.'

The old man hobbled back to his place, carrying the chit before him in triumph.

That was the beginning of the end. A silence had descended on them all. Thereafter there was a procession. It was all the same. The official had got his measure. He would just look up casually.

'How much? Thirty pounds?' Then he would bend his head and write. 'Thirty shillings,' he would say with finality.

So it went on for an hour. The last of them had gone. The official heaved a sigh of relief. He was packing away his papers.

'And Mr Tudor...' said the surveyor.

'Oh, yes! I had forgotten.'

Throughout it all Twmi had said no word. He stood there

at the back of the company, his head raised, hands clasped before him. He had not laughed when they had laughed. It seemed as though he had absorbed it all – *was* the company – in his sardonic lifted face and the drooping lines of his mouth.

The official had not looked up and he did not see Twmi. He had some idea that as he was using his house – for which payment would be made – things would be easy. And he was buoyant now with the buoyancy of a job well done.

'Let me see, Mr Tudor,' he went on, musing over the map, 'we want a lot from you.' He made some calculations. 'Yes, just half an acre.'

'That all?' said Twmi. The official looked up.

'How you haf it?' said Twmi in the same even voice. 'In a bag, or haf it sent?'

The official laughed pleasantly.

'We'll call for it,' he said. 'I'm afraid,' he went on, bending over the table, 'your garden will have to go – or most of it.'

'That all?' said Twmi.

'This line of beeches along the road.' He traced his hand casually along the line of crosses. 'They will have to come down, and then we traverse the lawn, so... Now Mr Tudor, name your price.'

'Nothing,' said Twmi.

'Nothing?' said the official, looking up. He was feeling uneasy.

'That's it,' said Twmi, 'nothing.'

'Come, come, Mr Tudor...'

'Come, come! Who the hell asked you to come? Me?' He

walked to the door and opened it. 'But you can go when you want.'

'Nonsense.' The official flung his pen down.

'Stay there,' said Twmi. 'All the same.'

'Mr Tudor. Half an acre is half an acre.' But he quailed under Twmi's eye. 'I ask you to name your price.'

'Ten thousand pounds,' said Twmi.

'Thirteen pounds ten,' said the official, bending over the table. He had had enough of this.

Twmi took a step forward.

'Take your hand up,' he said.

The official paused in the act of writing and then bent down again.

Twmi took his arm and snatched the pen from him. The man staggered back.

'What I say?' Twmi's eyes were narrowed and red. The man felt him rather than saw him.

'This is assault,' he gasped.

'Ay, and battery in a ploody minnit. Now – get out!' He nodded to the door. 'Once telling iss enough.'

The county surveyor ran between them.

'Mr Tudor! Have sense.'

'Too much,' said Twmi. 'Now pugair off – the both of you.' He jerked his finger to the door.

'What good?' said the county surveyor despairingly.

'You hear?' roared Twmi. 'Cod tamn it...' He took a step forward.

The two men hurried out into the yard.

'Madness!' shouted the official leaning through the open window of the car, his gills white, his face working. 'Madness,

Mr Tudor.' He beckoned to the county surveyor to wait while he got in his final words. 'General powers are conferred on local authorities...'

The county surveyor had raced up the engine in his anxiety to get away and the man's voice was drowned.

'... whereby a compulsory purchasing order can be made,' he got out. 'Pure obstruction! And – it will be dealt with!'

Twmi stood there at the door, his head lowered like an old bull set for the charge. The last words did it.

'Iesu mawr!' he snorted, his hands bent before him for a strangle hold. He came down the steps in a rush.

The surveyor slipped into gear and the car lurched out of the yard in one heave.

CHAPTER XXI

Evan stood in the room behind the little shop – the papers strewn about him. The grate was piled high with them and the burned flakes were wafted out and went floating round the room. The smoke blew down in gusts causing him to cough.

There was still an hour to go – the longest hour of his whole life. The time itself seemed dull and wingless – as though it had no contact with past or future; it lay heavy on him like the weight of death itself.

He went to the window and looked out. A cold weeping rain came down the valley, steady, unceasing in its pelting spears. There was no light in the sky and yet there were no clouds.

Beti's few things which she had brought over the night before were already packed. The old suitcase sagged outwards with the load and the cheap tin locks would not meet. It was one of brown paper composite, a poor thing at best and a threatening crack reached down its side.

It was as though Evan were holding communion with his dead self. This litter around him was the outward expression of all that he had been. It was himself that was going into the fire – but a self that no longer belonged to him. That he should care so little!

There were essays and philosophical tracts, long passages copied from the prophets in red ink, long eisteddfodic poems, odes and the smaller chiselled crystal clear things like the englyn, more elaborate than the sonnet itself, and untranslatable. It was in the englyn that the genius of his country found itself.

One sheet slipped out of a bundle and fluttered down beside the hearth. He reached for it and, without thought, flattened it out. It was a small thing, one of the few he had written in English, and that a good while back. He had scrawled 'Spring at Moelfre' across the folio head.

> If I could fresh be
> As this blown rose,
> Or the drapery
> The new Spring hangs about
> In quiet ways.
> Now does the new year flout
> A new virginity,
> Upon the tree
> Or in the steaming lane
> Where the last leaf lingers.
> Earth has forgot, nor knows,
> What she has ceased to be.

He carefully dropped it on to the fire and stove it in with a poker. But the poker went through it and this little piece of his was wafted round like a pennant. He scraped it off on the bars.

The old tiredness was coming on him again. It was becoming worse and worse: not physical, not mental but as though the whole life of him were tapped at the source. If he sat for long in a chair he would fall asleep. He was very thin, so thin that his shoulder blades showed through his jacket and his tall figure drooped in spite of himself.

But he was all right, he told himself. He needed a change, that was all. The worries and anxieties had worked in on him and now, with the new world Beti brought, he had lived beyond himself. Things would straighten themselves out in time. He would work hard at his uncle's shop, no matter what it cost him. If he had to 'live in' then Beti said that she could manage. She would find a job as a barmaid or something. It was all on Beti. Yet he had something to live for now... He tried to picture this other world as he sat there before the fire, hands on knees, head sunk forward, brooding.

A sudden gust blew out a cloud of smoke. He jumped up, choking and retching. He could not free himself, try as he would. His frame shook with the coughing.

There it was – a tiny speck of blood on his handkerchief, so small that he had to look twice to see it. But it *was* blood. The whole world fell away from him, slowly revolved into darkness deep as night itself. And then, as though in a turn, life returned.

It was nothing; it was nothing. He wanted to get a grip on himself, to quell the rising panic before it overwhelmed him. It was his teeth, his tonsils – anything. And a mere speck! He pooh-poohed it away but he kept walking and walking. He had to get out – to get away. He fastened the portmanteau and lifted it, breathless. He did not look back on the house as he left it – his home that was. He was away in the driving rain and along the road to where the trap that was to carry them to the junction was to pick them up. He would wait there for Beti. It would not be long now. He dared not look at the Red Lion as he passed.

Beti was upstairs. She had gone to her own room as a last act – to look out on the scene which had been hers all her life.

She did not want to think too much. She had prepared herself for it all. Deep down within her there was some well of courage – placid and unruffled as a well – on which she was able to draw. Her father had gone off to the town early to see his bank. She had watched him go – had run to get his stiff collar from behind the door, as always, had gone round him with the brush while he grunted and wheezed and reached his neck about. It had been her job ever since she could reach above his trouser tops, when with a back-handed reach he would finish off his back.

How she loved her father. Since as early as she remembered he had come between her and the world – the great weight of him, great beyond bulk. In all that bewildering world that had opened out before her he alone *was*. She had never been unfair to him, as her mother was, not in one moment's thought. Such a thing could never happen.

She had watched him lumber through the door and drop on to his pony from the horse-block. And as he moved off behind the corner of the barn it seemed that a great part of her life went with him.

It was different with her mother. But she remembered a younger and kinder mother in the old days. There were many things she remembered now – how kind and gentle she had been, how, in the long tossing nights of childhood, when the wind howled about the house and she cried out with the fear in her very soul, her mother had told her wonderful tales about the little tylwyth teg who ran about the mountains. Perhaps after all she had been unfair to her mother, for only Beti knew what a hard time she had had.

There were a hundred things that Beti remembered now – so long forgotten, and now they all came back. Her mother was not her father – but she was her mother. It was all going – father and mother and home – within the next half hour.

She was sure of herself – but she was not quite sure of herself. And she dared not think. She drew back the curtains from a little latticed window and looked out on to the lawn. It was the same – it had always been the same. It was February and the same clumsy cross and sceptre had shot up through the quiet rich crust of green. There were the snowdrops in their violent flowering of white. Beyond was the waterfall now coming down in an earth-coloured gush; the old beeches still with their ring of haws around the great boles, and that one that had been her swing with the bits of rope, rotted and worn, still on an outward bough.

It was her home. She looked out on it all and tried not to feel. But it seemed that she had gone beyond feeling. Never in all the world was there such a place as this. Wherever she went whatever happened to her – this was home. The tears came in a gush, but she fought against them. It was no use crying. There was a finer farewell to make.

As she stood there the door creaked and Gwenno came in on tip-toe.

'Beti...'

The two girls in a spontaneous act threw themselves into one another's arms.

'Beti fach...'

'Hush,' said Beti.

'I know!' said Gwenno. 'Tell me!'

'I am going.' Beti looked her straight in the eyes.

Gwenno bowed her head. What she wanted to say she could not say.

'Oh, Beti fach!' she said, and grasped her hand.

'When I haf gone you can say,' went on Beti.

'Oh, Beti! Such pals we been.'

'Never mind,' said Beti, biting her lips.

'Beti...'

'Go on.'

'Come unstuck I haf.' Gwenno burst out sobbing. It was Beti's turn to comfort her.

'Oh, Beti fach, help me: help me.'

Beti understood.

'What can I do?' went on Gwenno. 'What *can* I do?' she flopped into a chair and rocked herself backwards and forwards with a panic in her eyes.

257

'Tried everything,' she said. And then as the panic subsided a moment, went on: 'They say hot port is good.'

'Hush,' said Beti shocked to her heart.

'Hush?' Gwenno went on. 'What good saying hush?'

'Gwenno fach! Take care – do take care, I beg of you now. Promise?'

'Promise!' said Gwenno. 'Oh, Beti, I wish I wass you.'

'Oh, Gwenno, why did you?'

'Why arr *you*?' she said.

Beti bowed her head.

'Write to me, Beti. Only a line.' She went to the door and listened. 'I'll look out,' she said. Her fear had gone in Beti's trouble.

'Quick!' she beckoned.

Beti went to the door. She put her arms around her.

'Gwenno fach!'

'Quick,' said Gwenno, her head cocked.

She was down the stairs and out along the road. The trap was waiting; Evan was already up.

They had no word to say to one another until they were dropped at the junction, set among the fields. He was so white and still, his face grim and gone ash-grey that she felt that old dread – a dread right to the soul.

She went into the little buffet and bought some chocolate and raisins. The express came running down the valley under its load of steam, and then in a final curl ran into the station.

'Change for Brecon an' South Wales,' sang a porter running alongside the dripping carriages. 'For Brecon an' South Wales...'

258

They moved up to the last coach where the board overhead in a white streak across the roof bore the one word: PADDINGTON.

CHAPTER XXII

When Twmi got back it was past midday. The rain had blown off and there was a fitful sun shining.

Ben the Post was the only one in the bar. Twmi gave him one of his abrupt nods and looked down to his pot to see that he was served. They knew one another.

'Anybody come?' asked Twmi as an afterthought.

'Come?' said Ben.

'COME,' roared Twmi. 'Come iss come: went iss went. What the hell...'

The old man looked down at his feet and began to shuffle them. He bowed to the storm.

'Hi!' shouted Twmi. 'Have a look.' He caught hold of the old man's arm and dragged him to the window.

'You see...?'

The old postman pushed his spectacles back and looked out to the lawn and garden.

'Yess,' he said ruminating. 'I see all there iss to see for sure.'

'Well – take a look,' said Twmi. He had gone back into himself. 'Last time...'

'What you want?' asked Ben.

'Take a look,' roared Twmi.

'What iss there to see?' begged Ben.

'What there iss. There it iss,' Twmi shouted.' He cocked his thumb towards the window.

'Nothing...?' he asked with a glare.

'They been "rained off". Give them time man. You wait: you see! The gang iss on the way, neffer fear. Picks, shoffels and all.'

He stabbed his finger at the lawn.

'Up she goes,' he said with finality.

'Oh, dear me!' said Ben moved beyond himself. 'Come at last!'

'At last...?'

Ben never raised his eyes. Twmi stood there in the room and that was all.

'Pity,' said Ben. That was all he could say.

It was the same old sight. The lawn, sour green and shining with the rain, stretched away before them. The old beeches, dropped in the earth, stood there along the borders, the boles encumbered with moss. Around them were the haws, dropped around in a ring. Ben's name was on one of the trees, cut when he was a boy. A clumsy heart stood above it. He knew the tree but he had never troubled to look for the carving; it was so long ago. But it was still there – the bark blistered up around it. Up above them the branches were bare and lifeless: a nest or two showed, already mouldering and dropping.

Beyond was the waterfall: the rain had sent it into a roar. But there was no other sound. A flock of starlings had come down and went waddling off across the grass, picking here and there. Two or three tits had clamped themselves on an arbour and beyond, the bullfinches, their brilliant colours fired by the sun, were perched on the shrubs, picking away at the buds. The whole place seemed to come alight in the sunshine but there was no noise beyond the waterfall. Then the trees began to shake and creak in the wind and a shower of drops came down.

'Finished...?' said Twmi, in the flood-tide of his bitterness.

'Well, well,' said the old man, musing.

'Haf be!' answered Twmi savagely. 'But I tell you. They haf so much. Right! One step more...'

The old man felt him. He never once raised his eyes. Twmi stood there in the room, his voice no louder than a whisper. Ben was afraid to look up.

The tension loosened as suddenly. Twmi tilted his pint pot and said, himself again: 'Another wan?'

Ben, in the release, let himself go.

'Oh, tamn,' he began, 'listen now, Twm... more letters from the Post Office. What you think, ay? Can I drive a moto' van? Drive a moto' van! Engine of des-truckshun. Chuff-chuff-chuff, away we go...'

He got hold of an imaginary steering-wheel between his legs and gave it a vicious wrench.

'No stopping Tanygraig. Speed too fast. See you next week!'

He drove his feet down on to the stone floor and with a final wrench brought the engine of destruction up sharp.

'Drive a moto' van! You know what I say? I tell them to put the moto' van – you know!'

He bent over his mug and took a long draught.

'In the right,' said Twmi, paying no attention.

'Ay,' went on Ben. 'In the right! I got the sack all the same. No goot – finished! Pension now for me.'

'Wa-at? Shoved you out?'

'In a way, yess: in a way no. Same thing,' said Ben with a nod.

'No more hog nails,' said Twmi, his eyes shadowed.

'Oh,' went on Ben, 'light as slippers they iss to me.' He beat a tattoo on the floor. 'A man's feet iss all he got.'

Ben's eyes suddenly clouded with tears. He screwed up his wizened face to stave them off.

'A poss-card,' he said, fumbling in his pocket. 'Nearly forgot.'

Twmi took it between thumb and finger and went to the light.'

'St George's,' he said, musing. 'It looks like the House of Commons to me, whateffer.'

He took it back to Ben.

'House of Commons, this?'

Ben held it all ways up.

'Sure to be,' said Ben.

Twmi turned it over and read. Then he grunted. He went and put it up behind a bit of brass harness over the hearth.

'Ay,' he said, 'House of Commons it was. Two names for one thing. From Llew,' he added briefly.

263

Ben looked up.

'Went all through last Saturday.'

'Neffer, now!'

'So he says,' went on Twmi casually.

'See Lloyd George, I wonder.'

'Very like,' said Twmi dryly. Then he added: 'He got the job his uncle said.'

'Neffer!'

'Four quids a week to start.'

'Duw, Duw. He iss a wan, that lad.'

Twmi grunted.

'A man,' he said, and then went on bitterly. 'That's more than some.'

Twmi went to the window looking out on to the lawn. What he saw caused him to move out of the house. A lorry was debouching a load of gravel through the hedge, which they were cutting to ground level with billhooks. There was a cement mixer there, drawn on to the lawn and the wheels had cut ruts in it. A group of men stood around one of the beeches taking measurements.

'This one first,' shouted the foreman.

'You belong here?' asked the man, not moving his gaze from the tree.

'In a way,' said Twmi.

'Mr Tudor, then?'

'By Cod you arr right.'

'Sorry.'

'Don't menshun.' Twmi paced across the lawn. There was still some of it left to him.

'Listen,' he said. 'There's the line.' He finished his stride and faced them.

'Any pugair going over that...'

He raised his head like an old bull. And his eyes had that baleful red-rust glint like the fired eyes of a bull.

'I tell you...!'

They stood back in awe before him. Twmi walked back into the house.

He slumped into his chair.

'Beti!' he called.

His wife came running in.

'Where iss she, I like to know?'

The old man never raised his head.

'Beti!' His voice went through the house like a roar 'Beti...'

At the third shout Gwenno put her head through the door. The old man did not look at her. His eyes had gone up in a vacant stare, up to the ceiling.

'It iss no good,' said Gwenno, 'no good shouting.'

The old man dropped his eyes to her. That was the last word she could say.

'Wa-at?'

He made to get up. His baleful eyes glared like live coals. Gwenno trembled before him.

'Gone, sirr, on the express.'

He sat there staring before him, his eyes sightless. His great chest rising and falling was the only sign of life.

'Get out!' he said through his teeth. He fixed them with a glare.

The women ran out into the kitchen, screaming.

He caught hold of a chair in his great hand and swung it around him.

Ben the Post had scuttled through the door. He only heard the crash of it as he was halfway across the yard.

LIBRARY OF WALES
FUNDED BY

Llywodraeth Cynulliad Cymru
Welsh Assembly Government

**CYNGOR LLYFRAU CYMRU
WELSH BOOKS COUNCIL**

LIBRARY of WALES

The Library of Wales is a Welsh Assembly Government project designed to ensure that all of the rich and extensive literature of Wales which has been written in English will now be made available to readers in and beyond Wales. Sustaining this wider literary heritage is understood by the Welsh Assembly Government to be a key component in creating and disseminating an ongoing sense of modern Welsh culture and history for the future Wales which is now emerging from contemporary society. Through these texts, until now unavailable, out-of-print or merely forgotten, the Library of Wales brings back into play the voices and actions of the human experience that has made us, in all our complexity, a Welsh people.

The Library of Wales includes prose as well as poetry, essays as well as fiction, anthologies as well as memoirs, drama as well as journalism. It will complement the names and texts that are already in the public domain and seek to include the best of Welsh writing in English, as well as to showcase what has been unjustly neglected. No boundaries will limit the ambition of the Library of Wales to open up the borders that have denied some of our best writers a presence in a future Wales. The Library of Wales has been created with that Wales in mind: a young country not afraid to remember what it might yet become.

Dai Smith
Raymond Williams Chair in the Cultural History of Wales,
Swansea University

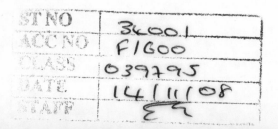

ST NO   36001
ACC NO   F1600
CLASS   039795
DATE   14/11/08
STAFF

Foreword by Katie Gramich

Katie Gramich is a Reader in English Literature at Cardiff University. Her recent publications include *Twentieth-Century Women's Writing in Wales: Land, Gender, Belonging* (University of Wales Press, 2007). She is the editor of *Almanac: A Yearbook of Welsh Writing in English* and chair of the Association of Welsh Writing in English. She was born in Ceredigion and has taught at several universities in England, Wales and Canada.

Cover image by Augustus John

Augustus John was born in Tenby in 1878. He and older sister Gwen studied at the Slade School of Art, UCL, in the 1890s, where Augustus was recognised as one of the most talented draughtsmen of his generation. Gwen John also went on to become an important artist who exhibited widely.

Augustus John's wife Ida, and his mistress – later his second wife – Dorelia McNeill, were an early focus for his art, and by the 1920s he was Britain's leading portrait painter. He died in Fordingbridge, Hampshire, in 1961.

LIBRARY OF WALES

SERIES EDITOR: DAI SMITH

'This landmark series is testimony to the resurgence of the English-language literature of Wales. After years of neglect, the future for Welsh writing in English – both classics and new writing – looks very promising indeed.'

M. Wynn Thomas

WWW.LIBRARYOFWALES.ORG

LIBRARY OF WALES titles are available to buy online at:

gwales.com
Llyfrau ar-lein
Books on-line

LLYFRGELL COLEG MENAI LIBRARY
SAFLE FFRIDDOEDD SITE
BANGOR GWYNEDD LL57 2TP